DATE DUE

THE LONG VIEW

Books by Robert Pack

The Long View

ESSAYS ON THE DISCIPLINE OF HOPE

AND POETIC CRAFT

ROBERT PACK

The University of Massachusetts Press

AMHERST

LC 91-13598
ISBN 0-87023-761-6
Set in Trump Medieval by Keystone Typesetting, Inc.
Printed and bound by Thomson-Shore, Inc.

Library of Congress Cataloging-in-Publication Data
Pack, Robert, 1929–
    The long view : essays on the discipline of hope and poetic craft
/ Robert Pack.
        p.   cm.
    Includes index.
    ISBN 0-87023-761-6
    I. Title.
PS3531.A17L66   1991
809.1—dc20   91-13598
                         CIP

British Library Cataloguing in Publication data are available

"The Idea in the Mirror" first appeared in *Kenyon Review* 9, no. 4
(1987); "The Long View" first appeared in *Kenyon Review* 12,
no. 4 (1990); "The Poetry of Inheritance" first appeared in
The Bread Loaf Anthology of Contemporary American Essays (Hanover, N.H.:
University Press of New England, 1989); "On Wording," "On
Sincerity and Skill," "On Experience," "On Prowess and Revision,"
"On Grace," and "On Fame" first appeared in *Writers on Writing:
A Bread Loaf Anthology* (Hanover, N.H.: University Press of
New England, 1991).

Acknowledgments for permission to reprint material under copyright
appear on the last printed page of this book.

For Stanley and Virginia Bates
and my colleagues
at the Bread Loaf Writers' Conference
who listened summer after summer and
from whom I have learned

CONTENTS

PREFACE

THE ESSAYS in *The Long View*, including the shorter meditations in the second section, are intended to be complete in themselves, and yet I hope that an attentive reader will feel that they are united by recurrent themes: the doubling of human awareness so that we know and, further, we know we know; the analogy between the discipline required in poetic craft and the imaginative discipline required in limiting what we allow ourselves to hope for in our quest for meaning and purpose; the consolations that help us to survive, which are to be found in the related pleasures of poetry, laughter, and music.

As in my earlier volume, *Affirming Limits*, this book also pays homage to those master poets whose high achievements have inspired my own efforts as a poet. I seek to honor them here, not to supersede them or substitute my reading of them for the original work. I try to honor these master poets, with special emphasis on the author of the Book of Job, by undertaking to read their poems with attentive care and to write about them with the greatest clarity and directness that I can manage, assuming that I am addressing the reader simply as another human being who wishes to live with dignity and die without fear in the face of a magnificent but indifferent universe. Following each of the essays in Sections I and III, the poems given extended discussion have been reproduced for the convenience of the reader.

The first section consists of three essays in which I deal with three themes: the poem as a form of the doubling of consciousness; poetic inheritance and the sense of tradition; poetic art as a form of laughter. In each of these essays, I examine poetic texts from an objective point of view as a critical observer, yet I end each of them with subjective reflections (in two cases, reflections of my family), implicitly acknowledging that we all bring our passions with us when we read, even when reading is given over to the discipline of reason and scrupulous interpretation. The personal reflections at the conclusion of these essays are, with all deliberateness, thematically related to the issues raised by the poems under discussion.

The second section of the book is composed of fourteen relatively short essays on various aspects of poetic craft, the sense of literary community, the relationship between poetry and music, between poetry and science, between one's psychology and one's imagination. These mini-essays are informal and anecdotal, stylistically kindred to the final sections of the first three essays, although they, too, contain passages of literary analysis. I hope that readers will find this book persuasive in its refusal to bifurcate impersonal analysis from personal revelation.

The third section consists of three essays, all grounded in my reading of Stephen Mitchell's lyrical new translation of the Book of Job. The first essay develops a comparison between Darwin's theory of evolution, based on his concept of ongoing creation, and the image of God as an amoral creator in the Book of Job. The essay explores the human need for comfort as it examines the imagery of Man on trial before an inscrutable God, and its reversal, God on trial in Job's moral imagination. The second essay traces the influence of the Book of Job on poems by William Blake, Gerard Manley Hopkins, Robert Frost, and Wallace Stevens. I offer an extended analysis of Stevens's late but difficult masterpiece, "The Auroras of Autumn," wherein Stevens confronts the "empty throne" which God seemingly has abandoned, leaving humankind with the burden of re-creating our own moral authority in an otherwise impersonal universe.

In the final essay, on the Book of Job and Shakespeare's *King Lear*, I explore the themes of betrayal and nothingness in meticulous detail. I regard these two overwhelming works as remarkably alike in their imagery, their themes, their tone, and, particularly, in their concerns with trial and judgment and the human need to create purpose out of nothingness, just as our physical universe was created ex nihilo out of the Big Bang explosion some fifteen billion years ago. Although I do not declare myself in my own personal voice in these final essays, I would be disappointed if the reader did not hear my own fears and longings, my own belief in the grandeur of "the long view," behind every word on the page.

PART ONE

ネ

The Idea in the Mirror:
Reflections on the Consciousness
of Consciousness

I

HAMLET'S SPEECH to the players in which he admonishes them to hold "the mirror up to nature" has given us one of the criteria for literary art that has prevailed to this day:

> the purpose of playing . . . was and is to hold, as 'twere the mirror up to nature, to show virtue her own feature, scorn her own image, and the very age and body of the time his form and pressure. (III.2.21–25)

By the nineteenth century, particularly in the poetry of Wordsworth, the emphasis on art as imitation was augmented by an equal emphasis on what the artist *added* to what he perceived. In *The Prelude*, Wordsworth describes the artist's fabricating power in relation to God:

> That through the growing faculties of sense
> Doth like an agent of the one great Mind
> Create, creator and receiver both,

3

Working but in alliance with the works
Which it beholds.

(II.256–60)

Wordsworth implies here that works of art are an extension
of nature and must be regarded as part of nature. Humankind's role as God's creation is fulfilled in imitating God as a
creator, and thus the creation of nature is not static, but
dynamic, because nature is always being enhanced by each
human being's description of it. Although physical nature is
a gift, *received* from God, nevertheless it is incumbent on
humans to interpret what has been divinely offered—physical reality—and thus to wed words to natural objects, creating a new and complex entity, the poem of existence extending itself through language.

In this definition of art, artists must necessarily become
conscious of their own selves, and of their own activity as
artists. In effect, the essential and inescapable work of the
mind becomes the mind's examination of itself. And thus
growth of the mind and the imagination becomes the central
theme of Wordsworth's great epic, *The Prelude*. When Wordsworth says, "often do I seem / Two consciousnesses, conscious of myself / And of some other Being" (II.31–33), he
takes as his subject both himself and the divinity inherent
within him, the "other Being" who is the author of both
nature and himself. Divinity must be regarded as an aspect of
himself, his own mind, and so the nature of imagination also
must be contemplated. Consciousness is, therefore, regarded
as an aspect of nature, and reflections upon his own consciousness become the thinking mode of the receiving and
the creating poet.

The particular form that structurally epitomizes this doubling of consciousness may be found in the poem that contains a work of art within itself, which the poem proceeds to
examine and speculate about. Wordsworth's "Elegiac Stanzas
Suggested by a Picture of Peele Castle" and Keats's "Ode on a

Grecian Urn" represent a new emphasis for poetry whereby
poets hold the mirror up to their own imaginations, showing
the pressure of their own minds both on themselves and on
the world they examine.

II

Wordsworth's poem "Elegiac Stanzas Suggested by a Picture
of Peele Castle, in a Storm, Painted by Sir George Beaumont"
dramatizes the process of grief that Wordsworth had to undergo after the drowning of his younger brother, John, on
February 5, 1805. Over a year after John's death, Wordsworth
has not completed his grieving, though he claims in the poem
(1806) that he now speaks with "mind serene." Having asserted earlier, in "Tintern Abbey" (1778), that "Nature never
did betray the heart that loved her," Wordsworth, in this
poem, now holds a radically different view of nature; the
difference between his earlier and his present state of mind
can be defined by the change in his attitude toward Beaumont's painting. In effect, Beaumont's painting of a storm, a
"sea in anger," is a mirror in which Wordsworth perceives the
anger in his own mind. Recognizing this anger as his own
defiance of nature and God is a necessary step he takes toward
allowing himself to mourn his deceased brother without false
consolation.

Let us, as readers, assume that the speaker of the poem is a
dramatic representation of Wordsworth, a literary character
who stands in relation to his author, just as Hamlet might
stand in relation to Shakespeare, so that we can examine the
self-deception of the poem's speaker without attributing it
completely to Wordsworth himself. As a poet, Wordsworth
may well be aware that he is objectifying his own emotional
confusion at the same time that he is suffering from it. Regarding the speaker of the poem as a character and the poem
as dramatic representation, not merely as philosophical doc-
trine, allows the reader to become aware that the poem is

about self-deception in an unusually complex way. Ostensibly, the poem is about Wordsworth's disillusionment in his earlier belief in the benevolence of nature. But this confession, though genuine on a philosophical level, nevertheless becomes a form of denial, a screen concealing emotions that the speaker is not yet ready to confront. This screen, blocking him from his own emotions, limits the speaker's capacity to mourn and thus to exorcise his repressed grief.

It is dramatically significant that in a poem of fifteen stanzas about the death of his brother, the speaker does not mention his personal grief, "The feeling of my loss," until stanza ten. The first half of the poem is spent describing Peele Castle, "thou rugged Pile," on a peaceful day, "Beside a sea that could not cease to smile; / On tranquil land, beneath a sky of bliss," as if that serene image were still a depiction that Wordsworth could cling to as a true representation of the spirit of nature. This nostalgic dwelling on the past reveals the speaker's emotional reluctance to relinquish his belief in an unbetraying nature, even as he claims that he now regards this view as an illusion. The description of the castle as "sleeping on a glassy sea" mirrors Wordsworth's view of his own optimistic philosophy which he now considers to be a false dream, a "sleep" from which his brother's death has jolted him awake. Wordsworth's cherished former belief that the poet, "an agent of the one great Mind," continues God's work as a creator by interpreting nature and thus creating art is intellectually disavowed through his ironic description of how, before his brother's death, he would have painted Peele Castle as a landscape of "perfect . . . calm."

> Ah! then, if mine had been the Painter's hand
> To express what then I saw; and add the gleam,
> The light that never was, on sea or land,
> . . . .
> I would have planted thee, thou hoary Pile
> Amid a world how different from this!

The referent of "this" is the stormy sea that Beaumont had actually painted, and this image now becomes Wordsworth's new emblem for a cruelly destructive nature. Wordsworth seems to have reconciled himself to a change of philosophical perspective in which a "humanised" self replaces divinity in nature as a source of consolation: "A deep distress hath humanised my Soul."

But this philosophical transformation in Wordsworth does not carry with it an equivalent emotional transformation. There are threatening feelings that Wordsworth has yet to acknowledge. Wordsworth's description of himself is accurate when he declares "Not for a moment could I now behold / A smiling sea, and be what I have been," but the subsequent two lines of the poem are contradictory and reveal more about the speaker than he himself realizes:

> The feeling of my loss will ne'er be old;
> This, which I know, I speak with mind serene.

To claim that one's grief will not age is to assert the work of grieving—which should in time relieve grief so that one can continue with life—has not succeeded. To commit oneself to endless and undiminished grief, as if that is the only way to remain loyal to the deceased, is surely an unconvincing and perverse form of serenity. Wordsworth, wishing not to betray his brother's memory as he feels nature has "betrayed" him, has constructed a spurious and self-defeating form of consolation.

Wordsworth's letters written at the time of his brother's death show the same patterns of contradiction and denial, the same desperate groping for consolation, that we find in "Elegiac Stanzas." Writing to his surviving brother, Richard, about the effect of John's death on their sister, Dorothy, Wordsworth says: "this loss of her beloved brother will long take deep hold. I shall do my best to console her." And on the very day that Wordsworth received the news of John's death, he wrote to George Beaumont about the "miserable affliction" of his sister and his wife, which he says he will do "all in my power to alleviate; but Heaven knows I want consolation myself." The form that consolation begins to take for Wordsworth, however, does not lie in the beauty or divinity of nature, but rather in stoical "fortitude." Now he articulates to his friend and fellow poet, Robert Southey: "As to fortitude, I hope I shall show that, and that all of us will show it, in a proper time, in keeping down many a silent pang hereafter. But grief will, as you say, and must, have its course." The sanity and virtue of fortitude is that it allows grief to take its "course" so that grief will diminish, but in a subsequent letter to Beaumont, Wordsworth writes: "I shall never forget him,—never lose sight of him: there is a bond between us yet, the same as if he were living, nay, far more sacred." Clearly, this is rationalization of an extreme kind in which Wordsworth virtually denies the fact of his brother's death, first by saying that their bond has not changed and then by insisting that this bond has become even stronger. Yet, in this letter, Wordsworth plunges into another vacillation that returns him to the realistic acknowledgment of his bereavement and the defense of fortitude which, in his poem, will find its expressive emblem in the image of Peele Castle: "I trust in God that I shall not want fortitude; but my loss is great and irreparable."

In another letter to Beaumont, written a little over a month after John's death, Wordsworth expresses what he calls his "monstrous" thoughts that reveal his anger against God for, in effect, betraying him by permitting John's death. Wordsworth's hostility here toward the God of nature demands a total change of faith and philosophy on his part, and "Elegiac Stanzas" does indeed entertain the possibility of such a change in belief. Here is Wordsworth's outcry that seems to go beyond any alleviating consolation:

Why have we sympathies that make the best of us afraid of afflicting pain and sorrow, which yet we see dealt about so

lavishly by the supreme governor . . . we have *more of love* in
our nature than he has? The thought is monstrous; and yet how
to get rid of it, except upon the supposition of *another* in a
better world, I do not see.

And yet by the end of this paragraph, in which he goes on to
praise his dead brother for his many good qualities, including
fortitude, Wordsworth, amazingly, plucks consolation out of
the air by describing him as "a noble person, with every hope
about him that could render life dear, thinking of, and living
only for, others—and we see what has been his end! So good
must be better; so high must be destined to be higher. . . ."
Wordsworth, the disillusioned poet of hope, is not able to
relinquish hope despite the evidence offered in this world.
Rather, he holds on desperately to his "supposition" of a
"better world."

Returning to the text of "Elegiac Stanzas," we see Wordsworth struggling to reconcile the antinomies of nature's cruelty and his own anger with his need for consolation and
hope. Having just claimed that he is now speaking with
"mind serene," Wordsworth praises Beaumont's painting for
its opposite quality—its lack of serenity—as a "passionate Work!", telling Beaumont that he "would have been the
Friend, / If he had lived, of Him whom I deplore." The ambiguous "Him" that Wordsworth refers to in this line is not God
but his dead brother, John, since Wordsworth's anger needed
to blame someone—God?—for his brother's dying. In saying
to Beaumont, "This work of thine I blame not, but commend," Wordsworth acknowledges his impulse to attribute
blame. Now he can express his own unresolved emotions
through the image of the "sea in anger," instead of denying
his anger by claiming he is serene of mind.

The attraction of the "huge Castle," for Wordsworth, however, is not simply that it is an emblem of fortitude. In describing Peele Castle as being "cased in the unfeeling armour
of old time," Wordsworth reveals another defense against loss
and grief, the defense of numbness or anesthesia. If only, like

the castle, he did not have to feel anything! And yet his feelings of anger, blame, and betrayal cannot be denied; they have, though inadvertently, been expressed. In acknowledging his change of heart, Wordsworth must reject and say "farewell" to his past "happiness" and his past self, "the heart that lives alone, / Housed in a dream." He is strangely excited now that he has woken from his illusion of a benevolent nature, and, having been "blind," he can finally see. The sudden elation in the line "But welcome fortitude, and patient cheer," however, is another grasp at consolation, a final fantasy of being in control of his emotional fate. This flare of elation instantly collapses, as it must, and the poem darkens into the somber tones of its concluding two lines: "Such sights, or worse, as are before me here.— / Not without hope we suffer and we mourn." These unrationalizing lines are the most forthright of the poem. Although Wordsworth can now see, he also sees what it is that he can see—"such sights, or worse," the afflictions of nature, the "pageantry of fear," extending beyond his own personal loss. His mind has held up the mirror to his own elusive self—the self that once believed the poet could "add the gleam" to nature's own light. The hushed and tentative statement, "Not without hope," is ambiguous in its implications: is it hope that "fortitude" will enable Wordsworth to endure his grief, or is it hope that a *better world* will redeem or replace the suffering of this world, as Keats will try to imagine in his depiction of eternity in "Ode on a Grecian Urn"? Going beyond philosophical uncertainty, Wordsworth ends his poem with the unmitigated fact that "we suffer," and, most significantly, he ends with the word "mourn," as if, with his confrontation of sorrow and his recognition of his own attendant anger, true mourning can begin.

III

The paradoxically realized goal of Keats's "Ode on a Grecian Urn" is to affect the reader exactly as Keats tells us the urn

affects him: to "tease us out of thought." The last two lines of
the poem, which are spoken by the urn, " 'Beauty is truth,
truth beauty,'—that is all / Ye know on earth, and all ye need
to know," to which generations of critics have tried to give
specific meaning, cannot be so pinned down. The lines, just
as Keats says, are a tease; they are designed to defy thought,
and indeed they do. The reason Keats dramatizes this collapse and negation of thought, however, is perfectly clear in
the context of the poem as a whole, for at heart the poem is
about the silence of eternity, and eternity, as Keats shows, is
an unthinkable thought—it is an idea that eludes us in its
very conception. To try to think about eternity brings the
mind to its own limit; at that border, the mind sees itself as
in a mirror, and must turn back to the mortal self and the
ephemeral world or lose itself in its own silence. By ironic
but inescapable implication, then, the urn's assertion of what
we "need to know" on earth is that we cannot know eternity
and that the mind must live within the limits of what is truly
thinkable.

From the beginning Keats presents us with an image that
might be considered paradoxical: the "unravish'd bride of
quietness"—though perhaps that image can better be described as absurd with a touch of the comic. This opening
tease is Keats's elusive way of introducing the theme of "silence" which, subsequently, will be equated with eternity.
The ability to create, to tell a "flowery tale" as sweetly as
possible, is presented as a competition between the urn and
the poet; immediately, the urn is imagined as a projection of
the poet's own resources, a mirror image of the poet's own
power to speculate. It seems that the urn's power to "express"
is superior to the poet's, precisely because its "legend" is uncertain and unknown. All the descriptions of the tableaux depicted upon the urn significantly take the form of questions.

The second stanza begins by continuing the competition
between the urn and the poet, basing it on the criterion of
whose singing is "sweeter." Again the urn wins because the
"pipes" represented on it literally cannot be heard, and thus

their silence evokes the infinite music of eternity to which, supposedly, the "spirit" alone can respond. Expressed by silence, the realm of eternity is depicted first as an instant of static and permanent frustration in which the singing lover (like the poem's speaker) never can kiss his beloved, but then a consolation is offered—apparently the consolation of eternity itself—in that the loved one "cannot fade" and will never cease to be "fair." In exhorting the lover "not [to] grieve," the speaker is addressing his own grieving at the ephemeral condition of mortality. Keats's poem is his attempt to confront and understand this generalized grief—the grief of all worldly lovers.

The consolation of imagining eternity as a condition beyond change, and thus beyond loss, is extended in stanza three, but the inherent absurdity of static eternity is also perceived by the reader. The speaker's continued but repressed grieving takes the form of denial; yet the assertion of unchanging happiness, through the excessive repetition of the word "happy," becomes a parody of the very idea of permanently "happy love." The speaker ends the stanza by describing mortal love as a kind of fever, accompanied by a "burning forehead," and asserts that human passion in its expression inevitably leaves the lover "cloy'd." However, the "piped," yet unheard, songs of eternity are even more surfeiting, as indicated by the repetition of "happy" six times in five lines. The hoped-for consolation implicit in the ideas of permanence and eternity deceives only for a moment; heaven is a concept that the mind, in confronting its own image, must reject. If there is any true consolation to be achieved, it must, ironically, be found in the mind's heroic rejection of its illusions.

Stanza four restates the relationship between the unheard and the heard in a correlative relationship between the unseen and the seen. Only two and a half lines in this stanza are assigned to describing the "mysterious priest" and the "heifer"—figures that appear on the urn. The "green altar,"

where supposedly the heifer will be sacrificed, exists merely
in a hypothetical future. Likewise, the "little town," from
which the priest may have departed, does not appear on the
urn and thus exists in a past that may never have existed. Both
the past and the future of the speaker's depiction of a conjec-
tured sacrifice are only speculation in the realm of the "silent." The urn's tale is a story that cannot be told because it
lacks the parameters of history, and its most significant content, therefore, is emptiness. The town, described as "desolate" because its people have left, becomes an image of the
futility of an impossible imagining. Keats has told a story
about a story that cannot be told, and the silence of that story,
like the story of eternity, finally yields nothing that the imagination can hold and possess.

The concluding apostrophe to the urn is replete with ironic
punning, Keats's own teasing resistance to being vexed by the
urn. The "brede / Of marble men" (with "brede" meaning
ornamental edging) describes men who cannot *breed*; and
the maidens who are "overwrought" as part of the urn's design are also *overwrought* with an unconsummated passion
which, as marble, they cannot feel. In what was probably
Keats's next-to-last letter (November 30, 1820), he wrote:
"even in quarantine, [I have] summoned up more puns, in a
sort of desperation, in one week than in any year of my life."
In returning to the literal fact that the urn is indeed a "silent
form," Keats effectively undermines and contradicts his earlier claim that the urn as a "Sylvan historian" can "express /
A flowery tale more sweetly than our rhyme," just as Wordsworth in "Elegiac Stanzas" had rejected the image of Peele
Castle beside a calm sea as a "chronicle of heaven." The
emotional climax of Keats's poem comes as a rejection of the
idea that the silence of the urn can tell the story of eternity.
Keats turns against his own earlier belief that earthly beauty
prefigures divine beauty ("Imagination and its empyreal reflection is the same as human life and its Spiritual repetition") in the same grieving spirit that Wordsworth had shown

in rejecting his earlier belief in the benevolence of an un-betraying nature. Keats's pained outcry, "Cold Pastoral!" as-serts the theological realization that a static eternity, though free of the sorrows of mortality, cannot be imagined as warm with passion, sweet with song, or happy. The specious idea of eternity expresses only the absurdity of history without time, passion without feeling. And so Keats focuses on the story that he *can* tell in the sweetness of his own sorrowful rhymes. It is the story of mortality and its "woe" which inevitably will go on to "waste" in every generation, thus, in a sense, binding everyone together in the consciousness of a shared fate.

The analogy between the urn and eternity, however, does not completely hold, despite the resemblance between the silence of the urn and the stasis of eternity, for the urn is a beautiful, mundane form, and its "slow time" means that it "remains" longer than the lifetime of a generation of lovers. It is tempting, therefore, to consider the urn's statement, "Beauty is truth, truth beauty," as a projection of Keats's own belief, particularly since the utterance of the urn is so close to Keats's language in his letter of November 22, 1817: "What the imagination seizes as Beauty must be truth—whether it existed before or not." But this letter was written almost two years before Keats composed "Ode on a Grecian Urn" in the middle of May 1819. In a letter written to his brother and sister over a two-and-a-half-month period, just preceding the writing of the ode, in which Keats speaks of the allegorical figures of Poetry, Ambition, and Love as seeming like "three figures on a greek vase," Keats expresses a radically changed attitude toward the role of Beauty in the world and the pos-sibility of human happiness.

In this letter of February 14–May 3, 1819, Keats hypothe-sizes that through the "persevering endeavours of a seldom appearing Socrates Mankind may be made happy," but then Keats turns against his own conjecture about human perfect-ability by saying: "I can imagine such happiness carried to an extreme—but what must it end in?—Death." The idea of death is inextricably bound to the idea of nature, and they impose a limit on human happiness. Keats goes on to reassert his point by saying: "in truth I do not at all believe in this sort of perfectability—the nature of the world will not admit of it," and he gives the example of a thinking rose:

> suppose a rose to have sensation, it blooms on a beautiful morning it enjoys itself—but there comes a cold wind, a hot sun—it cannot escape it, it cannot destroy its annoyances— they are as native to the world as itself: no more can man be happy in spite, the worldly elements will prey upon his nature. . . .

In this letter Keats does not try to imagine perfect happiness in eternity; rather, he focuses on the use of pain and suffering in this world in the humanizing process of creating "souls" here on earth, not in an afterlife. Keats says: "Call the world if you Please 'The Vale of Soul-making.'" For Keats, now, paradise cannot be imagined as having a comprehensible history; divinity can only be hinted at as some kind of spark as yet without embodiment. Keats says: "There may be intelligences or sparks of divinity in millions—but they are not Souls till they acquire identities." Keats's conception of the soul here is totally earthly and incarnate. The soul is not static, beyond change, and it does not preclude the suffering of death. Keats goes on to assert: "Do you not see how necessary a World of pains and troubles is to school an Intelligence and make it a Soul?" In thus insisting on the worldliness of the soul, its location in nature and time, and in affirming the necessity of worldly decay and sorrow in the soul's creation, Keats offers us what he calls "a faint sketch of a system of Salvation." Such a "sketch" is radically different from the earlier glib equating of Truth and Beauty, and, I believe, this rejection of his earlier view is the dramatized subject of "Ode on a Grecian Urn."

The earlier truth/beauty formulation is nostalgically re-

capitulated in the last stanza of the ode, mainly to be parodied, just as Wordsworth in "Elegiac Stanzas" dwells on a
remembered image of a peaceful ocean scene and then dismisses it as a false model for nature in what he calls the "fond
illusion of my heart." As a poem of grieving for the inevitable
loss of love and happiness, Keats's imagining of silence and
eternity, of the sweetness of unheard music, is a form of
denial, and the process of thought confronting thought that
the ode makes manifest is the strenuous overcoming of self-
deception. The end of the poem opens Keats and the reader to
a more realistic and honest acknowledgment that mortal
grief cannot be avoided. Grief is the very heart of the human
condition; as Wordsworth had said before him, "A deep distress hath humanised my Soul." The urn finally is "a friend
to man," but only because, like a mirror, it confronts the
speaker with an image of his own desperately rationalizing
mind and makes it possible for him to acknowledge his mortality in a dignified way, which, Keats says, "does not affront
our reason and humanity."

IV

Wordsworth's view of Beaumont's painting of Peele Castle
can be regarded as a reflection of the poet's changed and
darkened view of nature by means of which he sees himself
anew. Keats's urn gives dramatic representation to a parodied
and rejected belief in eternal happiness that is replaced by the
mind's acceptance of its own earthly limits. Likewise, the
mirroring shield in Auden's poem "The Shield of Achilles"
carries the artist's awareness of himself into the public arena
of social and political life. Auden retells Homer's story of
Thetis, Achilles' mother, who requested the armorer god,
Hephaestos, to design a shield for her son. Auden's description of what Hephaestos has forged onto the shield is exten-
sive and elaborate, just as in Homer's *Iliad*, but Auden's
Thetis (unlike Homer's) cries out "in dismay / At what the

god had wrought," because the imagery on the shield is ugly and depressing. The difference between what Thetis expected and what Hephaestos actually puts on the shield marks a realization for Thetis, and a change of belief for Auden, that is analogous to Keats's rejection of the urn's silent eternity and to Wordsworth's rejection of his view of nature as "calm" and benevolent.

Auden's shield of art functions as a mirror in which Thetis must confront her view of the world. But, since the shield is meant for Achilles to use in war, this central metaphor insists that the reader also ask how a work of art can serve or protect human life. The central irony of the poem is that the shield, as a weapon, cannot prolong Achilles' life or rescue him from death. The speculation inevitably follows as to whether art itself can perform any better service for human survival.

Auden's poem opens with Thetis excitedly looking over Hephaestos's shoulder to see what he has wrought on the shield; she assumes that he will have portrayed her ideas of fruitfulness and human order: "vines and olive trees, / Marble well-governed cities." The olive trees, like the olive branch, suggest the possibility of peace, and already a tacit irony emerges in the poem since the shield, of course, is an instrument of war. What Thetis sees on the shield, however, is distressing to her, for Hephaestos has depicted "wilderness," not order, and a "sky like lead" that evokes the dark futility of war despite the "shining metal" on which it is engraved.

Auden then gives the reader a close-up of the imagery on the shield, just as Keats had done with his urn, and although Auden's description seems neutral and objective, his choice of language strongly suggests that the scenes he portrays, the landscape itself, are replete with implications and thus require interpretation. The "plain without a feature," for example, which seemingly betokens nothing, lacks a "sign of neighborhood," and thus the image signifies that something is missing. From here on, everything in the poem is to be read as a "sign" of what is not immediately visible or apparent. The tableau of the soldiers is not given any particular location in historical time and place, and thus by implication can occur anywhere. Represented as "featureless," like the landscape, as a "million boots in line," the soldiers, expecting their marching orders, are "waiting for a sign" from their leader. But Auden's doubling back on the word "sign" causes the reader to see ironically that the soldiers are waiting for the wrong sign. The soldiers are "congregated," not in the spirit of worship in which responsible individuals are bonded together, but as an "unintelligible multitude" without understanding. For Auden's artist-god, Hephaestos, they are a sign of how morality can be lost in the anonymity of a crowd.

The motif of the misread sign is developed further in stanza three as a parody of divine revelation, when the soldiers are addressed by their leader "out of the air" by an unidentified "voice without a face," who speaks with the logic of statistics, not with compassion or morality. The soldiers march off virtually indistinguishable from the attendant "cloud of dust"—the dust to which they will return in death. They deny the "grief" that they will suffer, and they fail to confront the truth of their complicity in a war emptily defined as "some cause was just."

In his introductory essay to *The Portable Greek Reader*, Auden articulates what he takes to be the "assumption of the *Iliad*" about the unchanging condition of human affairs on earth:

> war is the normal condition of mankind and peace an accidental breathing space. In the foreground are men locked in battle, killing or being killed, farther off their wives, children, and servants waiting anxiously for the outcome . . . around them all indifferent and unchanging, the natural world of sky and earth. This is how things are; that is how they always have been and always will be. Consequently, there can be no moral or historical significance about the result of any conflict; it brings joy to

the victor and sorrow to the vanquished but neither could imagine raising the question of justice.*

Auden uses the Homeric model to represent the modern secularist view of our world in which people cannot successfully appeal to each other since no transcendent moral principles exist toward which they can aspire; so, too, they cannot confront their own behavior and find it faulty since *the self* has not taken on the conscience of its own consciousness. Thetis's expectation of harmonious order cannot be realized without the possibility of appealing to a conscience whose authority comes from beyond the world. Auden goes on to summarize that "the world of Homer is unbearably sad because it never transcends the immediate moment; one is happy, one is unhappy, one wins, one loses, finally one dies." This is indeed the sadness that Hephaestos makes manifest in the imagery of his shield.

The refrain of Thetis's looking over Hephaestos's shoulder is repeated, and this time her expectation is for meaningful religious worship, "ritual pieties," but again she is disappointed. A circumscribed world, like the one Homer portrays on Hephaestos's shield which shows the "Ocean River / which ran around the uttermost rim," cannot embody true worship or "sacrifice" because worldly aspiration alone cannot bring about change. Two stanzas later, Auden reinforces this point when he describes a wholly physical world, one "That carries weight and always weighs the same." Once again Thetis is given a scene by Hephaestos that could occur almost anywhere, "an arbitrary spot," with "ordinary decent folk" performing their banal activities—"one cracked a joke"—seemingly innocent in their quotidian routines. The import of what follows, however, is to be found precisely in what these people fail to see in the execution that subse-

*W. H. Auden, ed., *The Portable Greek Reader*, Viking Portable Library, no. 39 (New York: Penguin, 1960), 18–19.

quently takes place "As three pale figures were led forth and bound / To three posts driven upright in the ground." To the "bored officials" and the "crowd," this scene of crucifixion reveals only someone else's misfortune; it is an ordinary event.

The "decent folk" were there; they "watched" but they failed to see that this was a meaningful event that changed our understanding of history: it was the crucifixion of Christ (along with the two thieves), and it brought to the world, Auden suggests, a message of hope from beyond the world. Through the medium of Hephaestos's art, Auden has invited the reader of his poem to see what the crowd has failed to see—a spiritual sign—and in this sign of belief Auden has replaced his own earlier Marxist views for worldly reform and his own hope for a "cure" of social ills through psychoanalytic understanding (see Auden's "In Memory of Sigmund Freud"), with a belief in Christian salvation. Like Wordsworth's hope for a "better world" at a time of his deepest personal grief, Auden's poem finds hope in what appears to be hope's very absence. The subsequent imagery of his poem, which seems to portray a world that is devoid of spirit, defines that absence in such a way as to imply its opposite— the immanent presence of divinity. In the material world of "mass" and "weight," governed by the logic of "statistics," the victims remain victims, persecuted and unrescued: "they were small / And could not hope for help and no help came." But their pathetic hope, Auden's poem implies, has been misplaced as worldly hope, and thus necessarily it will remain unrealized. When Auden concludes the stanza with the sorrowful lines, "they lost their pride / And died as men before their bodies died," he makes a distinction between their defeated spiritual humanity—they "died as men"—and their mere physical existence—"their bodies died." In this distinction, however, lies the hope of the soul and the hope of another world for the reader of potential Christian faith.

Once again, the refrain of Thetis's expectation returns. Having expressed her wish for ordered government and pious sacrifice, Thetis now yearns for aesthetic grace, "athletes at their games, / Men and women in a dance," but Hephaestos offers her, instead, an image of uncultivated nature, "a weed-choked field." Auden follows this additional image of "vacancy" with a scene in which an "urchin, aimless and alone," tries, with no apparent motive, to kill a bird with his "well-aimed stone." Ironically, his "aimless" aim is to kill merely for the sake of killing. In the world of statistics and "axioms," through which this boy moves without purpose, "That girls are raped, that two boys knife a third" are inevitable events according to Auden's assumption about the Homeric, pre-Christian world: "This is how things are." And yet the world of moral responsibility and human compassion of which the boy has "never heard," the "world where promises were kept / Or one could weep because another wept," is given direct articulation as an idea by the narrator of the poem. Is such an idea merely an illusion, or does it exist as a verbal incarnation from another world, a divine world, just as Christ assumed the human body of Jesus? The idea of universal love, Auden suggests, awaits its further social incarnation in the form of human compliance with Jesus' commandment to love one another. Auden's poem insists through indirection that the crucial function of the shield is to show us, like a mirror, an image of ourselves as we are in a wholly secular and material world. In doing so, the shield and art itself protect us, not from suffering and death, but from the illusion of false optimism, the temptation of worldly hope. Auden's shield offers us the truth of the destructiveness of human nature and the indifference of the physical universe when they are seen as realities unto themselves.

In the Homeric myth, Hephaestos acknowledges himself as "being lame," yet Homer's epithet emphasizes his fame and his power, depicting him as the "renowned smith of the strong arms." Auden, however, in the last stanza tells us that Hephaestos, having completed his work, "hobbled away," as if he has been crippled by the pessimistic vision of life put

forth by his own art. When Thetis finishes looking at the
shield and "Crie[s] out in dismay," she no doubt realizes that
the shield cannot save her son and that her hopes for an
ordered and beautiful world are vain. In describing Thetis's
breasts as "shining," Auden stunningly links her body to the
"shining shield," suggesting that even nature in its nurturing aspect cannot protect us. Although Achilles is "man-
slaying," he cannot save himself by substituting the deaths of
other men for his own in brutal sacrifice. Killing is an il-
lusory form of omnipotence, and this is the last fantasy of the
poem to be discredited. Achilles' sacrifice of others is best
understood in ironic contrast with Christ's self-sacrifice.
Simply and factually, with five abrupt and stressed syllables,
the narrator sardonically tells us that this, indeed, is the
strong Achilles "Who would not live long." The shield of art
has done its work. Like Keats's urn and Wordsworth's re-
imagined painting of Peele Castle by Beaumont, the shield
has shown us the limits of our mortality and the inescapable
worldly conditions that necessitate human grieving.

V

The three poems I have examined express mourning and
disillusionment, and yet each has its own particular and
qualified form of consolation that derives from a heighten-
ing of consciousness. Each poet, in fact, examining his own
mind, becomes aware that consciousness is both an affliction
and a source of cure. Keats's urn is a "friend to man" because
it frees man from trying to imagine unimaginable thoughts
of eternity and returns him, appropriately, to earthly concerns. The urn's beautiful, artistic representation of unconsummated love makes manifest the limited consolation that
art can offer. Wordsworth's approval of Beaumont's painting
of a storm objectifies the end of Wordsworth's optimistic
view of nature as a gentle teacher of God's benevolence, yet
this disillusionment awakens a deepened sense of his own

humanity and a strengthening of his power of "fortitude."
Auden depicts his own view of the destructiveness of secular
humanity on Hephaestos's shield, but by holding that shield-
mirror before our faces, he enables us to see our own longing
for a "world where promises were kept," and to find in that
need a spiritual reality to which our moral yearning corresponds. In each case, the artist frees himself through his own
art by revising a former image of himself into a more painful
but also more realistic, credible, and courageous version of
himself and his world. Through the process of mourning,
disillusionment turns the poet from the danger of despair to a
modified and redirected version of hope.

Although I consider these three poems masterpieces of
lyric art, my own philosophical allegiance belongs with
Keats's dismissal of the ideas of eternity and paradise. To my
mind, the concept of heaven is an illusion, and I read the
history of religion as characteristic of human beings as fantasizing creatures—thinking animals who cannot accept the
thought of their own mortality. I am stirred by the heroic ring
of disenchantment in the name of an unflinching commitment to reality. Freud concisely articulates this world view in
The Future of an Illusion:

> [Man] will have to confess his utter helplessness and his insig-
> nificant part in the working of the universe; he will have to
> confess that he is no longer the centre of creation, no longer the
> object of the tender care of a benevolent providence. He will be
> in the same position as the child who has left the home where
> he was so warm and comfortable. But, after all, is it not the
> destiny of childishness to be overcome? *

I find something exciting about this call to tough-minded
maturity, something even consoling and hopeful. Yes, we can
make our way through the world without deceiving ourselves. We can examine our minds in the mirror of art and

---

* Sigmund Freud, *The Future of an Illusion* (New York: Doubleday, Anchor
Press, 1957), 88.

correct the distortions reflected there in our wished-for images of ourselves and our collective destiny.

Toward the end of Aeschylus's play, *Prometheus Bound*, the following terse exchange takes place between Prometheus and the chorus as Prometheus enumerates the benefits with which he has endowed the world:

P. I caused mortals to cease foreseeing doom.
C. What cure did you provide them with against that sickness?
P. I placed in them blind hopes.
C. That was a great gift you gave to men.
P. Besides this, I gave them fire.

Most readers remember Prometheus's gift of fire—which we might take to mean poetic inspiration—but forget his gift of "blind hopes," as if the need for human "blindness" is itself something we are compelled to deny. As human creatures, we are not able to live without "blind hopes," some measure of illusion, and since one cannot consciously believe in an illusion, it then follows that the power of reason must at some point give way to the power of wishing, the domain of the unconscious. Just as we are limited by our mortality, so, too, are we limited in our ability to examine our own consciousness. Honest self-awareness of human ambivalence, nevertheless, may reveal truths of self-understanding that can help us control our destructiveness, although individual confrontation of such truths may not be sufficient to save us collectively. It is my own hope, however, that through the poet's gift of the mirroring poem, these disillusioning but shared truths can indeed help us survive.

❧

William Wordsworth

ELEGIAC STANZAS

Suggested by a Picture of Peele Castle, in a Storm,
Painted by Sir George Beaumont

I was thy neighbour once, thou rugged Pile!
Four summer weeks I dwelt in sight of thee:
I saw thee everyday; and all the while
Thy Form was sleeping on a glassy sea.

So pure the sky, so quiet was the air!
So like, so very like, was day to day!
Whene'er I looked, thy Image still was there;
It trembled, but it never passed away.

How perfect was the calm! it seemed no sleep;
No mood, which season takes away, or brings:
I could have fancied that the mighty Deep
Was even the gentlest of all gentle Things.

Ah! then, if mine had been the Painter's hand,
To express what then I saw; and add the gleam,
The light that never was, on sea or land,
The consecration, and the Poet's dream;

I would have planted thee, thou hoary Pile
Amid a world how different from this!
Beside a sea that could not cease to smile;
On tranquil land, beneath a sky of bliss.

Thou shouldst have seemed a treasure-house divine
Of peaceful years; a chronicle of heaven;—
Of all the sunbeams that did ever shine
The very sweetest had to thee been given.

A Picture had it been of lasting ease,
Elysian quiet, without toil or strife;
No motion but the moving tide, a breeze,
Or merely silent Nature's breathing life.

Such, in the fond illusion of my heart,
Such Picture would I at that time have made:
And seen the soul of truth in every part,
A stedfast peace that might not be betrayed.

So once it would have been, —'tis so no more;
I have submitted to a new control:
A power is gone, which nothing can restore;
A deep distress hath humanised my Soul.

Not for a moment could I now behold
A smiling sea, and be what I have been:
The feeling of my loss will ne'er be old;
This, which I know, I speak with mind serene.

Then, Beaumont, Friend! who would have been the Friend,
If he had lived, of Him whom I deplore,
This work of thine I blame not, but commend;
This sea in anger, and that dismal shore.

O 'tis a passionate Work! —yet wise and well,
Well chosen is the spirit that is here;
That Hulk which labours in the deadly swell,
This rueful sky, this pageantry of fear!

And this huge Castle, standing here sublime,
I love to see the look with which it braves,
Cased in the unfeeling armour of old time,
The lightning, the fierce wind, and trampling waves.

Farewell, farewell the heart that lives alone,
Housed in a dream, at distance from the Kind!
Such happiness, wherever it be known,
Is to be pitied; for 'tis surely blind.

But welcome fortitude, and patient cheer,
And frequent sights of what is to be borne!
Such sights, or worse, as are before me here.—
Not without hope we suffer and we mourn.

John Keats

ODE ON A GRECIAN URN

I

THOU still unravish'd bride of quietness,
  Thou foster-child of silence and slow time,
Sylvan historian, who canst thus express
  A flowery tale more sweetly than our rhyme:
What leaf-fring'd legend haunts about thy shape
  Of deities or mortals, or of both,
    In Tempe or the dales of Arcady?
  What men or gods are these? What maidens loth?
What mad pursuit? What struggle to escape?
    What pipes and timbrels? What wild ecstasy?

II

Heard melodies are sweet, but those unheard
  Are sweeter; therefore, ye soft pipes, play on;
Not to the sensual ear, but, more endear'd,
  Pipe to the spirit ditties of no tone:
Fair youth, beneath the trees, thou canst not leave
  Thy song, nor ever can those trees be bare;
    Bold Lover, never, never canst thou kiss,
Though winning near the goal—yet, do not grieve;
    She cannot fade, though thou hast not thy bliss,
  For ever wilt thou love, and she be fair!

III

Ah, happy, happy boughs! that cannot shed
  Your leaves, nor ever bid the Spring adieu;
And, happy melodist, unwearied,
  For ever piping songs for ever new;
More happy love! more happy, happy love!
  For ever warm and still to be enjoy'd,
    For ever panting, and for ever young;
All breathing human passion far above,
  That leaves a heart high-sorrowful and cloy'd,
    A burning forehead, and a parching tongue.

IV

Who are these coming to the sacrifice?
    To what green altar, O mysterious priest,
Lead'st thou that heifer lowing at the skies,
    And all her silken flanks with garlands drest?
What little town by river or sea shore,
    Or mountain-built with peaceful citadel,
        Is emptied of its folk, this pious morn?
And, little town, thy streets for evermore
    Will silent be; and not a soul to tell
        Why thou art desolate, can e'er return.

V

O Attic shape! Fair attitude! with brede
    Of marble men and maidens overwrought,
With forest branches and the trodden weed;
    Thou, silent form, dost tease us out of thought
As doth eternity: Cold Pastoral!
    When old age shall this generation waste,
        Thou shalt remain, in midst of other woe
    Than ours, a friend to man, to whom thou say'st,
"Beauty is truth, truth beauty,—that is all
        Ye know on earth, and all ye need to know."

W. H. Auden

THE SHIELD OF ACHILLES

She looked over his shoulder
        For vines and olive trees,
Marble well-governed cities
        And ships upon untamed seas,
But there on the shining metal
        His hands had put instead
An artificial wilderness
        And a sky like lead.

A plain without a feature, bare and brown,
    No blade of grass, no sign of neighbourhood,
Nothing to eat and nowhere to sit down,
    Yet, congregated on its blankness, stood
    An unintelligible multitude,
A million eyes, a million boots in line,
Without expression, waiting for a sign.

Out of the air a voice without a face
    Proved by statistics that some cause was just
In tones as dry and level as the place:
    No one was cheered and nothing was discussed;
    Column by column in a cloud of dust
They marched away enduring a belief
Whose logic brought them, somewhere else, to grief.

                She looked over his shoulder
                    For ritual pieties,
                White flower-garlanded heifers,
                    Libation and sacrifice,
                But there on the shining metal
                    Where the altar should have been,
                She saw by his flickering forge-light
                    Quite another scene.

Barbed wire enclosed an arbitrary spot
    Where bored officials lounged (one cracked a joke)
And sentries sweated for the day was hot:
    A crowd of ordinary decent folk
    Watched from without and neither moved nor spoke
As three pale figures were led forth and bound
To three posts driven upright in the ground.

The mass and majesty of this world, all
    That carries weight and always weighs the same
Lay in the hands of others; they were small
    And could not hope for help and no help came:
    What their foes liked to do was done, their shame
Was all the worst could wish; they lost their pride
And died as men before their bodies died.

She looked over his shoulder
    For athletes at their games,
Men and women in a dance
    Moving their sweet limbs
Quick, quick, to music,
    But there on the shining shield
His hands had set no dancing-floor
    But a weed-choked field.

A ragged urchin, aimless and alone,
    Loitered about that vacancy; a bird
Flew up to safety from his well-aimed stone:
    That girls are raped, that two boys knife a third,
    Were axioms to him, who'd never heard
Of any world where promises were kept,
Or one could weep because another wept.

The thin-lipped armourer,
    Hephaestos, hobbled away,
Thetis of the shining breasts
    Cried out in dismay
At what the god had wrought
    To please her son, the strong
Iron-hearted man-slaying Achilles
    Who would not live long.

The Poetry of Inheritance

T HE DESIRE to write a will and leave behind something of value to an inheritor closely resembles the passion to write poetry. To give continuity and permanence to one's singular imagination, one needs to leave a testament of caring for the world. Many poems, in fact, assume the overt form of a written will. They formalize a scene in which the speaker says farewell, so that his or her departing advice conveys a sense of ongoing responsibility to the reader. In Yeats's poem, "The Tower," for example, the aging poet concludes:

> It is time that I wrote my will;
> I choose upstanding men
> That climb the streams until
> The fountain leap, and at dawn
> Drop their cast at the side
> Of dripping stones; I declare
> They shall inherit my pride.

After Yeats identifies his chosen inheritors, he leaves them the pride which he associates with his own creativity. In "Under Ben Bulben," the poem Yeats designed to be read as his last poem, Yeats explicitly admonishes his would-be successors:

> Irish poets, learn your trade,
> Sing whatever is well made,
> Scorn the sort now growing up
> All out of shape from toe to top,
> Their unremembering hearts and heads
> Base-born products of base beds.

Yeats's pride again shows through these lines. The values he asserts are those associated with creativity, mastering one's craft, and remembering, preserving the tradition out of which the poet has been born—a tradition that his own work will extend and revitalize. The element of hostility in Yeats's address to his audience of younger Irish poets is caused by his fear that his own values will be lost or rejected and that both he and the tradition that defined him, whose continuity alone can grant him immortality, will be forgotten. Without the covenant of tradition, death becomes absolute.

Scrutinizing poems that are true to their own principles of organization is the necessary way in which we, the inheritors, cherish these poems and keep their memory vital within us, creating a covenant that binds the generations together, despite the temptations of "unremembering hearts and heads" to neglect or destroy what has gone before. If we have the gratitude and uncompetitive generosity as writers to cherish and remember, so, too, may we hope that our own compositions will survive, bearing witness to what we have loved. Through patience and cultivated skill, we may provide the perspective that comes from composure—those expanded moments of stillness—to resist what Frost calls "the rush of everything to waste."

II

In defense against the noisy rush of time, moments when the landscape is silent and still are vital for Wordsworth because

they evoke a corresponding "calm" from his innermost being. God speaks to Wordsworth mainly during the pauses in
the normal flow of discordant and distracting sound. For
Wordsworth to respond fully to the imagery of nature—as if
nature were God's book—required that he respond as well to
the mystery of what God withholds. Just as Jesus used a
language of metaphor and mystery—"And he spake many
things unto them in parables"—so, too, the language of nature, for Wordsworth, was that of parable, and part of the
grammar of that language, even its essence, was silence. To
be in touch with the restorative power of divinity, Wordsworth needed to recollect and cherish the youthful experiences of silence that evoked in him a sense of the holy:

> Transcendent peace
> And silence did await upon these thoughts
> That were a frequent comfort to my youth.
>   (*The Prelude*, VI.139–41)

Wordsworth responds to a landscape as if he were a reader
perusing a text that invited his own interpretation. In the
education of the young, landscape and books are inextricably
linked, and Wordsworth wishes in behalf of all children:
"May books and Nature be their early joy!" A direct analogy
exists between the landscape as parable and the poem as
parable. The poem, in effect, becomes the landscape of the
mind, and God's presence is made manifest in the human
imagination as it responds to and interprets "Nature's self,
which is the breath of God, / Or His pure Word." The "Visionary power" that enables Wordsworth to have glimpses of
divinity abides in the "motions of the viewless winds, / Embodied in the mystery of words." For Wordsworth, the natural
landscape and the Bible are alike as symbolic forms and as
sources of revelation.

Wordsworth's masterpiece "Michael" is a framed story in
which the narrator first addresses the reader, then tells the
story of Michael and his son, Luke, who leaves home never

to return, and finally addresses the reader once again. The reader is invited *into* the story by being identified with the travelers on the "public way," who are given the choice to follow the narrator-guide into the "hidden valley" where Michael's story has been enacted. The relationship between the narrator-guide and the reader-traveler is crucial to the poem because it both parallels and contrasts with the relationship between Michael and Luke. The reader must decide whether to enter the landscape of the poem and listen to the story, and, finally, how to interpret the story. The poem opens with the word "If"—"If from the public way you turn your steps / Up the tumultuous brook"—and everything that follows is seen as the consequence of choices, though mysterious forces from the past affect the outcome of those choices.

The identity of the reader-traveler is doubly complex. At the end of the poem's first paragraph, which completes the prologue before the story itself begins, the narrator says that he will relate Michael's history "for the delight of a few natural hearts." Here, the narrator assumes that some special bond exists between himself and his self-chosen readers—it is like the bond Milton describes between himself and his reader when he says, "fit audience find, though few." But Wordsworth goes even further in identifying his reader by extending the image of his reader to include the "youthful poets" who will survive him. Thus, the narrator's story (and Wordsworth's poem) will be written "with yet fonder feeling, for the sake / Of youthful Poets, who among these hills / Will be my second self when I am gone." In telling Michael's story, the narrator is, in effect, writing his will, and he leaves his inheritance to the future generations of poets. The innermost issue of the poem lies in the question of how the narrator's telling of Michael's story will affect his readers and the poets yet to enter this landscape. If the story about Michael and his son describes the breaking of a covenant, how does the *relating* of the story provide the means for the reestablishment of the same covenant?

Wordsworth, through his narrator, tells the story of Michael as if it were a parable. The narrator-guide says of Michael and his wife that "they were as a proverb in the vale / For endless industry," and, most important, the entire poem is suffused with allusions to and echoes of the Twenty-third Psalm with imagery of green pastures, paths of righteousness, valley, staff, and dwellings.

Psalm 23: The Lord is my Shepherd
Wordsworth: There dwelt a Shepherd, Michael was his name

Psalm 23: He maketh me lie down in green pastures
Wordsworth: the tumultuous brook of Green-head Ghyll

Psalm 23: the paths of righteousness
Wordsworth: with an upright path / Your feet must struggle

Psalm 23: the valley of the shadow of death
Wordsworth: a hidden valley

Psalm 23: thy rod and thy staff
Wordsworth: a perfect shepherd's staff

Psalm 23: thy rod and thy staff they comfort me
Wordsworth: There is a comfort in the strength of love

Psalm 23: I will dwell in the house of the Lord for ever.
Wordsworth: at her death the estate was sold, . . . yet the
                    oak is left . . .

Psalm 23 is the underlying text of Wordsworth's poem, just as the presence of God is inherent in the very landscape that Wordsworth describes: "And in the open sunshine of God's love / Have we all lived." Michael never prays directly to God, for what he knows of divinity is to be found in physical nature. Even after Michael realizes that his son will not return, the narrator tells us that "Among the rocks / He went, and still looked up to sun and cloud, / And listened to the wind." Michael seeks "comfort" after his son goes to the "dissolute city" and "slacken[s] in his duty," then vanishes from the poem and from Michael's life, never to return. But that comfort depends upon an interpretation of what the landscape reveals. Consolation, for Wordsworth, is the work of man, yet nature, God's book, is always present to be read, to be beheld as a source of both beauty and comfort. The physical world itself and the story within the poem contain twin aspects of God's immanence. Both world and poem thus come together as a recorded parable in which the mystery of suffering and redemption is to be accepted and embraced. The actual landscape, the Bible, the story of Michael and Luke, and Wordsworth's poem, all form a continuum of divinity, flowing through time and history, and that divinity, Wordsworth hopes, is there to be received by the reader, who also is a traveler in "the valley of the shadow of death."

The reader-traveler, having entered the poem and its valley "hidden" from the "public way," is shown the "straggling heap of unhewn stones" which inspires the telling of Michael's story. Without the narrator-guide to interpret them, the stones would have no meaning, and the reader-traveler "might pass by, / Might see and notice not." To understand these stones is to remember and keep alive the story of the broken covenant, the separation of father and son. Through no fault of his own, Luke must leave home in order to earn money to help pay off a family debt from the forgotten past:

> . . . The Shepherd had been bound
> In surety for his brother's son, a man
> Of an industrious life, and ample means;
> But unforeseen misfortunes suddenly
> Had prest upon him; and old Michael now
> Was summoned to discharge the forfeiture.

The "patrimonial fields" that had bonded Michael and Luke together in love are now seen to carry a burden and an ancestral curse. Ominously, when Luke leaves home, he disappears into the same "public way" where the reader has entered the poem: "when he [Luke] had reached / The public way, he put on a bold face." The bond between father and son, the link between Michael's happy family and the landscape that nurtured them is broken, and Luke vanishes into a "hiding place beyond the seas."

What is the cause of this breaking of the family covenant? Who is at fault? Wordsworth has portrayed Michael's deep love for his son by depicting the motherly aspects of Michael's devotion and care-taking: "For oftentimes / Old Michael, while he [Luke] was a babe in arms, / Had done him female service, . . . and he had rocked / His cradle, as with a woman's gentle hand." Michael's physical powers ("His bodily frame had been from youth to age / Of an unusual strength") are enhanced and made complete by his tenderness and his capacity to express emotion, as when he and Luke together lay the first stone of the sheep-fold: "The old Man's grief broke from him; to his heart / He pressed his Son, he kissed him and wept." Michael has been an ideal father to Luke, nurturing him, teaching him, working with him, and the reader is likely to agree with Michael's own representation of himself to his son: "Even to the utmost I have been to thee / A kind and a good father." And yet might there have been a flaw in Michael's fathering? The narrator tells us that Luke had been "prematurely called" to help Michael with the herding of the sheep.

But we cannot demand inhuman perfection from Michael in the timing of the initiating process of his son in order for us to feel that Michael has been good to the "utmost." Wordsworth has portrayed Michael's humanness, but Luke's failure to maintain his father's values of loyalty and piety remains clouded in mystery. Wordsworth's description of Luke's fate is factual, without explanation, and astonishingly brief:

> Meantime Luke began
> To slacken in his duty; and, at length,
> He in the dissolute city gave himself
> To evil courses: ignominy and shame
> Fell on him, so that he was driven at last
> To seek a hiding-place beyond the seas.

The city is not the cause of Luke's fall—since Luke "gave himself"—but, rather, the city represents the unexplained presence of evil in the world. The city is a sign of the consequence of the broken covenant between man and the natural landscape, a manifestation of man's fallen condition.

Despite his goodness and his piety, Michael is not unaware of the fact that there is evil in the world. He is not a self-deceiving sentimentalist. The day before Luke must leave home, Michael takes him "Up to the heights," where the sheep-fold is to be built, and instructs him:

> Lay now the corner-stone,
> As I requested; and hereafter, Luke,
> When thou art gone away, should evil men
> Be thy companions, think of me, my Son, . . .

Michael's words are disturbingly prophetic, for beneath their ominous warning lies the suggestion that somehow Michael knows that "evil" will break the "links of love" that have "bound" father and son. Nevertheless, Michael takes hope, and he promises Luke that "When thou return'st, thou in this place wilt see / A work which is not here: a covenant / 'Twill be between us." The sheep-fold which Michael plans to complete during Luke's absence will symbolize this "covenant," binding together father and son, man and the landscape, the present and the future. The continuity of values from generation to generation is, precisely, what Wordsworth means by "hope," for it is the goodness of original creation itself that forever defines what is valuable and is to be cherished. And yet, despite the hope inherent in laying the first stone of the sheep-fold, Michael darkly concludes his last speech to Luke by saying that "whatever fate / Befall thee, I shall love thee to the last, / And bear thy memory with me to the grave." In a sense, Michael must take "fate" into his own hands, paradoxically, by accepting the fate of separation and loss, the fate that the covenant will be broken. But in accepting that fate, love ceases to be dependent on a happy outcome, on circumstances; rather, the emotion of love becomes its own fate.

To seek consolation in defeat, however, would be a form of perversity, and thus hope in the covenant must be paramount. The building of the sheep-fold is for Michael a testament to every value he has cherished. As the symbol of the covenant, it represents Michael's will, his inheritance. The original covenant, which is the model for Michael, was reaffirmed between God and Noah when God promised that he would never send another flood to punish humankind for disobedience.

> And I will establish my covenant with you; neither shall all flesh be cut off any more by the waters of a flood; neither shall there any more be a flood to destroy the earth. (Genesis 9.11)

And just as Michael needed a visible symbol of his covenant with Luke, so, too, the Lord before him had chosen to make visible his covenant with Noah in the image of the rainbow: "I do set my bow in the cloud, and it shall be for a token of a covenant between me and the earth."

Throughout Wordsworth's poetry, with the biblical covenant in mind, the presence of God is to be found in "natural objects." Every image in a landscape, as in a poem, is replete with symbolic implications.

In the biblical account, God continues to renew his covenant with his people throughout the generations. It is of particular significance in Genesis 17.4–5, when God says to Abram: "Behold, my covenant *is* with thee, and thou shalt be a father of many nations. Neither shall thy name any more be called Abram, but thy name shall be Abraham." Abram is renamed to indicate his role as a "father of many nations" and thus as the carrier of God's covenant. God then further instructs Abraham:

> And ye shall circumcise the flesh of your foreskin; and it shall be a token of the covenant betwixt me and you. . . . and my covenant shall be in your flesh for an everlasting covenant. (Genesis 17.11, 13)

Not only is God's covenant placed in nature, it is placed in the "flesh," so that the human body, like the landscape, also can be seen as revealing the immanence of God. Like God's reminder to Noah that he possesses destructive power to flood the earth that *he will not use,* God's decree of circumcision conveys the same message to Abraham: God could cut off the power of Abraham's paternity, but he chooses not to do so. God's covenant through the use of circumcision is the alternative to God's punishment, and God's blessing to Abraham, in treating Abraham as a chosen son, is to allow Abraham himself to become a father. Circumcision has the same function for Abraham as Michael's "threatening gestures" have for Luke; both are reminders of the potential aggression and destructiveness that love must overcome to make a covenant of continuity.

The story of father and son ends with Luke's disappearance to a "hiding-place beyond the seas." The covenant between them has been broken, and the cause of that rupture remains mysterious, even absurd. All we can say is that the cause seems to lie in the obscure family past as the result of an "evil choice" by an "evil man," whom Michael somehow must "forgive"; or the cause lies in the "burthened" fields, which seem to have a curse upon them like original sin. After the story's apparently hopeless conclusion, the narrator again addresses the traveler-reader who is still looking at the pile of stones. But at least the reader now knows the history of those stones and what they were intended to be. It is astonishing that the narrator's tone, despite the tragic tale, maintains an uncanny quality of tranquility, as if a long process of mourning has been completed.

The narrator begins the poem's epilogue by speaking of "comfort," when we might have felt that no comfort was to be found. He says: "There is a comfort in the strength of love," and we are reminded of Michael's last words to Luke, "I shall love thee to the last," as if we, too, are now able to partake of such love and, in turn, be strengthened by it. This comfort is grounded in communal memory, beginning with the narrator and Michael's neighbors—"I have conversed

with more than one who well / Remember the old Man"—
and now including the traveler-reader as well. Although the
story is one which, without the strength of love, can "overset
the brain, or break the heart," the telling of the story has an
opposite effect: it strengthens by releasing the source of human sympathy and compassion. The narrator asserts, " 'Tis
not forgotten yet / The pity which was then in every heart /
For the old Man!"

The poem's final image of Michael is of him "Sitting alone,
or with his faithful Dog," beside the sheep-fold, though we
are told that "from time to time" he did continue to work at
it. Nevertheless, it is not completed, and, looking at the pile
of stones, we are forced to face the fact that Michael "left the
work unfinished when he died." Michael's worst fears are
realized when, after the death of his wife, the land is sold,
their cottage is torn down, and "great changes" make the
neighborhood almost unrecognizable. Almost unrecognizable, but not totally so, for "the oak is left / That grew beside
their door," and, above all, the "straggling heap of unhewn
stones" is still there. We have left the "public way" and
entered the "hidden valley" in order to learn of the history
of these stones. The narrator-guide concludes without explicitly drawing a moral, that "the remains / Of the unfinished Sheep-fold may be seen," though his voice rises into
alliteration when he names the landscape in the final line,
"Beside the boisterous brook of Greenhead Ghyll." We are
left to make our own interpretation of what we have seen
and heard.

Without the narrator, the pile of stones would have appeared merely as a pile of stones without symbolic import.
We have paused in our traveling through Wordsworth's version of "the valley of the shadow of death" in order to see "the
remains / Of the unfinished Sheep-fold." "Remains" is the
absolutely crucial word here. First of all, it means ruins, but
after that another meaning of the word begins to resonate:
"remains" also implies that which endures and continues.

Just as Michael bears Luke's memory to the grave, the reader now carries with him the memory of Michael. In effect, the broken covenant is replaced by *the story of the broken covenant*, and it is now the reader's option to keep this story alive. Should the reader be a "youthful Poet," he will, indeed, become the narrator's "second self."

Wordsworth has given us a double story whose two lines are potentially parallel: Michael is to Luke as the narrator is to the reader. The covenant between Michael and Luke is broken, but the fate of the covenant between the narrator and the reader remains undecided. The reader or the youthful poet, should he so choose, can accept Michael's inheritance and thus replace Luke as the failed son, to become the son who does not break the continuity of the generations. By honoring the narrator's story, by electing to remember it and perhaps retell it, the reader, in effect, restores the covenant and completes the unfinished sheep-fold. By making this free choice—which is just as mysterious as Luke's giving himself to "evil courses"—not only is Wordsworth's own pastoral poem kept alive, but Michael's story within Wordsworth's poem is revivified as well. As we remember the shepherd Michael, with the "perfect Shepherd's staff" made by his own hand, the comforting words of the ancestral Bible are reflected in the landscape itself, in the enduring oak tree, the boisterous brook, and the stones:

> Yea, though I walk through the valley of the shadow of death, I will fear no evil: for thou *art* with me; thy rod and thy staff they comfort me.

III

Wordsworth's "Michael" is a model for Robert Frost's "Wild Grapes" in several significant ways. Both poems take as their protagonist an old person who is facing loss and death: the shepherd, Michael, and the old woman who is the narrator in "Wild Grapes." Both poems are framed stories in which the narrator first addresses the reader, then tells a story, and finally addresses the reader directly again. In Wordsworth's poem, the reader is identified with the travelers on the "public way" who are led into a "hidden valley," and in Frost's poem, the reader is identified with the friends who are attending the old woman's birthday party at which she recounts having picked wild grapes with her older brother when she was five years old. Both narrators tell their stories as if they were parables. Where the underlying text of Wordsworth's poem is the Twenty-third Psalm, that of Frost's poem is Luke 6.44: "For every tree is known by its own fruit: for of thorns men do not gather figs, nor of a bramble bush gather they grapes."

At the beginning of Frost's poem, in a spirit of enigmatic teasing, the old woman declaims to her friends who have gathered to celebrate her birthday:

> What tree may not the fig be gathered from?
> The grape may not be gathered from the birch?
> It's all you know the grape, or know the birch.

The point of her joke is that in New England wild grape vines climb up birch trees, so that it is possible for grapes to be gathered from birches. Thus, it seems, contrary to the Bible, not every tree can be known by its own fruit. To understand the metaphorical truth of the Bible, therefore, requires local interpretation. Beneath the old woman's natural lore, beneath her genial chiding, lies a serious need to tell a story and, finally, to make a statement about life and death, to sum up what she knows.

Her initiation into knowledge is achieved through a long process of self-projection and identification with others. This empathy commences with the old woman's depiction of her childhood self as if she were a grape:

> As a girl gathered from the birch myself
> Equally with my weight in grapes, one autumn,
> I ought to know what tree the grape is fruit of.

In relating how she was whisked up into the birch tree from which she was gathering grapes, couldn't get down by herself, and had to be rescued by her brother, she describes that historical day as if it were a second birthday, since her first "beginning" had been "wiped out in fear / The day I swung suspended from the grapes." In a sense her new life, which she comically calls her "extra life," finds its genesis in the fear that wipes out her first life, her innocence, since that fear will come to be seen as a source of rebirth into necessary knowledge. Continuing her joke, she says—"So if you see me celebrate two birthdays"—and, drawn into her circle of intimacy, we await her story which will become her gift to us.

The story of the grape gathering is a parable of the passing-on of knowledge in which the older brother, acting as a guide, leads the young initiate into a special landscape that she must learn to interpret. In his function as guide and teacher, the brother resembles Wordsworth's narrator in "Michael." Similarly, the bond between Frost's guiding brother and neophyte sister will develop into a covenant that, as in Wordsworth, will not be completed. The old woman's prologue address to her birthday party shifts abruptly back into the past which, in recollection, takes on the resonances of an anthropomorphic nature myth:

> One day my brother led me to a glade
> Where a white birch he knew of stood alone,
> Wearing a thin headdress of pointed leaves,
> And heavy on her heavy hair behind,
> Against her neck, an ornament of grapes.

The brother possesses knowledge of the landscape that the young girl desires, and the special "white birch he knew" is described as a kind of mother/earth goddess, a source of fertility and pleasure whose bounty the brother is willing to share with his sister, despite a measure of sibling reluctance. In "climbing" the tree, the brother seems to master it with proud male domination, just as in Frost's companion poem, "Birches," the boy "subdued his father's trees / By riding them down." In "Wild Grapes," however, oedipal competition between son and father for Mother Nature is, at most, implied, and the authoritative role played by the brother seems to combine father and brother in one. To further prove his prowess and mastery, the manifestations of his knowledge, the brother

> . . . climbed still higher and bent the tree to earth
> And put it in my hands to pick my own grapes.
> "Here, take a treetop, I'll get down another.
> Hold on with all your might when I let go."

With these resounding words of command, as if from the resident god of the mother tree, the brother has provided his sister with a holy text which, eventually, will require her own interpretation. She will have to make those words her own, and, indeed, the dialectical phrases, "hold on" and "let go," which seem so casual and colloquial when first uttered, will become the parabolic heart of the poem.

When her brother lets go of the tree branch the girl is holding, she is whisked up into the air like a caught fish. Her brother calls to her, "Let go! / Don't you know anything, you girl? Let go!" But the little girl, out of some primal instinct for survival not yet refined by knowledge, continues to hold on

> with something of the baby grip
> Acquired ancestrally in just such trees
> When wilder mothers than our wildest now
> Hung babies out on branches by the hands . . .

Again the tree is represented as a mother, but now, by analogy, the implication is that the child must learn *how* to let go, and we are told: "I held on uncomplainingly for life." What her brother teaches her about laughter is the next essential step in the process of her initiation:

> My brother tried to make me laugh to help me.
> "What are you doing up there in those grapes?
> Don't be afraid. A few of them won't hurt you.
> I mean they won't pick you if you don't them."

We must assume that the good-natured humor we see in the old woman at the poem's beginning is, at least in part, the gift of laughter she learned from her brother when in danger— the danger, it seemed, of being snatched off the face of the earth, "not to return," as Frost says of the boy in the same situation in "Birches."

The ability to confront fear with laughter is a revelation for the young girl, and it releases a new capacity for understanding in her that will enable her to comprehend her brother's next lesson—the concept of empathy which her brother introduces to her in comic form: " 'Now you know how it feels,' my brother said, / 'To be a bunch of fox grapes.' " Partaking of her brother's identification of her with the bunch of hanging grapes that "thinks it has escaped the fox / By growing where it shouldn't—on a birch" foreshadows the empathy the old woman will have for the distress of the "others" at the end of the poem. They wish they could be spared the burden of consciousness when they are facing death.

Clinging to the tree, not knowing how to let go, the young girl loses her "hat and shoes," and this image of her being stripped of her human vestments suggests a reversal of the image of her evolution from monkey ancestry earlier in the poem. Her reversal back toward nakedness reminds us of our creaturehood and our bodily vulnerability when confronted with natural danger. At first, her brother adds to the element of threat when he says, " 'Drop or I'll shake the tree and shake you down,' " but then he realizes that her fear is genuine, and for a moment he is puzzled: " 'Hold tight awhile till I think what to do. / I'll bend the tree down and let you down by it.' " This descent marks her second birth, and with it the fall into her first realization of mortality. The echo on the word, "down," in her brother's voice is sustained in the old woman's comment, "I don't know much about the letting down." However, when she feels the revolving earth again under her stocking feet, she knows now how to look deeply: "I know I looked long at my curled-up fingers." That quintessential image intimates her monkey ancestry, her future old age, and, above all, her power to hold on. Her brother, aware of his own responsibility in getting her up into the tree, and no doubt somewhat fearful himself, projects the blame onto her: " 'Don't you weigh anything? / Try to weigh something next time, so you won't / Be run off by birch trees into space.' " This frightening moment is remembered as comic from the distant perspective of present time, and the reader, too, enjoys the humor. The brother, however, has taken his sister as far as he can in his role of guide, and it remains for the old woman to make her own interpretation of her brother's crucial distinction between *weight* and *knowledge*, and her own interpretation of the symbolism inherent in "letting go" in the epilogue.

Once again she directly addresses her friends at the birthday party. Contrary to her brother's tease, "Try to weigh something next time," it was her weight that brought her back to earth, to her own "extra" life, which she now celebrates. What she lacked was not weight, but the knowledge of weight—the knowledge of mortality: "My brother had been nearer right before. / I had not taken the first step in knowledge." Learning here is likened to walking: the hike into the woods to gather grapes has its equivalent in an inner journey of the mind, making the literal landscape a symbolic one as well. The first step in knowledge, with its concomitant fear, is the awareness of death. To "let go with the hands" thus implies the necessity and inevitability of relinquishing one's own body back "down" to the "revolving" earth. Physically, one cannot hold on to life. The awareness of death does not require, however, that one stop loving life. Ceasing to

care should not be a defense against desiring to hold on to a
life that you must let go:

> I had not learned to let go with the hands,
> As still I have not learned to with the heart,
> And have no wish to with the heart—nor need,
> That I can see. The mind is not the heart.

The distinction that the old woman makes between the mind
and heart is that the mind must "let go" while the heart must
"hold on," but this apparent contradiction needs to be reconciled. Both attitudes toward life and death are necessary: the
mind must affirm the equally valid knowledge of the heart.
Her brother's words, "Hold on with all your might when I let
go," have assumed a deep meaning for her, she has made
them her own, and thus the covenant between them lives on
in her story.

The old woman's thoughts now turn in empathy to the
"others"—those who desire to escape thought in order not to
face the reality of death, those who wish for the oblivion of
"sleep." She knows that she, too, might yet suffer such a
failure of integrity and courage:

> I may yet live, as I know others live,
> To wish in vain to let go with the mind—
> Of cares, at night, to sleep.

Confronting this final fear, however, the fear of the loss of self
even in life, the old woman affirms her hard-won knowledge
that "nothing tells me / That I need learn to let go with the
heart." Just as the Bible says that "every tree is known by its
own fruit," so, too, the old woman becomes known to us, her
inheritors, by the fruit of her knowledge, by her taste of humankind's fall, embodied in her comic parable about her initiation into the knowledge of mortality. But it is not just the
mind's knowledge of mortality that matters; equally important is the attitude that the heart takes toward that knowledge. Her attitude is one of humor and sustained caring, and
that attitude remains with us as her enduring inheritance.

IV

Two summers ago I suffered my first angina attack while working in my garden. I was admiring the progress of my tomatoes toward succulent ripeness, and the late afternoon sun felt like a "savage source"—to use Wallace Stevens's phrase. Looking back, I like the appropriateness of that scene, since so many of my poems depend on garden imagery. My first thought, however, was one of denial: it was heartburn, surely, that afflicted me, my stomach had betrayed me, and I ignored the warning. But not for long. Within the next two weeks, whenever I tried to exert myself, I became breathless; I lacked the stamina that I have counted on all my life, and the pains in my chest were unmistakable. A stress test confirmed what I suspected, since I could not walk on the treadmill for more than a minute. Subsequently, an angiogram indicated that the four major arteries leading into my heart were almost entirely blocked. I was sent home to wait for an opening in the hospital's operating schedule, but two nights later I had another attack and was taken to the hospital in Burlington by ambulance. My wife was helping our oldest son move into his room at Yale, and the two of them drove through the night from New Haven to see me. I was stabilized with a nitroglycerin drip and scheduled for surgery three days later.

Those three days gave me time to prepare myself and collect my thoughts. My own father had died when he was only forty-six, after five years of debilitating illness, and I viewed myself as fortunate for having survived for fifty-seven vigorous years. Yes, I had enjoyed my life—I had relished my roles as husband, father, poet, and teacher. My reveries were interrupted, however, by my genial roommate, a Catholic priest, who felt obliged to cheer me up by assuring me of God's love and his promise of eternal life. Before he left, he insisted on blessing me, and because I was moved by the sweetness of his caring, I did not tell him that I was a confirmed atheist, that I wanted to face death without consolations that were false to me. I thought of Wallace Stevens whose whole body of poems affirms that we have only this life, but who, so it is rumored, called upon God in his last moments, and I took pride in realizing that I was not afraid, that I could remain true to my own beliefs.

The surgeon came in to introduce himself and outline his procedures. He was young and athletic-looking, and the moment we shook hands I trusted him. His fingers were long and thin, but his grip was firm, suggesting strength under control, and I said to him, "Remember that the heart is not just an organ, it's a metaphor as well." He informed me that he had been an English major at college, but that he didn't consider himself adept enough at dissecting poems, so had become a surgeon. I was determined to convey to him that although I loved life I did not want to survive the operation in a debilitated state as the result of a stroke and have my life dragged out as my father's had been. I wished to be remembered as vigorous and defiant. I did not want my family to be burdened with a prolonged and hopeless illness. The doctor indicated his understanding and assent to my request, and I felt relieved. Quoting Yeats, I declaimed that I chose to go "Proud, open-eyed and laughing to the tomb." Ah, those words felt good!

The next day the anesthesiologist visited me to explain his procedures. I was listening to my portable CD player when he arrived, and he asked me to show him how it worked. When he listened to the earphones, he was impressed. I asked him if he would be willing to hook me up to the earphones in the intensive care recovery room so that I could wake up listening to Mozart. "Since I'll be attached to so many tubes," I argued, "what difference will one more connection make?" "We've never done that here before," he said. "If I wake up to the music of Mozart," I replied, "whatever world I'm in will be just fine with me." I believe he surprised himself when he agreed, and I chose Mozart's complete piano sonatas for my hoped-for mundane resurrection.

The first thing that I remember in emerging dimly from the anesthetic was Mozart—Mozart whose music I had sung to myself a thousand times to assuage personal sorrow or to heighten jubilation. How much Mozartian time passed, I cannot know, but my next recollection is of my wife's voice telling me that the operation had gone well. I still could not open my eyes, but when my son took my hand—I knew it was *his* hand—I squeezed it as hard as I could. I must have drifted off again, but I recall that I thought of Wordsworth's Michael, how I wanted to be Wordsworth's "second self" in the Vermont landscape; I wanted to write more poems. I pictured the stone walls I had built with my son to frame our property, and I felt that palpable covenant between us. Weeks later, he told me that while he was holding my hand, he looked down at my feet and saw that I was trying to keep time to the music. "I knew then that you would be all right," he said.

My roommate in the recovery ward moaned during the night, and I resented the bastard. I wanted illness to be mine alone, unique and unforgettable. I told my attractive nurse that if she insisted on taking my temperature rectally at night she would have to marry me when I recovered, but she found my charm resistible. They allowed me to leave the hospital two days early, indicating that the breath of life was still strong within me. Two weeks after I got home I was walking a mile a day, but one afternoon my fever shot up, and my wife took me back to the hospital. I protested with what strength I had when they put me into a wheelchair, according to hospital rules, but I could see the tears in my wife's eyes as she watched me trying to assert myself. We were informed that I had developed an infection of the sternum, and the doctor wanted to admit me again to the hospital. But I refused. I wanted to be at home; I wanted to have my music and the view of my fruit trees and the Green Mountains.

My son left his job to return home and help my wife take care of me for the next ten days, since I had become too weak to lift myself out of bed, and twice a day I was required to sit in a hot bath to help the open wound in my chest drain. One evening, when the red maples had already begun to brighten, I asked my son to put on some Mozart. But I realized when the music began that I could not fully absorb its passionate beauty, that listening required strength to care as well as alertness of mind. I thought that having lost the energy to care perhaps I was ready to die. But there must have been enough caring left in me to hate the feeling of not caring, and I soon imagined myself splitting wood for the oncoming winter. I had learned something about the temptation of letting go, how the wish for release, "to cease upon the midnight with no pain," can flood your whole being.

By spring much of my strength had returned. I was happy to resume my routine of spring planting and tree-tending. But the infection seethed up again, and I had to return to the hospital for intravenous antibiotic treatments. I told my wife that I had begun to think of the Book of Job as a comedy. Before sending me home, the doctors decided to insert a catheter into my chest for administering antibiotics for the next six weeks. As I left the hospital, the attending physician advised me to take up meditation: "You need to empty your mind," she said, "for at least an hour a day. You need to relieve yourself of the pressures of thought." "How do you know that your mind is empty if you don't have a thought to tell you so?" I quipped. "Listen, Doctor," I then said, with professorial authority, "I've spent my whole life trying to fill my mind. I'm not going to try to empty it now. There's lots of Mozart in my mind. And lots of Shakespeare."

I'm restored to full health again, now that I have a normal flow of blood to the heart. Yet, having written a will for Clayfeld, the fictive protagonist of my recent book of narrative poems, I have decided to write a legal will of my own. My eighty-four-year-old mother sent me a copy of her will, which includes the following lines: "Where the application of life-prolonging procedures would serve only to artificially prolong the dying process, I direct that such procedures be withheld, and that I be permitted to die naturally." I have asked my lawyer to include the same statement in my will. "Naturally," for me is the key word; it implies "letting go" because an upright man must proudly continue to care about the dignity of life. I have instructed my lawyer, further, to put in my will that I want to be considered brain dead if a forty-eight-hour period elapses without my making a pun. I don't want to leave it to my doctors to decide when I have lost my humanity. Laughter, for me, is the truest index of our humanity in braving fate. I want to strut out "laughing to the tomb." A man should choose his own last gesture, his own last words:

> Here lies upright Bob Pack with his CD,
> Who thought will power could lighten gravity.

But there are many words to savor, cherish, and set forth before the last, and in our family there is the impediment of dyslexia. My mother is notorious among us for confusing words and names. Before she gets to "Bobby," she will often call "Tommy," her brother's name, or "Carl," the name of her first husband, which is also the name of my sister's son. A few years ago when my mother called to tell me that my sister's younger son was planning a trip to Africa, I asked her, "Where in Africa is he going? Africa is a big place." She paused for a moment, and then said, "Zabars, I think he's going to Zabars." I reminded her that Zabars is her favorite delicatessen in Manhattan. "Well," she replied, "I just hope that he eats well over there."

Although I was unhappy at college, my mother did not allow me to transfer to another college because, she insisted, my father had told her shortly before he died that he wanted me to go to Dartmouth. Though my spirits did not improve, I followed my father's wishes as my mother had conveyed them to me. Many years later, she apologized for having made me remain at Dartmouth against my wishes. "I don't think your father would have objected to your transferring," she speculated. "Let it go, Mom," I tried to console her; "I've

got new troubles now." More years went by. I had been di-
vorced and was now happily remarried with children of my
own. My mother and I were reminiscing. She was telling me
how dashing and energetic my father had been before he took
ill, how, as a state senator from the Bronx, he had worked
under Herbert Lehman when he was governor of New York
and how he would have been in line to run for governor
himself. Then her look darkened. "Bobby," she said, "it still
bothers me that I prevented you from changing colleges when
you wanted to." Astonished, I exclaimed, "For God's sake,
Mom, let it go; you can't hold yourself responsible for everything in the past." "But, Bobby," she went on, "I'm not sure
that your father said he wanted you to attend Dartmouth. I
think he might have said Williams."

Perhaps our family dyslexia in some inverse way has been
the source of my wanting to be a poet, to hold on to words, to
make the rhythm and sound of words convey the feelings of
their meanings. Perhaps all achievement has hidden roots
in the fear of vulnerability and of incompetence, and, above
all, in the dread of death—for everything we have learned to
love that death will take away. On her last birthday, my
mother took me aside to tell me that she is counting on me to
look after the family when she is gone. "A family is like
a hand," she said; "fingers are useless one by one." In my
mind she merged with the figure of the old woman in Frost's
"Wild Grapes," and I could see before me in my mother's
veined hands the image of the "curled-up fingers" of Frost's
woman when she was five years old and had just descended
from the birch tree. "Mom," I said, "don't you remember
that on her deathbed Grandma called us all in to hear her
prepared last words—"A family is like a hand." "I know," my
mother said, "it's easy to forget, but some words shouldn't
get lost. I wanted you to hear those words again. I want you
to remember."

જી

William Wordsworth

MICHAEL

A Pastoral Poem

If from the public way you turn your steps
Up the tumultuous brook of Greenhead Ghyll,
You will suppose that with an upright path
Your feet must struggle; in such bold ascent
The pastoral mountains front you, face to face.
But, courage! for around that boisterous brook
The mountains have all opened out themselves,
And made a hidden valley of their own.
No habitation can be seen; but they
Who journey thither find themselves alone
With a few sheep, with rocks and stones, and kites
That overhead are sailing in the sky.
It is in truth an utter solitude;
Nor should I have made mention of this Dell
But for one object which you might pass by,
Might see and notice not. Beside the brook
Appears a straggling heap of unhewn stones!
And to that simple object appertains
A story—unenriched with strange events,
Yet not unfit, I deem, for the fireside,
Or for the summer shade. It was the first
Of those domestic tales that spake to me
Of Shepherds, dwellers in the valleys, men
Whom I already loved—not verily
For their own sakes, but for the fields and hills
Where was their occupation and abode.
And hence this Tale, while I was yet a Boy
Careless of books, yet having felt the power
Of Nature, by the gentle agency
Of natural objects, led me on to feel
For passions that were not my own, and think
(At random and imperfectly indeed)
On man, the heart of man, and human life.
Therefore, although it be a history

Homely and rude, I will relate the same
For the delight of a few natural hearts;
And, with yet fonder feeling, for the sake
Of youthful Poets, who among these hills
Will be my second self when I am gone.

Upon the forest-side in Grasmere Vale
There dwelt a Shepherd, Michael was his name;
An old man, stout of heart, and strong of limb.
His bodily frame had been from youth to age
Of an unusual strength: his mind was keen,
Intense, and frugal, apt for all affairs,
And in his shepherd's calling he was prompt
And watchful more than ordinary men.
Hence had he learned the meaning of all winds,
Of blasts of every tone; and oftentimes,
When others heeded not, he heard the South
Make subterraneous music, like the noise
Of bagpipers on distant Highland hills.
The Shepherd, at such warning, of his flock
Bethought him, and he to himself would say,
'The winds are now devising work for me!'
And, truly, at all times, the storm, that drives
The traveller to a shelter, summoned him
Up to the mountains: he had been alone
Amid the heart of many thousand mists,
That came to him, and left him, on the heights.
So lived he till his eightieth year was past.
And grossly that man errs, who should suppose
That the green valleys, and the streams and rocks,
Were things indifferent to the Shepherd's thoughts.
Fields, where with cheerful spirits he had breathed
The common air; hills, which with vigorous step
He had so often climbed; which had impressed
So many incidents upon his mind
Of hardship, skill or courage, joy or fear;
Which, like a book, preserved the memory
Of the dumb animals, who he had saved,
Had fed or sheltered, linking to such acts
The certainty of honourable gain;

Those fields, those hills—what could they less? had laid
Strong hold on his affections, were to him
A pleasurable feeling of blind love,
The pleasure which there is in life itself.

   His days had not been passed in singleness.
His Helpmate was a comely matron, old—
Though younger than himself full twenty years.
She was a woman of a stirring life,
Whose heart was in her house; two wheels she had
Of antique form: this large, for spinning wool;
That small, for flax; and, if one wheel had rest,
It was because the other was at work.
The Pair had but one inmate in their house,
An only Child, who had been born to them
When Michael, telling o'er his years, began
To deem that he was old—in shepherd's phrase,
With one foot in the grave. This only Son,
With two brave sheep-dogs tried in many a storm,
The one of an inestimable worth,
Made all their household. I may truly say,
That they were as a proverb in the vale
For endless industry. When day was gone,
And from their occupations out of doors
The Son and Father were come home, even then,
Their labour did not cease; unless when all
Turned to the cleanly supper-board, and there,
Each with a mess of pottage and skimmed milk,
Sat round the basket piled with oaten cakes,
And their plain home-made cheese. Yet when the meal
Was ended, Luke (for so the Son was named)
And his old Father both betook themselves
To such convenient work as might employ
Their hands by the fire-side; perhaps to card
Wool for the Housewife's spindle, or repair
Some injury done to sickle, flail, or scythe,
Or other implement of house or field.

   Down from the ceiling, by the chimney's edge,
That in our ancient uncouth country style
With huge and black projection overbrowed

Large space beneath, as duly as the light
Of day grew dim the Housewife hung a lamp;
An aged utensil, which had performed
Service beyond all others of its kind.
Early at evening did it burn—and late,
Surviving comrade of uncounted hours,
Which, going by from year to year, had found,
And left, the couple neither gay perhaps
Nor cheerful, yet with objects and with hopes,
Living a life of eager industry.
And now, when Luke had reached his eighteenth year,
There by the light of this old lamp they sate,
Father and Son, while far into the night
The Housewife plied her own peculiar work,
Making the cottage through the silent hours
Murmur as with the sound of summer flies.
This light was famous in its neighbourhood,
And was a public symbol of the life
That thrifty Pair had lived. For, as it chanced,
Their cottage on a plot of rising ground
Stood single, with large prospect, north and south,
High into Easedale, up to Dunmail-Raise
And westward to the village near the lake;
And from this constant light, so regular,
And so far seen, the House itself, by all
Who dwelt within the limits of the vale,
Both old and young, was named The Evening Star.

Thus living on through such a length of years,
The Shepherd, if he loved himself, must needs
Have loved his Helpmate; but to Michael's heart
This son of his old age was yet more dear—
Less from instinctive tenderness, the same
Fond spirit that blindly works in the blood of all—
Than that a child, more than all other gifts
That earth can offer to declining man,
Brings hope with it, and forward-looking thoughts,
And stirrings of inquietude, when they
By tendency of nature needs must fail.

Exceeding was the love he bare to him,
His heart and his heart's joy! For oftentimes
Old Michael, while he was a babe in arms,
Had done him female service, not alone
For pastime and delight, as is the use
Of fathers, but with patient mind enforced
To acts of tenderness; and he had rocked
His cradle, as with a woman's gentle hand.

    And, in a later time, ere yet the Boy
Had put on boy's attire, did Michael love,
Albeit of a stern unbending mind,
To have the Young-one in his sight, when he
Wrought in the field, or on his shepherd's stool
Sate with a fettered sheep before him stretched
Under the large old oak, that near his door
Stood single, and, from matchless depth of shade,
Chosen for the Shearer's covert from the sun,
Thence in our rustic dialect was called
The Clipping Tree, a name which yet it bears.
There, while they two were sitting in the shade,
With others round them, earnest all and blithe,
Would Michael exercise his heart with looks
Of fond correction and reproof bestowed
Upon the Child, if he disturbed the sheep
By catching at their legs, or with his shouts
Scared them, while they lay still beneath the shears.

    And when by Heaven's good grace the boy grew up
A healthy Lad, and carried in his cheek
Two steady roses that were five years old;
Then Michael from a winter coppice cut
With his own hand a sapling, which he hooped
With iron, making it throughout in all
Due requisites a perfect shepherd's staff,
And gave it to the Boy; wherewith equipt
He as a watchman oftentimes was placed
At gate or gap, to stem or turn the flock;
And, to his office prematurely called,
There stood the urchin, as you will divine,

Something between a hindrance and a help;
And for this cause not always, I believe,
Receiving from his Father hire of praise;
Though nought was left undone which staff, or voice,
Or looks, or threatening gestures, could perform.

But soon as Luke, full ten years old, could stand
Against the mountain blasts; and to the heights,
Not fearing toil, nor length of weary ways,
He with his Father daily went, and they
Were as companions, why should I relate
That objects which the Shepherd loved before
Were dearer now? that from the Boy there came
Feelings and emanations—things which were
Light to the sun and music to the wind;
And that the old Man's heart seemed born again?

Thus in his Father's sight the Boy grew up:
And now, when he had reached his eighteenth year,
He was his comfort and his daily hope.

While in this sort the simple household lived
From day to day, to Michael's ear there came
Distressful tidings. Long before the time
Of which I speak, the Shepherd had been bound
In surety for his brother's son, a man
Of an industrious life, and ample means;
But unforeseen misfortunes suddenly
Had prest upon him; and old Michael now
Was summoned to discharge the forfeiture,
A grievous penalty, but little less
Than half his substance. This unlooked-for claim,
At the first hearing, for a moment took
More hope out of his life than he supposed
That any old man ever could have lost.
As soon as he had armed himself with strength
To look his trouble in the face, it seemed
The Shepherd's sole resource to sell at once
A portion of his patrimonial fields.
Such was his first resolve; he thought again,

And his heart failed him. 'Isabel,' said he,
Two evenings after he had heard the news,
'I have been toiling more than seventy years,
And in the open sunshine of God's love
Have we all lived; yet, if these fields of ours
Should pass into a stranger's hand, I think
That I could not lie quiet in my grave.
Our lot is a hard lot; the sun himself
Has scarcely been more diligent than I;
And I have lived to be a fool at last
To my own family. An evil man
That was, and made an evil choice, if he
Were false to us; and, if he were not false,
There are ten thousand to whom loss like this
Had been no sorrow. I forgive him;—but
'Twere better to be dumb than to talk thus.

   'When I began, my purpose was to speak
Of remedies and of a cheerful hope.
Our Luke shall leave us, Isabel; the land
Shall not go from us, and it shall be free;
He shall possess it, free as is the wind
That passes over it. We have, thou know'st,
Another kinsman—he will be our friend
In this distress. He is a prosperous man,
Thriving in trade—and Luke to him shall go,
And with his kinsman's help and his own thrift
He quickly will repair this loss, and then
He may return to us. If here he stay,
What can be done? Where every one is poor,
What can be gained?'
                    At this the old Man paused,
And Isabel sat silent, for her mind
Was busy, looking back into past times.
There's Richard Bateman, thought she to herself,
He was a parish-boy—at the church-door
They made a gathering for him, shillings, pence,
And halfpennies, wherewith the neighbours bought
A basket, which they filled with pedlar's wares;

And, with this basket on his arm, the lad
Went up to London, found a master there,
Who, out of many, chose the trusty boy
To go and overlook his merchandise
Beyond the seas; where he grew wondrous rich,
And left estates and monies to the poor,
And, at his birth-place, built a chapel floored
With marble, which he sent from foreign lands.
These thoughts, and many others of like sort,
Passed quickly through the mind of Isabel,
And her face brightened. The old Man was glad,
And thus resumed: —'Well, Isabel! this scheme
These two days has been meat and drink to me.
Far more than we have lost is left us yet.
—We have enough—I wish indeed that I
Were younger; —but this hope is a good hope.
Make ready Luke's best garments, of the best
Buy for him more, and let us send him forth
To-morrow, or the next day, or to-night:
If he *could* go, the Boy should go to-night.'

Here Michael ceased, and to the fields went forth
With a light heart. The Housewife for five days
Was restless morn and night, and all day long
Wrought on with her best fingers to prepare
Things needful for the journey of her son.
But Isabel was glad when Sunday came
To stop her in her work: for, when she lay
By Michael's side, she through the last two nights
Heard him, how he was troubled in his sleep:
And when they rose at morning she could see
That all his hopes were gone. That day at noon
She said to Luke, while they two by themselves
Were sitting at the door, 'Thou must not go:
We have no other Child but thee to lose,
None to remember—do not go away,
For if thou leave thy Father he will die.'
The Youth made answer with a jocund voice;
And Isabel, when she had told her fears,

Recovered heart. That evening her best fare
Did she bring forth, and all together sat
Like happy people round a Christmas fire.

With daylight Isabel resumed her work;
And all the ensuing week the house appeared
As cheerful as a grove in spring; at length
The expected letter from their kinsman came,
With kind assurances that he would do
His utmost for the welfare of the Boy;
To which, requests were added, that forthwith
He might be sent to him. Ten times or more
The letter was read over; Isabel
Went forth to show it to the neighbours round;
Nor was there at that time on English land
A prouder heart than Luke's. When Isabel
Had to her house returned, the old Man said,
'He shall depart to-morrow.' To this word
The Housewife answered, talking much of things
Which, if at such short notice he should go,
Would surely be forgotten. But at length
She gave consent, and Michael was at ease.

Near the tumultuous brook of Greenhead Ghyll,
In that deep valley, Michael had designed
To build a Sheep-fold; and, before he heard
The tidings of his melancholy loss,
For this same purpose he had gathered up
A heap of stones, which by the streamlet's edge
Lay thrown together, ready for the work.
With Luke that evening thitherward he walked;
And soon as they had reached the place he stopped,
And thus the old Man spake to him: 'My son,
To-morrow thou wilt leave me: with full heart
I look upon thee, for thou art the same
That wert a promise to me ere thy birth,
And all thy life hast been my daily joy.
I will relate to thee some little part
Of our two histories; 'twill do thee good
When thou art from me, even if I should touch

On things thou canst not know of. —After thou
First cam'st into the world—as oft befalls
To new-born infants—thou didst sleep away
Two days, and blessings from thy Father's tongue
Then fell upon thee. Day by day passed on,
And still I loved thee with increasing love.
Never to living ear came sweeter sounds
Than when I heard thee by our own fireside
First uttering, without words, a natural tune;
While thou, a feeding babe, didst in thy joy
Sing at thy Mother's breast. Month followed month,
And in the open fields my life was passed
And on the mountains; else I think that thou
Hadst been brought up upon thy Father's knees.
But we were playmates, Luke: among these hills,
As well thou knowest, in us the old and young
Have played together, nor with me didst thou
Lack any pleasure which a boy can know.'
Luke had a manly heart; but at these words
He sobbed aloud. The old Man grasped his hand,
And said, 'Nay, do not take it so—I see
That these are things of which I need not speak.
—Even to the utmost I have been to thee
A kind and a good Father: and herein
I but repay a gift, which I myself
Received at others' hands; for, though now old
Beyond the common life of man, I still
Remember them who loved me in my youth.
Both of them sleep together; here they lived,
As all their Forefathers had done; and, when
At length their time was come, they were not loth
To give their bodies to the family mould.
I wished that thou shouldst live the life they lived,
But 'tis a long time to look back, my Son,
And see so little gain from threescore years.
These fields were burthened when they came to me;
Till I was forty years of age, not more
Than half of my inheritance was mine.
I toiled and toiled; God blessed me in my work,

And till these three weeks past the land was free.
—It looks as if it never could endure
Another master. Heaven forgive me, Luke,
If I judge ill for thee, but it seems good
That thou shouldst go.'
                        At this the old Man paused;
Then, pointing to the stones near which they stood,
Thus, after a short silence, he resumed:
'This was a work for us; and now, my Son,
It is a work for me. But, lay one stone—
Here, lay it for me, Luke, with thine own hands.
Nay, Boy be of good hope; —we both may live
To see a better day. At eighty-four
I still am strong and hale; —do thou thy part;
I will do mine. —I will begin again
With many tasks that were resigned to thee:
Up to the heights, and in among the storms,
Will I without thee go again, and do
All works which I was wont to do alone,
Before I knew thy face. —Heaven bless thee, Boy!
Thy heart these two weeks has been beating fast
With many hopes; it should be so—yes—yes—
I knew that thou couldst never have a wish
To leave me, Luke: thou hast been bound to me
Only by links of love: when thou art gone,
What will be left to us! —But I forget
My purposes. Lay now the corner-stone,
As I requested; and hereafter, Luke,
When thou art gone away, should evil men
Be thy companions, think of me, my Son,
And of this moment; hither turn thy thoughts,
And God will strengthen thee; amid all fear
And all temptation, Luke, I pray that thou
May'st bear in mind the life thy Fathers lived,
Who, being innocent, did for that cause
Bestir them in good deeds. Now, fare thee well—
When thou return'st, thou in this place wilt see
A work which is not here: a covenant
'Twill be between us; but, whatever fate

Befall thee, I shall love thee to the last,
And bear thy memory with me to the grave.'

    The Shepherd ended here; and Luke stooped down,
And, as his Father had requested, laid
The first stone of the Sheep-fold. At the sight
The old Man's grief broke from him; to his heart
He pressed his Son, he kissed him and wept;
And to the house together they returned.
—Hushed was that House in peace, or seeming peace
Ere the night fell; —with morrow's dawn the Boy
Began his journey, and, when he had reached
The public way, he put on a bold face;
And all the neighbours, as he passed their doors,
Came forth with wishes and with farewell prayers,
That followed him till he was out of sight.

    A good report did from their Kinsman come,
Of Luke and his well-doing: and the Boy
Wrote loving letters, full of wondrous news,
Which, as the Housewife phrased it, were throughout
'The prettiest letters that were ever seen.'
Both parents read them with rejoicing hearts.
So, many months passed on; and once again
The Shepherd went about his daily work
With confident and cheerful thoughts; and now
Sometimes when he could find a leisure hour
He to that valley took his way, and there
Wrought at the Sheep-fold. Meantime Luke began
To slacken in his duty; and, at length,
He in the dissolute city gave himself
To evil courses; ignominy and shame
Fell on him, so that he was driven at last
To seek a hiding-place beyond the seas.

    There is a comfort in the strength of love;
'Twill make a thing endurable, which else
Would overset the brain, or break the heart:
I have conversed with more than one who well
Remember the old Man, and what he was

Years after he had heard this heavy news.
His bodily frame had been from youth to age
Of an unusual strength. Among the rocks
He went, and still looked up to sun and cloud,
And listened to the wind; and, as before,
Performed all kinds of labour for his sheep,
And for the land, his small inheritance.
And to that hollow dell from time to time
Did he repair, to build the Fold of which
His flock had need. 'Tis not forgotten yet
The pity which was then in every heart
For the old Man—and 'tis believed by all
That many and many a day he thither went,
And never lifted up a single stone.

     There, by the Sheep-fold, sometimes was he seen
Sitting alone, or with his faithful Dog,
Then old, beside him, lying at his feet.
The length of full seven years, from time to time,
He at the building of this Sheep-fold wrought,
And left the work unfinished when he died.
Three years, or little more, did Isabel
Survive her Husband: at her death the estate
Was sold, and went into a stranger's hand.
The Cottage which was named The Evening Star
Is gone—the ploughshare has been through the ground
On which it stood; great changes have been wrought
In all the neighbourhood; —yet the oak is left
That grew beside their door; and the remains
Of the unfinished Sheep-fold may be seen
Beside the boisterous brook of Greenhead Ghyll.

Robert Frost

Wild Grapes

What tree may not the fig be gathered from?
The grape may not be gathered from the birch?
It's all you know the grape, or know the birch.
As a girl gathered from the birch myself
Equally with my weight in grapes, one autumn,
I ought to know what tree the grape is fruit of.
I was born, I suppose, like anyone,
And grew to be a little boyish girl
My brother could not always leave at home.
But that beginning was wiped out in fear
The day I swung suspended with the grapes,
And was come after like Eurydice
And brought down safely from the upper regions;
And the life I live now's an extra life
I can waste as I please on whom I please.
So if you see me celebrate two birthdays,
And give myself out as two different ages,
One of them five years younger than I look—

One day my brother led me to a glade
Where a white birch he knew of stood alone,
Wearing a thin headdress of pointed leaves,
And heavy on her heavy hair behind,
Against her neck, an ornament of grapes.
Grapes, I knew grapes from having seen them last year.
One bunch of them, and there began to be
Bunches all round me growing in white birches,
The way they grew round Leif the Lucky's German;
Mostly as much beyond my lifted hands, though,
As the moon used to seem when I was younger,
And only freely to be had for climbing.
My brother did the climbing; and at first
Threw me down grapes to miss and scatter
And have to hunt for in sweet fern and hardhack;
Which gave him some time to himself to eat,
But not so much, perhaps, as a boy needed.

So then, to make me wholly self-supporting,
He climbed still higher and bent the tree to earth
And put it in my hands to pick my own grapes.
"Here, take a treetop, I'll get down another.
Hold on with all your might when I let go."
I said I had the tree. It wasn't true.
The opposite was true. The tree had me.
The minute it was left with me alone,
It caught me up as if I were the fish
And it the fishpole. So I was translated
To loud cries from my brother of "Let go!
Don't you know anything, you girl? Let go!"
But I, with something of the baby grip
Acquired ancestrally in just such trees
When wilder mothers than our wildest now
Hung babies out on branches by the hands
To dry or wash or tan, I don't know which
(You'll have to ask an evolutionist)—
I held on uncomplainingly for life.
My brother tried to make me laugh to help me.
"What are you doing up there in those grapes?
Don't be afraid. A few of them won't hurt you.
I mean, they won't pick you if you don't them."
Much danger of my picking anything!
By that time I was pretty well reduced
To a philosophy of hang-and-let-hang.
"Now you know how it feels," my brother said,
"To be a bunch of fox grapes, as they call them,
That when it thinks it has escaped the fox
By growing where it shouldn't—on a birch,
Where a fox wouldn't think to look for it—
And if he looked and found it, couldn't reach it—
Just then come you and I to gather it.
Only you have the advantage of the grapes
In one way: you have one more stem to cling by,
And promise more resistance to the picker."

One by one I lost off my hat and shoes,
And still I clung. I let my head fall back,

And shut my eyes against the sun, my ears
Against my brother's nonsense. "Drop," he said,
"I'll catch you in my arms. It isn't far."
(Stated in lengths of him it might not be.)
"Drop or I'll shake the tree and shake you down."
Grim silence on my part as I sank lower,
My small wrists stretching till they showed the banjo strings.
"Why, if she isn't serious about it!
Hold tight awhile till I think what to do.
I'll bend the tree down and let you down by it."
I don't know much about the letting down;
But once I felt ground with my stocking feet
And the world came revolving back to me,
I know I looked long at my curled-up fingers,
Before I straightened them and brushed the bark off.
My brother said: "Don't you weigh anything?
Try to weigh something next time, so you won't
Be run off with by birch trees into space."

It wasn't my not weighing anything
So much as my not knowing anything—
My brother had been nearer right before.
I had not taken the first step in knowledge;
I had not learned to let go with the hands,
As still I have not learned to with the heart,
And have no wish to with the heart—nor need,
That I can see. The mind—is not the heart.
I may yet live, as I know others live,
To wish in vain to let go with the mind—
Of cares, at night, to sleep; but nothing tells me
That I need learn to let go with the heart.

Laughter at the Abyss:
Hardy and Robinson

I

E. A. ROBINSON is the American inheritor of Thomas Hardy's unusual gift for the creation of dramas within the confines of lyric form. In both poets, the ability to tell stories, to create characters who reveal themselves under the pressure of circumstance, is enhanced by their expressive control of image, rhyme, meter, and stanzaic form. They are both able to epitomize a human life in the rendering of a particular incident and the behavior it elicits. Hardy and Robinson combine similar lyric and narrative techniques, and they are philosophically akin in their gloomy assessment of human endeavor: their main theme is failure—failure in love, failure to prevent or avoid violence, and failure to find ultimate consolation or happiness in an indifferent universe. Yet both employ laughter and comic effects in their poetic styles, and both envision laughter as a great human power, perhaps the last defense in the face of the existential void. Hardy wrote: "Life laughed and moved on unsubdued," and Robinson, de-

scribing the fatal weakness of spirit of a character named
Clavering, asserted that he "died because he couldn't laugh."

I must confess to a touch of mischief in choosing to write
about laughter in two of the gloomiest poets of the last hundred years, but my purpose is to reveal how laughter serves
not only as a defense against despair, but also as the positive
embodiment of poetic art. I have selected three poems for discussion in which laughter, combined with irony and parody,
leaves the speaker's voice before the ending of the poem—as
if laughter can take the poet only so far when confronting the
great sources of human despondency and despair, such as
human cruelty and war. In the fourth poem, however, laughter is sustained until the end. As I see it, this poem, Robinson's "Ben Jonson Entertains a Man from Stratford," which
imagines the character of William Shakespeare as the "father
of the world," is about the transfiguring power of art.

Sigmund Freud in his late essay "Humour" (1928) tells us
that in humor the superego speaks "words of comfort to the
intimidated ego." This is a remarkable statement since Freud
usually portrays the superego, which "inherits the parental
function," as severe, chastising, and constraining. In the case
of humor, however, it is as if the father, the superego, allows
the son, the ego, a moment of play exempt from the strictures
of reality. Freud calls this holiday from the demands of the
reality principle "a rare and precious gift." He makes a distinction between the holiday from reality that humor makes
possible in the momentary feeling of triumph that comes in
laughter and the unreality of dreams or insanity. Humor
carries within it a knowledge of the path back to reality, the
world in which the self is limited by nature. This gift of the
father to the son, interiorized as a benevolent dynamic between the superego and the ego, is a form of inner grace much
like that interim when we allow ourselves to inhabit the
timeless world of a poem, a novel, or a play. Although the
superego, according to Freud, is a "stern master," its tough
sense of reality includes the knowledge that we cannot en-

dure reality all the time; we require the respite of temporary illusion. Given this tolerance, the superego can remain true to its disciplining function even though, as Freud says, it may "wink at affording the ego a little gratification."

The forms that such humor takes in poems concerned with the most painful themes, such as old age, the rapaciousness of nature, human aggression and war, or the absence of moral purpose in a godless universe, are manifold. From outrageous punning to extravagant irony, the range of the poet's effects are designed to give readers the feeling that they also can confront whatever truths have to be faced through the power of laughter. In their capacities to laugh, poets allow themselves temporary illusions of being in control, but these illusions fabricate their own truths by virtue of the fact that they acknowledge themselves as illusions. Such laughter may also be seen as a form of reconciliation between father and son within the familial space of the mind, between the determination to see the world as it is and the acceptance of our vulnerability as creatures who cannot relinquish the need for pleasure. A laughing father may seem less remote, less an embodiment of intractable and repressive social or cultural forces if the son is able to partake of the father's spirit of humor.

II

The speaker at the opening of Thomas Hardy's poem "Channel Firing" is a skeleton lying in a cemetery beside a church, who has been awakened by the noise of "great guns." The skeleton first thinks that "Judgment-day" has arrived, and he sits "upright" in his coffin to converse with his fellow skeletons. Meanwhile, inside the church, the "mouse let fall the altar-crumb" as if interrupted in the act of communion. In order to assuage the skeletons' fears, God tells them that it is only "gunnery practice out at sea," not judgment day, and that the conditions of the world have not changed: as usual, men are preparing for war. This situation is grounded in farce, and the irony of God's supposedly consoling assurance that this is not judgment day extends this humor into theological comedy. Hardy offers his readers a parody of divine grace when God includes the gunners in his ironic consolation by saying that it would be a "blessed thing" to be merely dead, for if the gunners were resurrected on judgment day, surely they would be given the demeaning punishment of having to "scour / Hell's floor." God's malicious "Ha, ha" underscores the joke he has made at the expense of both the gunners and the befuddled skeletons.

This diabolical laugh may be read as the iconoclastic Hardy's parody of God's apparent indifference to human suffering. God's laughter here is the ironic equivalent of its opposite—God's creative laughter, as seen in the Book of Job, when God projects his own spirit onto the image of the horse that he has made: "He saith among the trumpets, Ha, ha! and he smelleth the battle afar off." If we assume, moreover, that God's laughter in this poem denotes the absence of a biblical God, then Hardy's creation of a fictive God who does not exist can be seen as a projection of Hardy's own defeated longing for a protecting God, and also as a protection against that longing. Because he cannot bring himself to believe in the traditional Hebrew or Christian God, and because he cannot find another belief to replace Christianity, Hardy only can defend himself through defiant laughter which makes ironic the very God in whom he cannot believe but to whom he wishes he could pray. God's sardonic "Ha, ha" is followed by his further taunting of the skeletons, suggesting capriciously that he may decide not to bring about the apocalypse and the day of resurrection: "It will be warmer when / I blow the trumpet (if indeed / I ever do; for you are men, / and rest eternal sorely need)." "Rest eternal" simply means that the skeletons will have to continue being dead, though even their restfulness is to be questioned, since we witness them sitting up in their coffins. The psychological effect of Hardy's own humor, projected and twisted into God's laughter and joking, is to hold in check Hardy's despair as he faces the human condition: warfare, mendacity, self-deception, and cosmic meaninglessness.

The response of the skeletons to God's ironic jesting is chillingly bland as one wonders, "Will the world ever saner be?" and another, revealing the hypocritical morality in his regrets about his career as a parson, replies: "I wish I had stuck to pipes and beer." The tone of the poem, however, changes radically in the last stanza from comic parody to something that might be described as mystical awe, when the poem's angry and defiant laughter dissolves into allusion and impersonal wonder.

The voice that speaks the poem's last stanza is not the original voice of the skeleton, but a distant consciousness that has borne witness to human strife throughout his story: "Again the guns disturbed the hour, / Roaring their readiness to avenge." Such disturbance, it seems, always has been the inclination, "the readiness," of human nature, and yet by this late date in human history, the original source of human violence—some primal act that evoked the passion for revenge—has been forgotten or repressed. The speaker of this final stanza cannot name what needs to be avenged. Vengeance has ceased to be a response to a specific affront; it has become a condition of the human mind, a cause of further vengeance.

The final two lines of the poem are even more mysterious as they plunge us back into mythic-historical time to evoke a sense of origins and perhaps destiny: "As far inland as Stourton Tower, / And Camelot and starlit Stonehenge." The heavy alliteration of the "st" and "t" sounds sharpens the speaker's breath as it speeds from the teeth to become the stark, highly stressed final phrases. The word, "inland" (like Wordsworth's, "though inland far we be") suggests that early civilization has come from the sea where life first emerged and that some originating force still is taking its course. Stourton Tower refers to Alfred the Great who fought the Vikings and unified England in the ninth century, while Camelot evokes the myth of order and chivalry associated with King Arthur. Stonehenge is a 350-foot wide circle in England's Salisbury Plain that was built about four thousand years ago, no one knows how, as an astronomical calendar that perhaps enabled the priests of the time to make human sacrifices or calculate eclipses and other heavenly events.

What might these priests have witnessed in the configurations of the stars in "starlit Stonehenge"? Might they have seen disaster, the inevitability of human destructiveness, or might they have seen the possibility of human order and civilization? Likewise, does Camelot suggest the potential for an ordered and graceful society, or the inevitable collapse of attempts for order and grace? Does Stourton Tower offer a model in King Alfred, the early champion of Christianity, of social cohesion and purpose, or does it reveal the inevitability of warring forces? Are these images of hope or of despair? Deliberately, Hardy evokes these questions to leave them unresolved, to shock the reader's mind into speculation about both human origins and human endings. This is the final form that Hardy's laughter takes—openness of thought in the face of dread, detachment so profound that it becomes its own kind of passion, as if one could say "Ha, ha" even to a universe in which God is only a fiction to whom no appeal for peace and pity can be made.

Hardy's poem, "God-Forgotten," is even more extreme in its use of parody and comic irony to achieve its effect of depicting human irrationality and meanness by projecting these attributes onto the figure of God. The title of the poem itself cuts both ways in equivocating as to whether man has been forgotten by God or God forgotten by man. The opening tone is mock heroic: the speaker, with a rhetorical flourish, "lo!", assumes the role of the representative of humankind who journeys to heaven to confront God with the "sad" condition of the human race. The speaker is like Job in calling

God to account for human suffering that appears to be undeserved, with no connection between transgression and punishment. Hardy's iconoclastic humor is immediately height-
ened as God's first reply to the moralistic speaker is one of
defensive denial:

> —"The Earth, sayest thou? The Human race?
> By Me created? Sad its lot?
> Nay: I have no remembrance of such place:
> Such world I fashioned not."—

Employing the tactic of claiming that one has no memory of
an event or action for which one could be held responsible,
God immediately reveals that he possesses the human traits
of evasiveness and convenient amnesia.

Not having done anything wrong, but sensing that he is in
danger of God's disapproval, the speaker obsequiously asks
for forgiveness as he reminds God, alluding to the beginning
of the Gospel according to Saint John, "In the beginning was
the word," that God did indeed create the Earth when he
spoke "the word that made it all." God and the speaker are
uncomfortably alike in their hypocrisy, the only difference
between them being God's power and the speaker's deference
to that power. Somewhat placated by the speaker's humbling
of himself, God now feels freer to admit that he did create
humankind, though he covers himself by diminishing the
importance of this particular creation, since there were so
many, and thus rationalizing his initial lapse of memory:
"The Earth of men—let me bethink me. . . . Yea! / I dimly do
recall / Some tiny sphere I built long back / (Mid millions of
such shapes of mine)." God's boasting reminds the speaker
where the power lies in this confrontation. This is Hardy's
parodic version of God's question to Job, "Where wast thou
when I laid the foundations of the earth?" God gets carried
away in depicting his busyness as a creator and the relative
unimportance of one small sphere of life, Earth, when he
says, "It lost my interest from the first," but immediately he

turns his own callousness into blame of human beings for causing what he presumes to be their own self-destruction. When the speaker timidly replies, "Lord, it existeth still," God then accuses humankind of not having stayed in touch with him and delivers a tirade in which his hissing sibilants make him sound suspiciously like Satan in Milton's *Paradise Lost*:

> "It used to ask for gifts of good,
> Till came its severance, self-entailed,
> When sudden silence on that side ensued,
> And has till now prevailed."

Once God gets caught up in the spirit of castigation, he cannot stop himself, and the reader surely recognizes in him the human trait of self-justification. "All other orbs have kept in touch," God accuses, and then God's indulgent reasoning circles round to his first claim that really, he is too busy to be expected to concern himself with human need. It is sad, God argues, that "Earth's race should think that one whose call / Frames, daily, shining spheres of flawless stuff / Must heed their tainted ball. . . ." The reader who is not offended by blasphemy will savor the subtlety of God's contradiction of himself in claiming that he creates, "flawless stuff," yet describes the Earth as "tainted," just as the objective reader will enjoy the broad and aggressive humor in Hardy's portrayal of the pomposity of authority, even divine authority. Hardy's parody of God expresses his own frustration and anger at not being able to find true authority in the universe—an active God who authorizes mercy and justice. The qualities that God lacks in Hardy's version of him are in reality the qualities that Hardy sees lacking in human beings. Hardy projects self-absorption onto God to create a metaphor to show the consequences of the human failure to empathize.

The motive behind Hardy's portrayal of God's failure to assume responsibility and to be compassionate emerges in the poem's next lines in which God's tone begins to change:

> "But sayest it is by pangs distraught,
>   And strife, and silent suffering?—
> Sore grieved am I that injury should be wrought
>   Even on so poor a thing!

Hardy's introducing a note of sympathy in God's psychology reflects his own empathy for the human condition, what elsewhere he calls the "Spirit of Pity." The poem's comedy is right on the edge of heartbreak, yet Hardy is able to look into what he takes to be the cosmic abyss with the aid of laughter. God's moment of pity then leads to another kind of rationalization. Having boasted earlier that he was too busy to concern himself with the human "cry" of pain and need, God now acknowledges his own weakness and limitation when he says to the speaker: "Thou shouldst have learnt that *Not to Mend* / For Me could mean but *Not to Know*." In acknowledging that he is neither omniscient nor infallible, God almost merges with the figure of the speaker; they now partake of the same pathos. In a last attempt to be helpful, God commands his messengers to "straightway put an end / To what men undergo." But even this suggested cure is a failure, since it is ambiguous as a potential source of hope for humankind: does it mean that God will put an end to human suffering, or does it mean that God will solve the problem of suffering by putting an end to life on earth? The irony of the uncertainty is crushing, and it leads the speaker in the last stanzas to the awareness of his own incapacity to imagine God as anything other than a projection of his own weaknesses.

As in "Channel Firing," the relief of comic parody drops from the poem at the end, and the speaker confronts his own fantasy of a heroic journey to heaven that seemed to result in God's sending a messenger to Earth to help relieve the suffering of the human race: "Homing at dawn, I thought to see / One of the Messengers standing by." Even so absurd an illusion as the one Hardy has contrived for this poem is able to deceive the speaker who desperately seeks consolation. Yet, finally, the illusion cannot work. Reality, not God, must have the final word in Hardy's poem when the speaker exclaims, "Oh, childish thought! . . . Yet often it comes to me / When trouble hovers nigh." Hardy's courage resides in his ability both to recognize his own childishness—the poem has been a kind of tantrum in defiance of a father-god who does not exist and therefore cannot protect—and to recognize the human susceptibility to childish fantasy in times of "trouble." The last two lines of the poem, coming after all that bravura parody, are remarkably tender and touching, evoking, I believe, a comprehensive sympathy for humanity that has been latent throughout the poem.

In acknowledging the childish aspect of himself, Hardy, in effect, splits himself into two psychic parts: father and son. It is as if the father allows the child-son to be free, for a time, to indulge in a comic fantasy, to enjoy a respite of laughter, and through that laughter to express his hostility toward the universe which cannot respond to his contorted prayer for attention and understanding. Ironically, Hardy's imagination depends (as Hardy himself is fully aware) upon a god in whom he does not believe—a god, therefore, he can parody and blaspheme and, like the devil, against whom he can vent his moral outrage for the lack of moral authority in the world.

The son's freedom to enjoy and find relief in fantasy and laughter is made possible by the fatherly aspect of Hardy's imagination, which allows the "childish thought" to run its course. Laughter, then, functions as a kind of holiday from reality, when the father relaxes the supervision of his son, which in its serious mode would hold the son to the painful dictates of an indifferent universe. In accepting the son's need, the father also embraces laughter in the face of a cosmic void. Generated out of desperation, laughter serves survival by expressing the mind's need for imagining some form of human victory, some form of power beyond abject helplessness. If the fatherly part of the mind allows the son-child

part of the mind an interval of play, then what is enacted is a
benevolent form of authority that replaces the absent authority of God. For the adult with a child's needs still within him,
permissible play may be manifested in the art of poetry.

III

Robinson's poem "Mr. Flood's Party" tells the story of an old
man who is returning home at night after going to town to fill
up his jug with liquor. Since all his friends are dead and he is
alone, he talks to himself, pretending that he and his imagined double are having a party. The poem's speaker at first
appears to be omniscient, and yet there is a hint of person-
ality in the speaker's introduction of the full name, "Eben
Flood," which in the context of a poem about drinking reads
as a pun on *ebb* and *flow*. The stressed vowel sound "o" in
"old" is almost immediately picked up in the crucial word,
"alone," repeated in the opening syllable of the second line in
"Over," and then carried further in the rhyme of "below" and
"know." This lugubrious "o" sound dominates the poem;
though we become less aware of it in the poem's comic
passages, it returns as the poem's final rhyme in "below" and
"ago." The effect of this repeated pattern turns the narrator
from a neutral figure into an emotionally involved witness.

The ironies of Mr. Flood's condition become immediately
apparent in the details given by the speaker to describe his
circumstances. Mr. Flood is living at an "upland hermitage"
that is so lonely that even the hermits have "forsaken" it, just
as Mr. Flood himself seems to have been forsaken. Since Eben
Flood is now without work or occupation, to describe him as
"having leisure" reminds us that involuntary leisure is not a
blessing but a burden and a source of nostalgic regret.

Quoting "The bird is on the wing" from the Rubaiyat,
whose message is to seize pleasure since time is fleeting, Mr.
Flood addresses himself by proposing a toast. He answers
"huskily" in the voice of his agreeable double, but the reader

does not know whether Mr. Flood's voice is husky because of his drinking or because it is thick with emotion. The speaker then describes Mr. Flood through two comparisons, one implicit, the other explicit, both of which are designed to elevate our sense of Mr. Flood, but both of which must be read ironically when we remind ourselves that Mr. Flood is a drunken old man. The speaker's sympathetic wish in behalf of Mr. Flood is revealed in his depiction of his being "Alone, as if enduring to the end" if we hear in those words the echo from the Gospel according to St. Matthew (10.22), "he that endureth to the end shall be saved." Since Mr. Flood is indeed enduring to the end, why can't he, too, be saved? The implied comparison with Jesus' faithful disciples passes immediately into a comparison with Roland, who blew his horn and died sacrificially in battle to protect the retreating troops of Charlemagne. But Roland's "horn," Oliphant, has become Mr. Flood's "jug," and as readers we are uncertain as to whether we are being asked to regard Mr. Flood as heroic or to see his drinking as a parody of heroism, suggesting that he is not worthy of salvation. The speaker goes on to inform us that the "salutations" of his friends that had "honored" him in the past now "Rang thinly till old Eben's eyes were dim." Once again, the speaker offers a descriptive detail that is ambiguous: are Eben's eyes dim because of too much drinking, or are they dim with the tears of his loneliness? There appears to be a distance between us, the readers, and Mr. Flood that cannot be bridged. We ourselves do not know whether to laugh or cry.

Eben's imagining of his jug as Roland's horn is quickly transformed into the narrator's portrayal of him as a mother and of the jug as a "sleeping" child being put to bed. The speaker partakes of Eben's maternal dramatization of himself in this stanza without any distancing irony as if he (the speaker) does not want to wake Eben from his illusion any more than Eben wants to let his imaginary child wake to the reality of a world in which "most things break." But Eben, to protect himself from the pathos of his own "trembling care,"

interrupts his spell of heavy melancholy with another comic
gesture of offering himself one more drink, pretending that he
and his double have not seen each other for some time and
need to get caught up on what has happened in the interim. In
saying "Welcome home!" to his double, however, Mr. Flood
recovers his comic mode of addressing himself as a drinking
partner, this time with an exaggerated flourish of formal
respect: "No more, sir; that will do." The illusion that he is in
control of his life because he is in control of his drinking
offers its moment of equivocal consolation: "So, for the time,
apparently it did, and Eben evidently thought so too."

The speaker's empathetic identification with Eben no
longer can be sustained, and he draws back from him, acknowledging that his imagining of what Mr. Flood is imagining is merely a matter of conjecture. The telltale word,
"apparently," reveals that the speaker can only surmise why
Mr. Flood pauses in his drinking, and, furthermore, the word
"evidently" indicates that outward behavior, what we see
others do, is an imperfect index of what they think and feel.
Even for the poem's would-be omniscient speaker, Mr. Flood's
inner life must remain a mystery, remote and untouchable.

And yet the speaker enjoys one more moment of humor in
response to Mr. Flood's singing. Indulging briefly in his last
romanticizing of Mr. Flood, describing him with the ornate
imagery of "the silver loneliness / Of Night," the speaker
permits himself relief from his empathetic sorrow with his
joke about Eben's drunkenness: "he lifted up his voice and
sang, / Secure, with only two moons listening, / Until the
whole harmonious landscape rang." Such harmony, based on
illusion, cannot be sustained, nor can the laughter that the
play of illusion makes possible.

In the last stanza, the speaker's tone becomes unrelievedly
sad with the ending of Mr. Flood's song: "The weary throat
gave out; / The last word wavered, and the song was done."
Eben raises his jug to resume drinking, and the illusion that
he can resist his need for liquor and keep himself company is

abandoned with the shaking of his head, the recognition that his defenses are inadequate to assuage the brutal fact of his being completely alone. Trapped in the fate of his old age, not even the speaker's sympathy can reach him. For the fleeting duration of a single line, "There was not much that was ahead of him," the speaker flinches in the face of the tough reality that there is in fact no comfort for Eben to be found. The crushing word, "nothing," appears necessarily in the next line as the speaker is forced to acknowledge the inescapable loneliness that has been assigned to Mr. Flood: "And there was nothing in the town below— / Where strangers would have shut the many doors / That many friends had opened long ago." The poem ends with the wailing "o" sounds of "below," "opened," and "ago"—the same sounds with which this mournful poem began.

For all his imaginative sympathy, the speaker is hardly different from the "strangers" who now shut their doors to Mr. Flood. The speaker's failure to invite Mr. Flood to his own house, I believe, represents Robinson's view of the limit of art itself. The artist must remain an observer; he cannot enter into the world of his narration to help mitigate the sorrow that he can so movingly describe. Although Mr. Flood makes a gesture of need with his "hand extended," the speaker cannot respond to the gesture with his own hand as in the poem by Robert Burns, "Auld Lang Syne," which Mr. Flood quotes: "And here's a hand my trusty frien', / And gie's a hand o' thine."

The reason, of course, that the artist cannot enter into the world he describes is that this is merely a world of words, a fictive world. Keeping his distance is not a moral failure, but an acknowledgment of the distinction between life and art. Robinson reminds his readers repeatedly in his poems that even though his characters may be based on his observations of real people—just as Tilbury Town in his poems is based on the real Gardiner, Maine, where Robinson lived—those characters must become fictions in his poems because there is a limit to how deeply we can see into other people's lives. For example, in "Eros Turannos," Robinson's poem about an unhappy marriage where "passion lived and died," the seemingly omniscient narrator interrupts his analysis of the couple by stepping forward in the poem to parody himself in his role of the wise, all-knowing poet: "We tell you, tapping on our brows, / The story as it should be,— / As if the story of a house / Were told, or ever could be." We cannot tell other people's stories; we can only imagine them and express our imaginings. Robinson as poet seeks to expose not only the illusions of his characters, but the danger of illusion to artists who forget that they are dreamers of words. At best, poets can remind us of the real world from which their fictions have sprung, and to which they must return, and thus the poets' laughter and the poets' tears may relieve us in our holiday from actuality, and strengthen us in our return to reality. "But there's a time / For most of us," Robinson said, "when words are all we have / To serve our stricken souls."

Just as Hardy asserted "If way to the better there be, it exacts a hard look at the worst," Robinson depicted his heroes as figures under extreme circumstantial stress—like Aunt Imogen who, though saddened by not having children of her own, nevertheless "made everybody laugh," or like Rembrandt's wife, Saskia, who, before she died, Rembrandt tells us, "with a guile / Of kindliness that covered half her doubts / Would give me gold, and laugh" (about the worth of his paintings), or like Abraham Lincoln who "Met rancor with a cryptic mirth." But the figure who best exemplifies the heroic power of laughter in the face of sorrow is William Shakespeare in Robinson's "Ben Jonson Entertains a Man from Stratford." This poem is structured as a monologue spoken by Jonson to an alderman who has recently seen Shakespeare, their mutual friend. Jonson is eager to express his wonder at what seems to him the unlikely combination of Shakespeare's artistry, his ability to create imaginary realms, and Shakespeare's worldliness, in particular his interest in money and in his house. The poem opens: "You are a friend then, as I make it out, / Of our man Shakespeare, who alone of us / Will put an ass's head in Fairyland / As he would add a shilling to more shillings." Jonson goes on: "he'll have that house— / The best you ever saw," and with the double image of Shakespeare in mind—a man who is equally at home in Fairyland and in the actual town of Stratford—Jonson cries out: "Good God! / He makes me lie awake o'nights and laugh."

The portrait of Shakespeare that Ben Jonson paints is of a tormented man with "diverse and inclement devils [who] / Have made of late his heart their dwelling place," and yet, astonishingly, he has achieved a mysterious detachment from his own life, as well as from the human condition in general. This is not a detachment in which nothing matters, but rather a detachment of acceptance that derives from a sense of what is inevitable in nature and in human behavior. Although Shakespeare is only "five and forty" in the poem, Jonson has a sense of him as being timeless, as if he had lived many lives in many places within his own single life:

> He's old enough to be
> The father of the world, and so he is.
> "Ben, you're a scholar, what's the time of day?"
> Says he; and there shines out of him again
> An aged light that has no age or station—
> The mystery that's his—a mischievous
> Half-mad serenity that laughs at fame
> For being won so easy.

As the supreme creator of fictive worlds, Shakespeare epitomizes to Jonson the very essence of fatherhood, and in this imagining Jonson thus depicts himself as the son who receives the father's blessing: the gift of detached laughter—laughter as a paradoxical form of passionate detachment.

When Shakespeare teases Jonson by asking him the banal question—"what's the time of day?"—the implication is that to the artist "time" has a different meaning than to the "scholar" since artistic fictions are only true if they reveal what is constant in human behavior irrespective of historical location. Shakespeare's "aged light that has no age or station" places him everywhere and anywhere in historical time. That is his mystery. And thus his "half-mad serenity" and his laughter reveal him to be simultaneously both in and out of his own life, both within and beyond his own historical moment in a place called Stratford.

Jonson sees Shakespeare as a man whose relationships with women have not been successful, who has become wary of the outcome of sexual love: "They've had him dancing till his toes were tender, / And he can feel 'em now, come chilly rains." In particular, Jonson interprets Shakespeare's publication of his sonnets as having a confessional aspect about the hurt caused him by the betraying lady in that sequence of poems: "He's put one there with all her poison on, / To make a singing fiction of a shadow / That's in his life a fact." Yet even in Jonson's glimpse into Shakespeare's private life, he emphasizes Shakespeare's power to transform individual experience into art—a "singing fiction." Jonson sees Shakespeare's failure in marriage, as well as in romance, and he describes Shakespeare's wife as someone "Who seems to have decoyed him, married him, / And sent him scuttling on his way to London." But these disappointments are merely part of a general process of disillusionment, of bearing steady witness to the human failure to live up to human ideals, and so Jonson declares that Shakespeare "has dreams / Were fair to think on once, and all found hollow. / He knows how much of what men paint themselves / Would blister in the light of what they are." And thus the mystery remains: how can Shakespeare, the genius of disillusionment in whose brain there is "a worm at work," become a source of laughter?

Jonson recounts one meeting when Shakespeare seemed particularly downcast. He "gloomed and mumbled," and Jonson tells us how he tried to cajole him: " 'What is it now,' said I,—'another woman?' " Shakespeare's response, however, is not the banter that Jonson had expected. Rather, Jonson says, "That made him sorry for me, and he smiled." Jonson's error was to assume that Shakespeare's gloomy mood was directly related to something in his own experience rather than to the human condition of disappointment and disillusionment. Shakespeare's smile—just once removed from laughter—is tenderly condescending; he is "sorry" that Jonson cannot rise to a more impersonal view of human failure and suffering. Shakespeare's reply indicates that what is on his mind is the moral meaninglessness of nature itself and the vanity of human endeavor:

> "No, Ben," he mused; "it's Nothing. It's all Nothing.
> We come, we go; and when we're done, we're done.
> Spiders and flies—we're mostly one or t'other—
> We come, we go; and when we're done, we're done."

Once again Ben Jonson tries "cheering" Shakespeare, for he has not yet fully accepted that Shakespeare's is an impersonal sorrow, and he asks, "what ails ye?" but Shakespeare, trusting in Jonson's final sympathy and understanding, continues in the same lugubrious vein:

> "Your fly will serve as well as anybody,
> And what's his hour? He flies, and flies, and flies,
> And in his fly's mind has a brave appearance;
> And then your spider gets him in her net,
> And eats him out, and hangs him up to dry.
> That's Nature, the kind mother of us all.
> And then your slattern housemaid swings her broom,
> And where's your spider? And that's Nature, also.
> It's Nature, and it's Nothing. It's all Nothing.
> It's all a world where bugs and emperors
> Go singularly back to the same dust,
> Each in his time; and the old, ordered stars
> That sang together, Ben, will sing the same
> Old stave tomorrow."

Nature may not reveal meaning or purpose that is congenial
to human wishes and human needs, but in Shakespeare's
bleak vision of human mortality and the transience of all
matter, there is design—the "ordered stars / That sang together," and Shakespeare's singing art is thus in harmony
with the indifferent order of the cosmos.

Jonson's strategy of dealing with Shakespeare's refusal to
find consolation when "he talks like that" in such "dreams"
as immortality beyond Nature is to take him to a pub and
"make him drink." Shakespeare is no more successful, however, as a drinker than he is as a lover or husband. In the spirit
of friendship Jonson says, "He'll drink, for love of me, and
then be sick," but Jonson goes on to comment: "The great /
Should be as large in liquor as in love— / And our great friend
is not so large in either." Only one subject, it seems, can break
Shakespeare's gloom in contemplating Nature as "Nothing,"
and that is Shakespeare's management and caring for his
"damned House" in Stratford. Jonson's probing comment is
that he and Shakespeare "laugh here at his thrift, but after
all / It may be thrift that saves him from the devil." The devil
Jonson has in mind is the spirit of despair.

Despite their mutual laughter about Shakespeare's "thrift"
in such a worldly concern as his house, Shakespeare directs
the conversation back to the theme of how human beings
cannot accept reality, how, in particular, they are addicted to
the illusion of immortality:

> "Ben, what's 'immortal'?
> Think you by any force of ordination
> It may be nothing of a sort more noisy
> Than a small oblivion of component ashes
> That of a dream-addicted world was once
> A moving atomy . . . ?"

Having received the gift of laughter from Shakespeare, thinking of how he makes him "lie awake o'nights and laugh,"

thinking of Shakespeare's "Half-mad serenity that laughs at fame," Jonson seeks to return the favor now and "make him laugh." In the spirit of play, Jonson calls Shakespeare a "mad mountebank," and to Jonson's surprise those words have a completely different effect from what he expected: "And by the Lord I nearer made him cry." The cause of Shakespeare's astonishing reaction is not, I believe, that he feels insulted or misunderstood, but precisely the opposite: Jonson has got him absolutely right. Shakespeare is indeed mad to have stripped himself of illusions. The human mind was not designed to survive without fabricated consolations. And, yes, Shakespeare knows full well that his art cannot cure the ills of the world; it is itself the medicine of dreams in a "dream-addicted world." But the response that Shakespeare's near-weeping evokes in Jonson does not diminish his authority or grandeur in Jonson's eyes, nor does it reduce him to an image of personal vulnerability; rather, it completes the vision of Shakespeare as the humane "father of a world," the world of art. Jonson sees Shakespeare as godlike in his comprehensive attributes: "And I say now, as I shall say again, / I love the man this side idolatry." Though Shakespeare is godlike to him, Jonson insists that he loves him, not as an idol, but as a man.

Jonson is quick to clarify to the alderman the possible misimpression that he thinks Shakespeare has completed his work: "He may not be so ancient as all that." And Jonson goes on then to predict what Shakespeare's next creations will be, presumably on the basis of conversations they have had about projected plays. Jonson says: "Just wait a year or two for Cleopatra, / For she's to be a balsam and a comfort." Although Cleopatra is another of Shakespeare's destructive and fatal women, the cause of Antony's downfall and death, she is capable of both worldly and transcendent love, and in this respect she is a "comfort" to Shakespeare's imagination and a compensation for the love that was lacking in Shakespeare's own life. Yet even beyond the imagining of woman's love,

Shakespeare will create his last plays of forgiveness and reconciliation, the healing of family wounds, which Jonson describes as "a last great calm / Triumphant over shipwreck and
all storms."

The "last great calm" is the consummation of Shakespeare's art, the triumphant illusion of a "mad mountebank"
to provide a necessary dream for human yearning to dwell
upon. Shakespeare, in effect, both believes and disbelieves
his own visions; he is both illusioned and disillusioned. Although Jonson describes Shakespeare's final disaffection for
"a phantom world he sounded and found wanting," Jonson
also reminds us again of Shakespeare's worldliness, his desire
for "those egregious shillings." The poem ends with an ex-
clamatory passage expressing Jonson's wonder at the paradox
of Shakespeare's nature in which he balances two oxymo-
ronic phrases: "mad"/"careful" and "proud"/"indifferent."
Shakespeare, like all people, loves and suffers in his own life;
his uniqueness lies in his artistic capacity to be passionately
detached from his individual history, and thus capable of
living in imaginary worlds of his own creation:

>   Tell me, now,
>   If ever there was anything let loose
>   On earth by gods or devils heretofore
>   Like this mad, careful, proud, indifferent Shakespeare!
>   Where was it, if it ever was? By heaven,
>   'Twas never yet in Rhodes or Pergamon—
>   In Thebes or Nineveh, a thing like this!
>   No thing like this was ever out of England;
>   And that he knows. I wonder if he cares.
>   Perhaps he does. . . . O Lord, that House in Stratford!

Jonson's final astonishment comes with his consideration
that Shakespeare may even be indifferent to his own genius.
He knows—how could he not?—that nothing like him has
appeared before "out of England," but Jonson, the deliberate
artist himself, is dumbfounded before the mystery of Shake-

speare's indifference to his own art: "I wonder if he cares." All Jonson can be sure about—as his final, laughing, exclamation makes clear—is Shakespeare's attachment to his house: "O, Lord, that House in Stratford!" And on that note of laughter, Shakespeare, the "father of a world," the father of both illusion and disillusionment, is fixed in Jonson's mind as a paradoxical author of consolation: to care and not to care, to weep in laughter and to laugh in tears.

IV

I did not take it personally at the time of my Bar Mitzvah service that God had neglected to bring about the lowering of my voice. When I intoned in my clear soprano, "Boruch attoh Adonoi Elohenu . . ." and the rabbi proclaimed, "Today you are a man!" the laughter from the congregation was unmistakable. I was mature enough to be tuned to the nuances of humiliation, but if God wanted to have a joke at my expense, well, I could handle it. My father's gift to me that spring of 1942 was a huge cardboard map of Europe, Asia, and Africa, which we hung on the wall of the playroom in the basement. My father bought pins with round, colored heads, and we kept track of the positions, by nationality, of the Allied and the Axis soldiers. To learn the importance of geography, we read the newspapers together and moved the pins across the board as the German armies advanced. It was like a game to me, and it seemed that my father, too, enjoyed our shared activity.

The German armies continued to advance. Late in May, General Rommel won a major victory in North Africa. In June he entered Egypt, and it appeared as if he would be able to seize the oil fields in the Middle East and proceed to join the German armies that were now moving deeper into Russia. By the end of August, German forces were encamped by the Volga River outside of Stalingrad. For the first time the unthinkable dawned on me—the Germans actually might win the war. And I became afraid. I wondered if they might try to invade the United States. The black German pins were spread all over our map, and our family was filled with talk about the persecution of the Jews. My father tried to assure me that the Jews were God's chosen people: they suffered because God expected so much from them, but they—we— had always managed to survive and, despite the Nazis, we would continue to survive.

In the summer of 1943 my father was recovering from the first of a series of strokes that would kill him two years later at the age of forty-six. I remember his embarrassment at his physical disability and slowness of speech and that he seemed to be more at ease in the less demanding company of my younger sister. And I remember my own embarrassment with my friends when my father tried to have a game of catch with us but could not hold on to the ball. Though I may have projected my own discomfort onto him, I think my father was aware of how my view of him had changed. I suspected that was why he had planned a special fishing trip for us to Maine, where he used to go, so he claimed, with his best friend. My mother was not happy about his driving so far, and she made him promise to drive slowly. We camped out, and, except for our taking turns in wondering out loud why nei- ther of us had gotten even a nibble, there were long pauses in our conversation.

By evening of the third and last day of our trip, we had decided to head back to the campsite when my father said he wanted to try one more cast. His fly dropped on a dark spot of still water near a fallen tree that had become lodged between the rocks, and immediately the water broke as a huge trout twisted into the air and then plunged down beneath the rotting tree. My father held the line taut while giving the fish sufficient play, and I saw him standing there in the orange light as if miraculously restored to perfect health. Just as he had taught me, he reeled in the fish without rushing, keeping the curve of the rod in front of him. He called to me to make ready the net, and I stepped into the shallow and got him. To my father's astonishment, as well as my own, I began shouting, "Let's put him back! I want to put him back!" But my father insisted that we keep him. Expertly he cleaned the glistening trout, and we ate him for dinner that night by the campfire.

While the fish cooked in the popping bacon grease, my father removed from his knapsack a silver flask with his initials on it and began to take long, gurgling swigs. I had never seen that flask before, nor could I even remember my father taking a drink, but that night he slurped from the flask which reflected the firelight whenever he lifted it to his lips. He told me that he did not remember his own father very well, except that the family had come from Germany when he was a boy to escape that nation's hostility toward the Jews. His father had died when my father was a child; his mother raised him. She wanted him to become a lawyer, and he had worked nights to put himself through school. He had continued to help support his mother even after he was married and I was born.

My father had become a state senator from the Bronx, and we lived in a mixed neighborhood of Italians, Irish, and Jews. Periodically he drove to Albany to consult with Herbert Lehman, the governor of New York State, and he took me with him so that I could play with the cairn terriers which Governor Lehman raised on his estate. But now I watched his worn eyes as, between swigs and with an animated fluency that I had not heard in years, my father told me a story about myself—as if, though fifteen and a baritone, I needed to be instructed in my own history. When I was about ten, he took me to a meeting of the Senate and arranged for me to sit beside the speaker as he conducted the legislative meeting.

On that particular day an antivivisection bill was up for debate on the Senate floor, and when I realized that the bill was designed to protect animals from suffering from human cruelty, I asked the speaker if I could say something to the assembly, and he approved. I declared that someone has to protect animals who can't protect themselves, and that God loves every living "orgasm" under the sun. I remember my father's telling the story with absolute clarity, although I had blocked it out myself. My father laughed and rocked beside the fire and turned his flask upside down above his raised head to get the last few drops. I have come to suspect that for some mischievous purpose of his own, he invented the part about my Freudian slip, and yet that remains my most cherished image of my father—drinking and laughing. He put the flask back in his knapsack, took out a book, opened it, looked at me darkly, and read out loud: " 'The worst returns to laughter'; Shakespeare assures us that 'the worst returns to laughter.' "

Many years later I came across those words, which were already emblazoned in my mind, when I read *King Lear* at college. And it was later still when I realized that those lines, spoken by Edgar, are immediately followed by the entrance of Edgar's blinded father, Gloucester, so that Edgar cries out: "O gods! Who is't can say, 'I am at the worst?' / I am worse than e'er I was. . . . And worse I may be yet. The worst is not, / So long as we can say, 'This is the worst.' " Nor does the ending of the play with the deaths of Cordelia and King Lear offer the relief of showing the worst returning to laughter. But in this most painful of Shakespeare's plays there is, nevertheless, a treasured moment of laughter. King Lear and his daughter have reconciled, but they have been captured by the enemy armies of Cordelia's cruel sisters. In despair, and mysteriously echoing the words of Edgar, the play's other wronged child, Cordelia, says, "We are not the first / Who, with best meaning, have incurr'd the worst." Lear, however, disdaining the fate that has overtaken them, replies ecstatically:

> Come, let's away to prison.
> We two alone will sing like birds i' the cage.
> When thou dost ask me blessing, I'll kneel down,

And ask of thee forgiveness. So we'll live,
And pray and sing, and tell old tales, and laugh
At gilded butterflies, and hear poor rogues
Talk of court news; and we'll talk with them too:
Who loses and who wins, who's in and who's out;
And take upon's the mystery of things,
As if we were God's spies; and we'll wear out
In a wall'd prison, packs and sects of great ones
That ebb and flow by th' moon.

I don't know of a passage that better illustrates Shakespeare's "half-mad serenity," or one that is closer in spirit to
the everlasting "mystery of things" that Hardy evokes. King
Lear remains interested in the news, the politics of the fleeting world, but from a great psychological distance. Events
have become the substance of tales, and conversation has
become ritualized and made aesthetic so that it takes on the
quality of song. Above all, to look at the world in the spirit of
what I have called "passionate detachment" is to see the
unfolding of human history as a source of laughter, to see
nature, not in its cruelty, but epitomized in the delicate
image of a gilded butterfly. This is indeed a form of innocence, really a form of illusion, though it is grounded here in
the believable reunion of a consoling parent and a needful
child. This ecstatic moment of laughter with Lear and Cordelia reunited, however, is not the image with which Shakespeare chooses to end his play. I believe, nevertheless, biased
as I am in behalf of the wish for survival, that such a note of
laughter, an image of a gilded butterfly, would please my
father's ghost as the conclusion to my fleeting recollection of
our last happy time together. I'll bet he'd drink to that!

FATHERING THE MAP

In May of nineteen-hundred forty-two,
    my father's birthday gift to me
        was a long, cardboard map,

extending from green England in the west,
    past purple Germany,
  beige Russia, east to red Japan.
We hung it in the basement playroom where
    I tended my aquariums
of turtles, salamanders, frogs, and kept
    my pen of flop-eared rabbits,
my wood hutch of guinea pigs who slept
    within my tended peace.
  My father's plan was that together
we would track the progress of the war.
  He bought a box of colored pins
to represent each country's tanks and troops
    so that we could "keep score"
of Allied victories, but I recall
    the black pins spreading out
    across two darkened continents.
By August, cricket calls contending in the night,
    my father's faulty health turned bad
    as German armies camped
beside the Volga River outside Stalingrad,
    and it occurred to me
for the first time that we might lose—
    that purposes beyond
my comprehension might have chosen us
    to know defeat: we Jews,
    even here in America,
would be exterminated when the Nazis came.
    In nineteen forty-five,
we moved because my father died: two strokes
    had left him speechless,
    though his eyes were still alive
    when I last sat with him.
I had to give my turtles to the zoo,
    my salamanders and my frogs,

my flop-eared rabbits and my guinea pigs,
        and every loss I knew
went with them as if loss could be restored
        in a protected place.
    The day the moving truck arrived,
I cleared our cluttered map, pin by cold pin,
        from yellow Naples up to Finland,
orange Normandy to rainbow-hued Berlin,
        but left it on the basement wall
            in case the kid who came
    to live there in my house could find
some other use for it, some other game.
    But that was forty years ago.
        I never met the boy
who moved in after me, and I don't know
        what he did with our map—
perhaps his father threw it out, replaced
        it on the wall when we sent troops
to South Korea, or they might have traced
        the torrid Gaza wars
so they could bear and understand
        the unchanged passions of
the shifting borders of the Holy Land.
    Maybe the boy who moved in next
received a birthday map of the whole world—
        as if his father were to say:
            keep count of oil spills
        and each rain forest, stripped of trees,
whose species we exterminate each day;
        remember the first covenant
            Jehovah made with Noah
following the flood: *Neither shall flesh
    be cut off to destroy the earth.*
        Maybe his father's eyes
    were fresh with tears as if he meant
        to keep a vow: "Mute death

is unredeemable; I can't accept
  our breaking of the covenant."
    The map I'll leave my son
will look like moonlight seething on the sea—
  all blank but for a single pin
     to represent an ark,
in hope another covenant to save the earth
    may find words in the dark.

Thomas Hardy

CHANNEL FIRING

That night your great guns, unawares,
Shook all our coffins as we lay,
And broke the chancel window-squares,
We thought it was the Judgment-day

And sat upright. While drearisome
Arose the howl of wakened hounds:
The mouse let fall the altar-crumb,
The worms drew back into the mounds,

The glebe cow drooled. Till God call, "No;
It's gunnery practice out at sea
Just as before you went below;
The world is as it used to be:

"All nations striving strong to make
Red war yet redder. Mad as hatters
They do no more for Christes sake
Than you who are helpless in such matters.

"That this is not the judgment-hour
For some of them's a blessed thing,
For if it were they'd have to scour
Hell's floor for so much threatening. . . .

"Ha, ha. It will be warmer when
I blow the trumpet (if indeed
I ever do; for you are men,
And rest eternal sorely need)."

So down we lay again. "I wonder,
Will the world ever saner be,"
Said one, "than when He sent us under
In our indifferent century!"

And many a skeleton shook his head.
"Instead of preaching forty year,"
My neighbour Parson Thirdly said,
"I wish I had stuck to pipes and beer."

Again the guns disturbed the hour,
Roaring their readiness to avenge,
As far inland as Stourton Tower,
And Camelot, and starlit Stonehenge.

GOD-FORGOTTEN

I towered far, and lo! I stood within
The presence of the Lord Most High,
Sent thither by the sons of Earth, to win
Some answer to their cry.

—"The Earth, sayest thou? The Human race?
By Me created? Sad its lot?
Nay: I have no remembrance of such place:
Such world I fashioned not."—

—"O Lord, forgive me when I say
Thou spakest the word that made it all."—
"The Earth of men—let me bethink me. . . . Yea!
I dimly do recall

"Some tiny sphere I built long back
(Mid millions of such shapes of mine)
So named. . . . It perished, surely—not a wrack
    Remaining, or a sign?

"It lost my interest from the first,
My aims therefor succeeding ill;
Haply it died of doing as it durst?"—
    "Lord, it existeth still."—

"Dark, then, its life! For not a cry
Of aught it bears do I now hear;
Of its own act the threads were snapt whereby
    Its plaints had reached mine ear.

"It used to ask for gifts of good,
Till came its severance, self-entailed,
When sudden silence on that side ensued,
    And has till now prevailed.

"All other orbs have kept in touch;
Their voicings reach me speedily:
Thy people took upon them overmuch
    In sundering them from me!

"And it is strange—though sad enough—
Earth's race should think that one whose call
Frames, daily, shining spheres of flawless stuff
    Must heed their tainted ball! . . .

"But sayest it is by pangs distraught,
And strife, and silent suffering?—
Sore grieved am I that injury should be wrought
    Even on so poor a thing!

"Thou shouldst have learnt that *Not to Mend*
For Me could mean but *Not to Know*:
Hence, Messengers! and straightway put an end
    To what men undergo." . . .

Homing at dawn, I thought to see
One of the Messengers standing by.
—Oh, childish thought! . . . Yet often it comes to me
    When trouble hovers nigh.

E. A. Robinson

MR. FLOOD'S PARTY

Old Eben Flood, climbing alone one night
Over the hill between the town below
And the forsaken upland hermitage
That held as much as he should ever know
On earth again of home, paused warily.
The road was his with not a native near;
And Eben, having leisure, said aloud,
For no man else in Tilbury Town to hear:

"Well, Mr. Flood, we have the harvest moon
Again, and we may not have many more;
The bird is on the wing, the poet says,
And you and I have said it here before.
Drink to the bird." He raised up to the light
The jug that he had gone so far to fill,
And answered huskily: "Well, Mr. Flood,
Since you propose it, I believe I will."

Alone, as if enduring to the end
A valiant armor of scarred hopes outworn,
He stood there in the middle of the road
Like Roland's ghost winding a silent horn.
Below him, in the town among the trees,
Where friends of other days had honored him,
A phantom salutation of the dead
Rang thinly till old Eben's eyes were dim.

Then, as a mother lays her sleeping child
Down tenderly, fearing it may awake,
He set the jug down slowly at his feet
With trembling care, knowing that most things break;
And only when assured that on firm earth
It stood, as the uncertain lives of men
Assuredly did not, he paced away,
And with his hand extended paused again:

"Well, Mr. Flood, we have not met like this
In a long time; and many a change has come

To both of us, I fear, since last it was
We had a drop together. Welcome home!"
Convivially returning with himself,
Again he raised the jug up to the light;
And with an acquiescent quaver said:
"Well, Mr. Flood, if you insist, I might.

"Only a very little, Mr. Flood—
For auld lang syne. No more, sir; that will do."
So, for the time, apparently it did,
And Eben evidently thought so too;
For soon amid the silver loneliness
Of night he lifted up his voice and sang,
Secure, with only two moons listening,
Until the whole harmonious landscape rang—

"For auld lang syne." The weary throat gave out;
The last word wavered, and the song was done.
He raised again the jug regretfully
And shook his head, and was again alone.
There was not much that was ahead of him,
And there was nothing in the town below—
Where strangers would have shut the many doors
That many friends had opened long ago.

BEN JONSON ENTERTAINS
A MAN FROM STRATFORD

You are a friend then, as I make it out,
Of our man Shakespeare, who alone of us
Will put an ass's head in Fairyland
As he would add a shilling to more shillings,
All most harmonious,—and out of his
Miraculous inviolable increase
Fills Ilion, Rome, or any town you like
Of olden time with timeless Englishmen;
And I must wonder what you think of him—
All you down there where your small Avon flows

By Stratford, and where you're an Alderman.
Some, for a guess, would have him riding back
To be a farrier there, or say a dyer;
Or maybe one of your adept surveyors;
Or like enough the wizard of all tanners.
Not you—no fear of that; for I discern
In you a kindling of the flame that saves—
The nimble element, the true caloric;
I see it, and was told of it, moreover,
By our discriminate friend himself, no other.
Had you been one of the sad average,
As he would have it,—meaning, as I take it,
The sinew and the solvent of our Island,
You'd not be buying beer for this Terpander's
Approved and estimated friend Ben Jonson;
He'd never foist it as a part of his
Contingent entertainment of a townsman
While he goes off rehearsing, as he must,
If he shall ever be the Duke of Stratford.
And my words are no shadow on your town—
Far from it; for one town's as like another
As all are unlike London. Oh, he knows it,—
And there's the Stratford in him; he denies it,
And there's the Shakespeare in him. So, God help him!
I tell him he needs Greek; but neither God
Nor Greek will help him. Nothing will help that man.
You see the fates have given him so much,
He must have all or perish,—or look out
Of London, where he sees too many lords.
They're part of half what ails him: I suppose
There's nothing fouler down among the demons
Than what it is he feels when he remembers
The dust and sweat and ointment of his calling
With his lords looking on and laughing at him.
King as he is, he can't be king *de facto*,
And that's as well, because he wouldn't like it;
He'd frame a lower rating of men then
Than he has now; and after that would come
An abdication or an apoplexy.

He can't be king, not even king of Stratford,—
Though half the world, if not the whole of it,
May crown him with a crown that fits no king
Save Lord Apollo's homesick emissary:
Not there on Avon, or on any stream
Where Naiads and their white arms are no more,
Shall he find home again. It's all too bad.
But there's a comfort, for he'll have that House—
The best you ever saw; and he'll be there
Anon, as you're an Alderman. Good God!
He makes me lie awake o'nights and laugh.

And you have known him from his origin,
You tell me; and a most uncommon urchin
He must have been to the few seeing ones—
A trifle terrifying, I dare say,
Discovering a world with his man's eyes,
Quite as another lad might see some finches,
If he looked hard and had an eye for Nature.
But this one had his eyes and their foretelling,
And he had you to fare with, and what else?
He must have had a father and a mother—
In fact I've heard him say so—and a dog,
As a boy should, I venture; and the dog,
Most likely, was the only man who knew him.
A dog, for all I know, is what he needs
As much as anything right here today,
To counsel him about his disillusions,
Old aches, and parturitions of what's coming,—
A dog of orders, an emeritus,
To wag his tail at him when he comes home,
And then to put his paws up on his knees
And say, "For God's sake, what's it all about?"

I don't know whether he needs a dog or not—
Or what he needs. I tell him he needs Greek;
I'll talk of rules and Aristotle with him,
And if his tongue's at home he'll say to that,
"I have your word that Aristotle knows,
And you mine that I don't know Aristotle."

He's all at odds with all the unities,
And what's yet worse, it doesn't seem to matter;
He treads along through Time's old wilderness
As if the tramp of all the centuries
Had left no roads—and there are none, for him;
He doesn't see them, even with those eyes,—
And that's a pity, or I say it is.
Accordingly we have him as we have him—
Going his way, the way that he goes best,
A pleasant animal with no great noise
Or nonsense anywhere to set him off—
Save only divers and inclement devils
Have made of late his heart their dwelling place.
A flame half ready to fly out sometimes
At some annoyance may be fanned up in him,
But soon it falls, and when it falls goes out;
He knows how little room there is in there
For crude and futile animosities,
And how much for the joy of being whole,
And how much for long sorrow and old pain.
On our side there are some who may be given
To grow old wondering what he thinks of us
And some above us, who are, in his eyes,
Above himself,—and that's quite right and English.
Yet here we smile, or disappoint the gods
Who made it so: the gods have always eyes
To see men scratch; and they see one down here
Who itches, manor-bitten to the bone,
Albeit he knows himself—yes, yes, he knows—
The lord of more than England and of more
Than all the seas of England in all time
Shall ever wash. D'ye wonder that I laugh?
He sees me, and he doesn't seem to care:
And why the devil should he? I can't tell you.

I'll meet him out alone of a bright Sunday,
Trim, rather spruce, and quite the gentleman.
"What ho, my lord!" say I. He doesn't hear me;
Wherefore I have to pause and look at him.

He's not enormous, but one looks at him.
A little on the round if you insist,
For now, God save the mark, he's growing old;
He's five and forty, and to hear him talk
These days you'd call him eighty; then you'd add
More years to that. He's old enough to be
The father of a world, and so he is.
"Ben, you're a scholar, what's the time of day?"
Says he; and there shines out of him again
An aged light that has no age or station—
The mystery that's his—a mischievous
Half-mad serenity that laughs at fame
For being won so easy, and at friends
Who laugh at him for what he wants the most,
And for his dukedom down in Warwickshire;—
By which you see we're all a little jealous. . . .
Poor Greene! I fear the color of his name
Was even as that of his ascending soul;
And he was one where there are many others,—
Some scrivening to the end against their fate,
Their puppets all in ink and all to die there;
And some with hands that once would shade an eye
That scanned Euripides and Aeschylus
Will reach by this time for a pot-house mop
To slush their first and last of royalties.
Poor devils! and they all play to his hand;
For so it was in Athens and old Rome.
But that's not here, or there; I've wandered off.
Greene does it, or I'm careful. Where's that boy?

Yes, he'll go back to Stratford. And we'll miss him?
Dear sir, there'll be no London here without him.
We'll all be riding, one of these fine days,
Down there to see him—and his wife won't like us;
And then we'll think of what he never said
Of women—which, if taken all in all
With what he did say, would buy many horses.
Though nowadays he's not so much for women.
"So few of them," he says, "are worth the guessing."

But there's a worm at work when he says that,
And while he says it one feels in the air
A deal of circumambient hocus-pocus.
They've had him dancing till his toes were tender,
And he can feel 'em now, come chilly rains.
There's no long cry for going into it,
However, and we don't know much about it.
But you in Stratford, like most here in London,
Have more now in the *Sonnets* than you paid for;
He's put one there with all her poison on,
To make a singing fiction of a shadow
That's in his life a fact, and always will be.
But she's no care of ours, though Time, I fear,
Will have a more reverberant ado
About her than about another one
Who seems to have decoyed him, married him,
And sent him scuttling on his way to London,—
With much already learned, and more to learn,
And more to follow. Lord! how I see him now,
Pretending, maybe trying, to be like us.
Whatever he may have meant, we never had him;
He failed us, or escaped, or what you will,—
And there was that about him (God knows what,—
We'd flayed another had he tried it on us)
That made as many of us as had wits
More fond of all his easy distances
Than one another's noise and clap-your-shoulder.
But think you not, my friend, he'd never talk!
Talk? He was eldritch at it; and we listened—
Thereby acquiring much we knew before
About ourselves, and hitherto had held
Irrelevant, or not prime to the purpose.
And there were some, of course, and there be now,
Disordered and reduced amazedly
To resignation by the mystic seal
Of young finality the gods had laid
On everything that made him a young demon;
And one or two shot looks at him already
As he had been their executioner;

And once or twice he was, not knowing it,—
Or knowing, being sorry for poor clay
And saying nothing . . . Yet, for all his engines,
You'll meet a thousand of an afternoon
Who strut and sun themselves and see around 'em
A world made out of more that has a reason
Than his, I swear, that he sees here today;
Though he may scarcely give a Fool an exit
But we mark how he sees in everything
A law that, given we flout it once too often,
Brings fire and iron down on our naked heads.
To me it looks as if the power that made him,
For fear of giving all things to one creature,
Left out the first,—faith, innocence, illusion,
Whatever 'tis that keeps us out o' Bedlam,—
And thereby, for his too consuming vision,
Empowered him out of nature; though to see him,
You'd never guess what's going on inside him.
He'll break out some day like a keg of ale
With too much independent frenzy in it;
And all for cellaring what he knows won't keep,
And what he'd best forget—but that he can't.
You'll have it, and have more than I'm foretelling;
And there'll be such a roaring at the Globe
As never stunned the bleeding gladiators.
He'll have to change the color of its hair
A bit, for now he calls it Cleopatra.
Black hair would never do for Cleopatra.
But you and I are not yet two old women,
And you're a man of office. What he does
Is more to you than how it is he does it,—
And that's what the Lord God has never told him.
They work together, and the Devil helps 'em;
They do it of a morning, or if not,
They do it of a night; in which event
He's peevish of a morning. He seems old;
He's not the proper stomach or the sleep—
And they're two sovran agents to conserve him
Against the fiery art that has no mercy

But what's in that prodigious grand new House.
I gather something happening in his boyhood
Fulfilled him with a boy's determination
To make all Stratford 'ware of him. Well, well,
I hope at last he'll have his joy of it,
And all his pigs and sheep and bellowing beeves,
And frogs and owls and unicorns, moreover,
Be less than hell to his attendant ears.
Oh, past a doubt we'll all go down to see him.

He may be wise. With London two days off,
Down there some wind of heaven may yet revive him:
But there's no quickening breath from anywhere
Shall make of him again the poised young faun
From Warwickshire, who'd made, it seems, already
A legend of himself before I came
To blink before the last of his first lightning.
Whatever there be, there'll be no more of that;
The coming on of his old monster Time
Has made him a still man; and he has dreams
Were fair to think on once, and all found hollow.
He knows how much of what men paint themselves
Would blister in the light of what they are;
He sees how much of what was great now shares
An eminence transformed and ordinary;
He knows too much of what the world has hushed
In others, to be loud now for himself;
He knows now at what height low enemies
May reach his heart, and high friends let him fall;
But what not even such as he may know
Bedevils him the worst: his lark may sing
At heaven's gate how he will, and for as long
As joy may listen, but *he* sees no gate,
Save one whereat the spent clay waits a little
Before the churchyard has it, and the worm.
Not long ago, late in an afternoon,
I came on him unseen down Lambeth way,
And on my life I was afear'd of him:
He gloomed and mumbled like a soul from Tophet,

His hands behind him and his head bent solemn.
"What is it now," said I,—"another woman?"
That made him sorry for me, and he smiled.
"No, Ben," he mused; "it's Nothing. It's all Nothing.
We come, we go; and when we're done, we're done.
Spiders and flies—we're mostly one or t'other—
We come, we go; and when we're done, we're done."
"By God, you sing that song as if you knew it!"
Said I, by way of cheering him; "what ails ye?"
"I think I must have come down here to think,"
Says he to that, and pulls his little beard;
"Your fly will serve as well as anybody,
And what's his hour? He flies, and flies, and flies,
And in his fly's mind has a brave appearance;
And then your spider gets him in her net,
And eats him out, and hangs him up to dry.
That's Nature, the kind mother of us all.
And then your slattern housemaid swings her broom,
And where's your spider? And that's Nature, also.
It's Nature, and it's Nothing. It's all Nothing.
It's all a world where bugs and emperors
Go singularly back to the same dust,
Each in his time; and the old, ordered stars
That sang together, Ben, will sing the same
Old stave tomorrow."

               When he talks like that,
There's nothing for a human man to do
But lead him to some grateful nook like this
Where we be now, and there to make him drink.
He'll drink, for love of me, and then be sick;
A sad sign always in a man of parts,
And always very ominous. The great
Should be as large in liquor as in love,—
And our great friend is not so large in either:
One disaffects him, and the other fails him;
Whatso he drinks that has an antic in it,
He's wondering what's to pay in his insides;
And while his eyes are on the Cyprian

He's fribbling all the time with that damned House.
We laugh here at his thrift, but after all
It may be thrift that saves him from the devil;
God gave it, anyhow,—and we'll suppose
He knew the compound of his handiwork.
Today the clouds are with him, but anon
He'll out of 'em enough to shake the tree
Of life itself and bring down fruit unheard-of,—
And, throwing in the bruised and whole together,
Prepare a wine to make us drunk with wonder:
And if he live, there'll be a sunset spell
Thrown over him as over a glassed lake
That yesterday was all a black wild water.

God send he live to give us, if no more,
What now's a-rampage in him, and exhibit,
With a decent half-allegiance to the ages
An earnest of at least a casual eye
Turned once on what he owes to Gutenberg,
And to the fealty of more centuries
Than are as yet a picture in our vision.
"There's time enough,—I'll do it when I'm old,
And we're immortal men," he says to that;
And then he says to me, "Ben, what's 'immortal'?
Think you by any force of ordination
It may be nothing of a sort more noisy
Than a small oblivion of component ashes
That of a dream-addicted world was once
A moving atomy much like your friend here?"
Nothing will help that man. To make him laugh,
I said that he was a mad mountebank—
And by the Lord I nearer made him cry.
I could have eat an eft then, on my knees,
Tail, claws, and all of him; for I had stung
The king of men, who had no sting for me,
And I had hurt him in his memories;
And I say now, as I shall say again,
I love the man this side idolatry.

He'll do it when he's old, he says. I wonder.
He may not be so ancient as all that.
For such as he, the thing that is to do
Will do itself,—but there's a reckoning;
The sessions that are now too much his own,
The roiling inward of a stilled outside,
The churning out of all those blood-fed lines,
The nights of many schemes and little sleep,
The full brain hammered hot with too much thinking,
The vexed heart over-worn with too much aching,—
This weary jangling of conjoined affairs
Made out of elements that have no end.
And all confused at once, I understand,
Is not what makes a man to live forever.
O no, not now! He'll not be going now:
There'll be time yet for God knows what explosions
Before he goes. He'll stay awhile. Just wait:
Just wait a year or two for Cleopatra,
For she's to be a balsam and a comfort;
And that's not all a jape of mine now, either.
For granted once the old way of Apollo
Sings in a man, he may then, if he's able,
Strike unafraid whatever strings he will
Upon the last and wildest of new lyres;
Nor out of his new magic, though it hymn
The shrieks of dungeoned hell, shall he create
A madness or a gloom to shut quite out
A cleaving daylight, and a last great calm
Triumphant over shipwreck and all storms.
He might have given Aristotle creeps,
But surely would have given him his *katharsis.*

He'll not be going yet. There's too much yet
Unsung within the man. But when he goes,
I'd stake ye coin o' the realm his only care
For a phantom world he sounded and found wanting
Will be a portion here, a portion there,
Of this or that thing or some other thing

That has a patent and intrinsical
Equivalence in those egregious shillings.
And yet he knows, God help him! Tell me, now,
If ever there was anything let loose
On earth by gods or devils heretofore
Like this mad, careful, proud, indifferent Shakespeare!
Where was it, if it ever was? By heaven,
'Twas never yet in Rhodes or Pergamon—
In Thebes or Nineveh, a thing like this!
No thing like this was ever out of England;
And that he knows. I wonder if he cares.
Perhaps he does. . . . O Lord, that House in Stratford!

PART TWO

೭☙

On Wording

No matter how sorrowful the subject matter of one's story or poem, no matter how grim one's vision of human existence, every serious artist brings to his or her creation a similar kind of loving care for detail and form. In this sense all true art is life enhancing, for it affirms the virtues of precision and the goodness of design. If nihilists give themselves over to the absence of purpose and order, artists commit themselves to the structuring of chaos and the filling of the existential void.

The love of verbal order, which Yeats describes as "speech wrought of high laughter, loveliness and ease," is at the heart of each artist's motivation to create, and it demands that he or she regard the craft as seriously as the chosen subject. Thus every poem also celebrates itself by demonstrating the power of the human mind to create design, adding to nature where nature is seen as barren of human purpose. When we, as readers, peruse a poem, we regard it as a presence and as an event, as well as consider its meaning. This is what Williams asserts when he says: "A poem which does not arouse respect for the technical requirements of its own mechanics . . . will be as empty as a man made of wax or straw . . . technique means everything. . . . The importance lies in what the poem is. Its existence as a poem is of first importance, a technical matter." Yeats warns, "The greatest temptation of the artist is creation without toil," and Blake insists, "Invention depends altogether upon execution or organization; as that is right or wrong, so is the invention perfect or imperfect. Whoever is set to undermine the execution of art is set to destroy art."

In a 1945 letter to a friend, Dylan Thomas wrote: "It is only the texture of a poem that can be discussed at all. Nobody wants to talk about how a poem FEELS to him: he finds it emotionally moving or he doesn't: and, if he does, there's nothing to discuss except the means, the words themselves, by which this emotional feeling was aroused." In the same sense, an experienced writer cannot instruct a beginner in how to be imaginative or how to become inspired. The writer can, however, exhort the beginner to be deliberate in the choice of words, in the conviction that without the right wording, without the appropriate rhythms, without design, an essential aspect of what one feels does not get communicated. It is as if Shakespeare, having written "This thou perceiv'st, which makes thy love more strong, / To love that well which thou must leave ere long," might have expressed what he felt by saying: "You can see that what makes your love stronger is that you must leave life pretty soon." For the artist, the choice of words is not a matter of mere ornament; it is a matter of conveying the *feeling* of what one thinks.

In his poem "Adam's Curse," Yeats compares the difficulty of writing a poem with the difficulty of making oneself into a humanely beautiful person. The poem's central idea is that art cannot be created without labor and that spontaneity, paradoxically, is something that must be achieved, through discipline, as the effect of the completed poem. Both in art and in love, Yeats claims, the experience of grace comes, not first, but last. In Adam's fallen world only labor and control can liberate instinct. Such is the condition and burden of our inheritance from Adam. Yeats's poem begins:

> We sat together at one summer's end,
> That beautiful mild woman, your close friend,
> And you and I, and talked of poetry.
> I said: A line will take us hours maybe;
> Yet if it does not seem a moment's thought,
> Our stitching and unstitching has been naught.

Yeats's poem ends convincingly because it creates the *illusion* that its words have flowed naturally and inevitably from the poem's innermost emotions of weariness: Yeats's pessimism about winning the love of Maud Gonne, the woman he addresses. The poem is successful in contriving to express—and thus to relieve—an immediate feeling of emotional failure—a failure redeemed through the very act of its deliberate and organized articulation.

ಜಿ

On Sincerity and Skill

IN HIS ESSAY "Politics and the English Language," George Orwell states that "the great enemy of clear language is insincerity."* There are, I believe, two kinds of insincerity: the insincerity of the scoundrel whose intent is to deceive and manipulate and for whom language is powerful precisely because it can conceal the truth; and the variant of insincerity that, not exactly intentional, is partly unconscious and into which we all slip from time to time. We might call the latter the insincerity of failed self-knowledge; it comes from laziness or lack of courage. Auden portrays this kind of insincerity deftly in his parody of the social worker who exclaims: "We are all here on earth to help others; what on earth others are here for I don't know." Montaigne says: "If falsehood, like truth, had only one face, we would be in better shape. For we would take as certain the opposite of what the liar said. But the reverse of truth has a thousand shapes and a limitless field. . . . We are men, and hold together only by our word."

---

* George Orwell, *A Collection of Essays* (New York: Doubleday, Anchor Books, 1954), 173.

Good writers need good readers, and good readers must be good listeners. Caring listeners must be as sensitive to rhythm and voice tone as they are to image and to meaning. Robert Frost declared in a letter to E. A. Robinson: "Good writing is good speaking caught alive. The speaking tones are all there on the printed page."

Whatever claims we might conjecture or dispute for the political or moral effects of literature upon society, we would agree, I assume, that literature must perform the essential cultural function of keeping the language "alive," rescuing it from abstractions that are devoid of image or feeling. Orwell goes on to say that "in our time, political speech and writing are largely the defense of the indefensible," yet Orwell's modest political optimism was rooted in his further statement that "the present political chaos is connected with the decay of language; and one can probably bring about some improvement by starting at the verbal end." Language is most effective *and* truthful when it refers concretely to the physical world of common experience and when it evokes a human voice whose intonation conveys the nuances of emotion.

The poet James Wright told the story of a candidate for mayor who promised his potential voters that under his administration the city would rise to "new platitudes of achievement." Wright's remark in response to this political promise was that he could almost hear the language crying out: "Save me! Save me!" We must continue to try to listen to each other and to learn to use words precisely, so that heartfelt and imaginative writing, free of sloppiness and quackery, will not become merely an oddity of our civilization like the duckbilled platitude.

As writers and readers we share a love for language, for how words sound, for the rhythms they can dance out, for the patterns they can be made to form; but we also share the unending responsibility for guarding language so that it remains accurate as a means by which human truths may be sought and expressed in order that we can hold together. If the enemy of honest language is insincerity and if even the writer of the most firm integrity can lie a little, out of the human weakness that desires attention or influence, then it follows that we need each other not just as audience, but as critics, helping each other to know ourselves better.

Commenting on Shelley's claim that poets are the "unacknowledged legislators of the world," Auden says that the "unacknowledged legislators of the world" describes, more appropriately, not the poets, but the secret police. He is right. There are limits to what artists can do through their art to improve the human condition. Were this not so, Shakespeare surely would have cured us many griefs ago. Perhaps the beginning of artistic integrity is simply humility: a poem is, first and last, merely a poem. As Yeats admits: "We do not have the gift to set a statesman right." I do not think I am being pessimistic in suggesting that all that literary art can do is help keep our language fresh, heartfelt, and honest, and rescue discourse from excessive abstraction and propaganda. Human history, as I imagine its mythic origin, begins with the serpent's lie to Eve in the Garden of Eden. The fork-tongued devil—the principle of deception for the sake of power and of self-deception for the sake of pride—still contends for the ownership of the world. We need each other's support in the endeavor to tell a fuller truth than the comfortable indignations that confirm our own self-righteousness. Telling the complex truth requires skill as well as sincerity. Or, perhaps, I might say, it requires the patience to develop skill as a necessary aspect of sincerity.

Theodore Roethke describes himself as a "perpetual beginner." And Yeats, in the last year of his life, wrote to Dorothy Wellesley: "I am beginning to learn how to write." The talent to learn how to write honestly and well demands the patience to accept limited success and to endure failure. In a hundred years, most current writers are likely to be forgotten. What keeps us trying against the odds must be our belief in the power of language: the value of order that verbal design can add to the world it describes. William Carlos Williams asserts his poetic commitment to the creating of design: "The birds twitter now anew, but a design / surmounts their twittering. / It is a design of a man / that makes them twitter. It is a design." If such lasting design—design that both enhances and surmounts nature—is difficult to achieve, at least we may choose to feel with Robert Frost that "what is worth succeeding in, is worth failing in." Our best hope, of course, is that our sincere failures will be instructive, that we will grow in skill by acknowledging and understanding them.

On Experience

For every literary artist the impulse to write derives, at least in part, from something rooted in his or her own experience. Some element of that originating impulse will become manifest in the work of art, though it may be transformed significantly in the process of creation and revision. And yet the activity of creation must include its own emotion, independent of the artist's initiating subject. Every true poem contains and expresses the delight of its own creation, thus possessing what Wallace Stevens calls the "gaiety of language."

Because of this aspect of the poem, in which the poem celebrates itself as a model of the human power of artistic creation, the effect of the poem differs radically from the emotion that the poem is about. No matter how sorrowful their subjects, all good poems bring pleasure. A bad poem about a beautiful landscape leaves an impression of ugliness. No poetic attempt can be redeemed by the poem's worthy subject or the poet's sincerity. Because poems often are complex, they may puzzle us at first and reveal their emotional force upon contemplation. Gutsy emotions may be evoked by a poem, but no poem is written directly from the gut. A poet does not write about death at his father's funeral, nor about desire when aroused to make love. A human statement may be directly and deeply moving, but we do not value it as a poem, no matter how affected we are, unless it has the passion of poetic design as well as the passion appropriate to its own chosen subject. Ultimately, we love poems for being poems, though we demand that they be serious and intelligent in the way they bear witness to human emotion and behavior.

An entry in Yeats's diary of September 1909, preparatory to his writing the poem "The Fascination of What's Difficult," reads as follows:

> Subject: To complain of the fascination of what's difficult. It spoils spontaneity, and pleasure, and wastes time. Repeat the line ending difficult three times and rhyme on bolt, exalt, colt, jolt. One could use the thought that the winged and unbroken colt must drag a cart of stones out of pride because it is difficult, and end by denouncing drama, accounts, public contests and all that's merely difficult.

This passage is revealing in its self-consciousness; it is hardly language conveying the immediacy of experience or even conviction of belief. Although it does allude to the experience of getting his plays produced, Yeats needed to relive the experience in the imaginative process of writing his poem before the completed poem could convey his feelings of anger, before he could find in the poem itself a voice with the energy to utter a real curse:

> The fascination of what's difficult
> Has dried the sap out of my veins, and rent
> Spontaneous joy and natural content
> Out of my heart. There's something ails our colt
> That must, as if it had not holy blood
> Nor on Olympus leaped from cloud to cloud,
> Shiver under the lash, strain, sweat and jolt
> As though it dragged road-metal. My curse on plays

> That have to be set up in fifty ways,
> On the day's war with every knave and dolt,
> Theatre business, management of men.
> I swear before the dawn comes round again
> I'll find the stable and pull out the bolt.

Yeats's "curse on plays / That have to be set up in fifty ways" expresses his frustration, yet poetic inspiration, symbolized by the horse, Pegasus, has been liberated into flight within the poem's formal design.

There is a story about Pablo Picasso, perhaps apocryphal, yet, like a parable, convincing in conveying a danger inherent in the artistic process. An art dealer owned three paintings attributed to Picasso, but he was only sure that one of them had been painted by Picasso. And so he arranged a test by inviting Picasso to his gallery to assign dates to the paintings. "That's a fake," said Picasso when shown the first painting. "That too is a fake," Picasso said when shown the second, and, again with the third, Picasso asserted, "that also is a fake." The puzzled art dealer stated that he knew for certain that the third painting had indeed been painted by Picasso himself. "Let me assure you," Picasso replied, "that I can paint a fake Picasso as well as anyone." Imitating one's own success may be the most subtle form of artistic fakery. The experience of writing, no matter what one's poem or story is about, always must include the experience of venturing anew into the fresh possibilities of verbal design, the gaiety of language, even in the face of the most profound sorrow.

꧁

On Prowess and Revision

Form both controls and releases energy in literary art and in sports. Frost is right, I believe, in arguing that these talents—what he calls "prowess"—are alike whether one is disciplining the mind or the body. Frost describes prowess as the "ability to perform with success in games, in the arts and in battle." Sometimes, possessed no doubt by the Muse of Poetry, athletes, not usually eloquent, burst into metaphor. I offer two favorite examples: when asked what it was like to face the great hitter, Rod Carew, one pitcher replied, "Trying to get a fast ball past Rod Carew is like trying to sneak the sunrise past a rooster"; when a running back was asked what it was like to be tackled by the crushing linebacker, Dick Butkus, he replied, "Butkus is an accident looking for a place to happen." The theme is always energy and its marvelous transforming power. Blake tells us that "Energy is eternal delight."

All sport lovers know that the poet laureate of baseball is Yogi Berra, for the ordinary laws of linguistic logic never have been able to inhibit Yogi—as when Yogi proclaimed, transforming what was once a cliché, that "ninety percent of the game of baseball is one-half mental." And when manager

Casey Stengel instructed Yogi to swing only at balls within the strike zone, after which advice Yogi fanned on three straight pitches, he complained: "Casey, I can't think and hit at the same time." The literary translation of that remark might be found in one experienced writer's reply to a novice: "Yes, I do think about craft much of the time—except when I'm writing." One may begin with literary potential, but real "prowess" comes through achieved control: discipline is needed to release power and give energy its focus in performance.

There is a cartoon in which Patrick Henry, having just declared "Give me liberty or give me death!" is sentenced by the judge to be shot. As two sergeants are about to lead him from the courtroom, Henry turns to the judge and says, "Your Honor, let me try rephrasing that." This cartoon, of course, is a parable of the writer's special prerogative—his or her liberty to revise a poem even at the last minute. In this respect, the consequences of actual life most differ from the consequences of writing. We are not free to revise historical events. The closest we come in life to the artist's ability to revise is through the power to forgive and to ask for forgiveness. In "Asphodel that Greeny Flower," William Carlos Williams says: "What power has love but forgiveness? In other words / by its intervention / what has been done / can be undone." The artist's freedom to revise, to begin again, to try to do better, is a kind of grace—the special privilege of the life of the imagination.

Revision means learning through the acknowledgment of limitation and failure. Creation in its largest sense, then, must be thought of as a process of creation, destruction, and re-creation. In this process we may become aware of powers we did not know we possessed. In a practical sense—since the human mind is agile in its capacity for rationalization—whenever a friendly critic says to us, "that poem can be improved; its language can be more precise, more visual, more musical; its structure can be more dramatic, more expressive," he can help us overcome the powerful wish to have completed the poem. The critic, or his interiorized admonishing voice, can help us find the strength to destroy what has been only partially realized, and to begin again. Such self-discipline, incorporating the critical and revising intelligence into a larger creative enterprise, is expressed in Picasso's advice to a young painter:

> When you begin a picture, you often make some pretty discoveries. You must be on guard against these. Destroy the thing, do it over several times. In each destroying of a beautiful discovery, the artist does not really suppress it, but rather transforms it, condenses it, makes it more substantial. What comes out in the end is the result of discarded finds. Otherwise, you become your own connoisseur. I sell myself nothing.

A famous American poet offered his audiences of aspiring poets the following formula for composition: "First idea, best idea," he said. How could they possibly go wrong by following such advice? Successful writing must be easy if one can count on the Muse, on instant inspiration, to do the work. But how does one know the first idea is the best idea if one does not have a second idea with which to compare it? In a perverse mood, one might imagine Galileo declaring: "First hypothesis, best hypothesis, and so of course, the sun must revolve around the earth." The rationalizing wish to write without revision belies the deeper delight of sustained concentration, of accumulating detail and shaping particulars into an informing design. Artistic pleasure requires the fidelity to return and reconsider. Yeats claimed in his autobiography: "Is it not certain that the Creator yawns in earthquake and thunder and other popular displays, but toils in rounding the delicate spiral of a shell?" Such toil frees the imagination to consider the further possibilities of its own designs and, of equal importance, it rewards the artist's consideration of the reader in the meticulously communicated sharing of his or her vision.

❧

On Grace

In 1932, Sidney Cox, Frost's intimate friend, sent Frost his biography of him in which Cox took pains to relate what he knew about Frost's life to his poetry. Cox's assumption was that a direct connection was to be found between Frost's historical experience and his art. With a severity that risked destroying their friendship, Frost wrote back to Cox: "To be too subjective with what an artist has managed to make objective is to come on him presumptuously and render ungraceful what he in pain of his life had faith he had made graceful."*

No biographer can describe the leap an artist makes between his or her life and art. That particular transformation is the very mystery of art. The ability to fabricate is, in part, a power we create out of pure potentiality. This power to create grace from disorder derives from the cultivation of a discipline, the learning of a skill; its potential is inherent, but its realization must be earned. No aspect of craft is beneath the concern of the serious artist—as suggested by the cartoon that shows a novelist working at his desk, apparently in frustration, who looks up to see the Muse descending, harp in hand. She smiles benevolently and says: "I before E except

---

*William R. Evans, *Robert Frost and Sidney Cox: Forty Years of Friendship* (Hanover, N.H.: University Press of New England, 1981), 204.

after C." The commitment to achieve graceful form, to master a craft, and thus to be worthy of the Muse always has needed the reinforcement of a tradition that honors serious art and of a community that supports the process of learning. The love of words and patterns of words and the belief in the reality of the illusion that words can create constitute the writer's essential bond with the reader.

It is difficult to define what Frost meant when he spoke of giving to words a form that possesses "grace." Perhaps grace comes when the mind holds onto something precious, when the distraction of "getting and spending" falls away and we achieve a clarification of what we value or what we love. Or perhaps grace comes when performance is in harmony with intention, and, paradoxically, we feel free of the limitation of being a singular individual bound by a single life. As artists, we become more than ourselves; we become what we have made. "All that is personal soon rots," Yeats said, knowing that the artist's inevitable argument against nature is to preserve his or her words of shared caring, words cared into graceful form from what time would obliterate.

We do not invent language; we inherit it. Language has its own genius which re-creates itself through our use of it. We are the means by which it grows and keeps itself alive. Like a god, it speaks through us and survives us. Our minds are created by language; our thinking is made possible by the structure it provides, just as our bodies know only what our senses are capable of perceiving. And if we give ourselves to the language, embracing it, cherishing it word by word, laughing as we name the world, we may take on something of its grandeur and its majesty. I want to say that we receive its "grace," for we enter into the community of mind that crosses time and place, containing them. Every true poem, by its very nature, is a celebration of its inheritance—the language—which is never ours, though we, in our passing, partake of its ongoing grace.

❧

On Fame

TWO EVENTS—a remark at breakfast by my younger son and a dream I had—teased me into thinking about fame. Trying to prepare himself for school, but still sleepy and distracted, my son asked me: "Dad, was it you or the other Vermont poet who wrote 'Birches'?" With a flourish of gracious acknowledgment appropriate to his accolade, I reminded him that "Birches" was written by Robert Frost. My moment of fame had come and gone, and I went to my study, wondering if the wish to be remembered is indeed an essential aspect of a writer's motivation—as if in some psychological sense the fear of death and oblivion could be mitigated by the thought that something we have made survives us in our culture.

Last May, having taught my final class and turned in my grades, I was seized with what Frost calls "A springtime passion for the earth." I did not need another metaphor to connect me to my place, my Vermont landscape; I needed the earth itself—the actual touch of things, and so I decided on the project of expanding my rock garden. This work involves hauling the largest rocks I can lift and arranging them in curves and circles within which flowers and shrubs can be planted. The rocks must be placed so as to support and hold each other as if they had been destined to fit together. For the whole month rocks were the center of my thoughts and the sufficient pleasure of my days. Having completed my work, seeing that it was good, I had the following dream. I was sitting in a familiar auditorium, and we were waiting for the speaker to arrive at the podium. A distinguished, white-haired man—perhaps it was William Butler Yeats himself—glided to the microphone and said: "Will Robert Pack please come up from the audience?" Amid great applause, I left my seat, and with firm strides I walked along the aisle, up the steps to the platform where Yeats awaited me. He took my hand, held it, and then announced: "I am proud to inform all of you gathered here tonight that Robert Pack is this year's recipient of the Nobel Prize for outstanding achievement—in the building of rock gardens." The shocking aspect of the dream was the exquisite clarity of my awareness of disappointment. Yes, I was delighted to have won fame, and yet I knew that it was not exactly the fame I had hoped for.

In thinking about this dream, it seemed apparent to me that a sense of specific accomplishment could be separated from the wish for approval and public reward. As much as I love my rock garden, I do that work, not to connect myself with someone else, or with an audience, but for its intrinsic pleasure. The element of intrinsic pleasure is no less in the fitting together of words to make a poem, but the further criterion of wishing to be understood, to reach into another's life, defines, for me, what is essential to the desire for artistic accomplishment. This definition is important in its practical emphasis on communication, touching through words, sharing a sense of human worth with an actual audience of caring listeners.

Literary communication, however, includes more than ideas and conscious structures; it also includes the feelings that accompany ideas and the knowledge both of things and of people. For such communication we need more than accu-

rate description; we need metaphors and stories, and thus indirection—Dickinson's "Tell all the Truth but tell it slant."
In his sequence of dream songs, where Berryman declares,
"these poems are not meant to be understood, you understand," he is seriously joking (another form of indirection).
And when Stevens states that "a poem must resist the intelligence almost successfully," he, too, is reminding us that
poems speak from mysterious or unconscious depths, yet
finally they must be gathered into the structures of consciousness through the discipline of craft. Out of the poet's
silences, into his or her words, and finally into the reader's
silences, might be one way of charting the process of artistic
reaching out. Such a process does not need the validation of
fame, for it bespeaks the universal human need to touch and
be touched. Wherever an audience chooses to assemble, art
takes on the quality of holiness—not because it is divine,
but because it issues from the endless struggle against separation and loneliness. It matters only a little now who wrote
"Birches." What does matter is that such a poem has become
part of our collective inheritance, for also we need art in order
to be more compassionately conscious of the sources of our
own joys and sorrows. Perhaps in a thousand years, after who
knows what wars and cataclysms, "Birches" will still survive
in some anthology under the heading "Circa 1900, author
anonymous." If so, not knowing the name of the author will
not be an unbearable loss to the living.

⁊⁊

On Looking

Rᴏʙᴇʀᴛ Fʀᴏsᴛ asserted in a letter that "poetry is a fresh look and a fresh listen." The cadences implied by the sequences of words on a page is what Frost meant when he said, "I can't keep up any interest in sentences that don't sʜᴀᴘᴇ on some speaking tone of voice." The willingness to listen constitutes the literary bond that holds us together, and the shared love for the names of things. For example, in August in Vermont the fields and woods will be brimming with flowers in bloom: fireweed, black-eyed Susans, purple vetch, bird's-foot trefoil, tiger lilies, hawkweed, asters, chickory, thistle, purple loosestrife, daisy fleabane, small sundrops, joe-pye-weed, wood-sorrel, and jewelweed. The names themselves are a cornucopia of delights. And on Bread Loaf Mountain, following the constellations of the zodiac on a clear night, one can become dizzy with stars. Chances are good at this time of the year that we will get our first display of northern lights. The sense of awe, both wonder and dread, that comes from the feeling of human finitude in the presence of cosmic space ties us to our first ancestors and reminds us of our mere creaturehood, our vulnerability, and, thus, our need for language to assert our momentary presence on this planetary stage. This world of lights and images, witnessed and named, is indeed the theater, as Stevens says in "The Auroras of Autumn," in which we play out the obscure dramas of our lives:

> It is a theatre floating through the clouds,
> Itself a cloud, although of misted rock
> And mountains running like water, wave on wave,
> Through waves of light. It is of cloud transformed
> To cloud transformed again, idly, the way
> A season changes color to no end,
> Except the lavishing of itself in change,
> As light changes yellow into gold and gold
> To its opal elements and fire's delight,
> Splashed wide-wise because it likes magnificence
> And the solemn pleasures of magnificent space.

Surely, at the heart of literary ambition, there lies the wish to name things in their passing, cherishing them more powerfully, precisely because they *are* passing. We are most centered in our lives when we apprehend ourselves in our own vanishing—as Shakespeare's Antony does in a passage that is the literary source of Stevens's description above of the northern lights. Shakespeare's key word, "pageant," becomes Stevens's key word, "theatre."

ANTONY: Eros, thou yet behold'st me?
EROS: Ay, noble lord.
ANTONY: Sometimes we see a cloud that's dragonish;
         A vapor sometimes like a bear or lion,
         A towered citadel, a pendant rock,
         A forked mountain, or blue promontory
         With trees upon't that nod unto the world
         And mock our eyes with air. Thou hast seen these signs;
         They are black Vesper's pageants.
EROS: Ay, my lord.
ANTONY: That which is now a horse, even with a thought
         The rack dislimns, and makes it indistinct
         As water is in water.

EROS: It does, my lord.
ANTONY: My good knave, Eros, now thy captain is
           Even such a body: here I am Antony,
           Yet cannot hold this visible shape. . . .

As Shakespeare's vision informs Stevens's poem, so, too, Stevens's words become part of the natural landscape, part of the spectacle of the northern lights, and those words enable us to see more clearly, more humanely, what already is there in the physical world, our home, our place.

Samuel Butler quipped that "a chicken is an egg's way of producing another egg," and, likewise, for us, creatures of culture as well as of nature, it is probably meaningless to assign priority to the things of this world over our names for them. We are now preceded both by trees and by the names of trees—oak, maple, ash, poplar, birch, basswood. Throughout recorded looking, the place we inhabit is always being expanded as the natural fact of the newly rooted poem becomes, in its turn, both precedent and cause for the worded nature that follows in the flare of its inevitable passing.

On Humility

THERE IS a story about Albert Einstein that reads as a parable of artistic, as well as scientific, ambition. A promising physicist was described to Einstein as a very humble young man. Einstein reputedly replied: "How can he be humble? He hasn't discovered anything yet!" Humility, like modesty, is a dangerous virtue, for, as Einstein suggested, one must have some accomplishment to be modest about. And if one's modesty exceeds one's achievements, one risks being hypocritical—one's humility becomes an invitation to flattery. The parable also implies that a physicist probably needs a measure of presumptuous ambition if he or she sets out to do original work. So, too, the serious artist must venture forth against discouraging odds in the attempt to create a poem, a story, or a novel that will survive and become part of an enduring tradition. In effect, every artist must prepare himself, through trial and repeated effort, to wake up one morning and say, "Today I will begin work on my masterpiece which, perhaps, I will call *Paradise Lost.*" There can be no substantial ambition without arrogance in the face of the task to be accomplished, and, of course, such animating arrogance—"I have presumed," Milton confesses, carries with it, inevitably, the fear of unworthiness: humility, not as a manifestation of virtue but as a form of uneasiness. Most serious writers will acknowledge *worry* as a symptom of ambition, but the anxiety inherent in ambition may be regarded as both necessary and good; anxiety need not result in the denial or distortion of influences.

And yet to argue in behalf of the healthy and grateful aspect of tradition and influence necessitates also the acknowledgment of the anarchic wish for the breaking of constraints that are associated with parental power. At a public reading, a Vermont poet recited a poem in which he shoots Robert Frost so that his own poetic style would supersede the supposedly old-fashioned diction of Frost. The audience nervously applauded, though one saucy wit remarked afterward that he thought Frost would have been faster on the draw than his would-be assassin. Yes, the Oedipus and the Electra complexes have their equivalents in the arena of literary ambition. But it is also possible that sons can reconcile with their fathers, daughters with their mothers, and that gratitude for what the parents have embodied—tradition seen as a gift, an enabling inheritance—can become the bond that replaces an adversarial sense of generational competitiveness. Thus, also, the compulsive pursuit of the eccentric and the new may give way as an avant garde aesthetic to a more stable emphasis on substance and quality.

All writers must celebrate what Yeats called "monuments of unaging intellect," the society of readers and writers that forms when literary values and ambitions are shared. The conception of quality and literary seriousness, as exemplified in models of past achievement, should strengthen a writer's resolve to do his or her best, without diminishing the sense of self or individual style. In his late poem "Under Ben Bulben," Yeats leaves his inheritance to the next generation of poets, exhorting them: "Irish poets, learn your trade, / Sing whatever is well made, / Scorn the sort now growing up / All out of shape from toe to top, / Their unremembering hearts and

heads / Base-born products of base beds." The devoted reader
of Yeats may feel that Yeats has earned the right to indulge in
his own grouchiness that derives both from defiance of death
and from generational tension, but the dominant passion of
Yeats's poem that moves us here includes his injunction to
preserve the commitment to artistic excellence and the personal wish to be remembered. To resent the past is to repress
the certain knowledge that the present generation—for all
our innovations and reforms—soon becomes the past. A serious writer's only hope lies in the power of a literary tradition
that remains relevant and alive, in which the bond between
parent and child is a source of power, rather than a threat to
individuality.

Another parabolic story tells of a monk who is lying on his
death bed, hoping that he will be inspired with some final
words for his fellow monks to remember. The grieving monks
circle about him, enumerating his talents and his virtues:
"He had the truest tenor voice in our choir," said one. "He was
the best interpreter of the philosophy of Aquinas," said another. A third added: "You could always count on him for a
sympathetic look and a kindly word." "His poetry flowed so
gracefully within the constraints of sonnet form," said the
literary monk among them. The dying monk managed to lift
his head a little from his pillow as they bent to catch his final
words: "Don't forget my humility!" he whispered. One can
imagine a pious gasp suppressed collectively by the surviving
monks, yet one also can imagine that in their official de-
corum they fail to notice the dying monk's exaggerated wink
as he points across the room to the desk where, later, they
will find his poems, meticulously inscribed, carefully arranged by theme, and bound in the finest Florentine leather
to be preserved as his inheritance for his posterity.

ॐ

On Lying and Nonsense

In SHAKESPEARE'S *As You Like It,* an exchange between Audrey, a country wench, and Touchstone, the clown, reads as follows:

TOUCHSTONE: Truly, I would the gods had made thee poetical.
AUDREY: I do not know what "poetical" is. Is it honest in deed and word? Is it a true thing?
TOUCHSTONE: No, truly, for the truest poetry is the most feigning; and lovers are given to poetry, and what they swear in poetry may be said as lovers they do feign.

Shakespeare's view of love, particularly in his comedies, is that it must be regarded as a fiction, an invention, an illusion, and yet, like poetry, the idea of love is a lie that contributes something valuable to reality. In *A Midsummer Night's Dream,* Theseus declares, "The lunatic, the lover, and the poet, / Are of imagination all compact," and though each of them deals in deception, including self-deception, each of them has the power to give such palpable embodiment to their lying, that the lies take on a truth of their own. Theseus goes on to describe the poet's imagination which "bodies forth / The forms of things unknown. . . . and gives to airy nothing / A local habitation and a name." So, too, Wallace Stevens asserts the human need for such "lying" when he cries out: "Unreal, give back to us what once you gave, / The imagination which we spurned and crave." Yeats also insists on the connection between the imagination's power to create fictions and the human capacity for love when he says that "love itself would be no more than an animal hunger but for the poet." As lovers and poets, by the lunatic light of our nocturnal minds, we dream ourselves back into wakefulness.

Lying for the sake of love or for the sake of poetry assumes that lying can have a benevolent effect. The belief in the "white lie" places human need for consolation or avoidance of pain above the literalness of reality—reality as unmitigated fact. Plato, in barring poets from his ideal Republic, chooses strict truthfulness, beyond fictive imagination, as his highest value. And, as in the writings of Freud, nobility of mind is to be found when the pleasure principle gives way through reasoning to the intractable dictates of the reality principle. Our ambivalence toward lying, even in its most benign forms, is characteristic of our psychology. We can see this ambivalence, for example, in such words as "fabricate," which means both to make, to create, and to make up or deceive; and "fabulous," which means both legendary, pertaining to a fable, and barely credible, straining belief. Plato, finally, has Socrates relent and allow what he calls the "honeyed muse" to return from exile upon the condition that "she make a defense of herself in lyrical or some other metre."

In his essay "The Lie Detector," Lewis Thomas, a biologist, takes delight in the fact that human beings cannot lie without the lie's having an actual effect on our bodies. Thomas expounds: "A human being cannot tell a lie, even a small one, without setting off a kind of smoke alarm somewhere deep in a dark lobule of the brain, resulting in the sudden discharge of nerve impulses. . . . Lying, then, is stressful, even when we do it for protection, or relief, or escape, or profit. . . . We are a moral species by compulsion, at least in the limited sense that we are biologically designed to be truthful to each other."* The inability to lie with physiological impunity demonstrates to Thomas that we are not moral beings merely by social necessity or conditioning.

In reflecting on the counterclaims of artistic lying, on the one hand, and the tough-minded adherence to the truth, on the other, I decided to perform an experiment on myself. When giving a poetry reading, I would have myself strapped to a lie detector and I would find out what effect my own lying—for the sake of creating images and poetic fictions— had on my own body. Would my body respond as if I were guilty of some crime against instinctual morality, the morality of literal truthfulness? Would the ghost of Plato rise from the audience and gesticulate with a sweeping gesture of banishment?

I could, of course, excuse myself by pleading the Fifth Amendment or by claiming poetic license. The Examination Center in Waterbury, Vermont, informed me that the police do not give lie-detector tests to heart patients or to pregnant women because such tests are dangerously stressful. Since I am repeatedly pregnant with new poems, I ought to be exempt. But a bolder strategy, I think, would be to recite an hour-long nonsense poem—a poem of pure sounds. Nonsense, like music, is free of content—except for the feeling of its vowels and consonants—and such feeling cannot lie because it cannot be measured by anything outside itself. How it sounds is what it is. Its creation embodies the spirit of play in that it lives and moves by the rules of its own making. Nonsense defies the tyranny of reason, of logic, and of meaning by liberating itself from the preexistent structures of reality. Nonsense expresses the triumphant anarchy of the mind, the lover's expansive sense of possibility.

*Lewis Thomas, *Late Night Thoughts on Listening to Mahler's Ninth Symphony* (New York: Viking, 1983), 128.

And yet, though beyond lying and the truth, beyond morality and guilt, my nonsense poem, I fear, would leave me
standing before the microphone rather lonely. If anyone in
the audience remained after an hour of my declaiming pure
and meaningless sounds, no matter how expressive or mellif-
luous, they would, I am sure, miss the basic pleasure of
human communication. Human sharing is so precious that
we easily forget we cannot live without reaching out to touch
each other through language, meaningful language. A little
lying, a little illusion, to hold us together is to be desired, I
would say, since our vulnerable natures require both intimacy and protection from intimacy at the same time.

There is no phrase more exuberantly happy than one that
appears in Lewis Carroll's poem "Jabberwocky." After his son
has slain the monstrous Jabberwock, the father cries out: "O
frabjous day!" His jubilation carries him virtually beyond the
limits of language, not only in the round note of the rush of
breath in the vowel, "O," but also in the invented adjective,
"frabjous," which has its own stressed grab and grip and lip-
ful juiciness. And yet "frabjous" is not totally beyond meaning, for it suggests the words *fabulous* and *joyous*, with an
extra "r" thrown in free for the pleasure of rolling it up from
the throat and over the teeth while the whole phrase presses
itself against the norm of iambic meter—a pleasure fabricated for the love of its invention.

On Ecstasy

Our modern word *ecstasy* has come to indicate a condition of exalted delight in which normal or mundane understanding is felt to be transcended. The etymology of the word, going back to the Greek, *ecstasis,* means to be driven out of one's place, out of one's senses, beyond oneself. I like to think that a contemporary version of ecstasy, one induced by the combination of imagination and science, not by drugs, manifests itself in the contemplation of and indeed in the attempt to communicate with intelligent life from outer space. It would be bliss to know that we are not alone in the vastness of the universe. But if we are to beam out messages to a civilization that would have to be at least a hundred light years away, we must turn inward first, to ask ourselves: What greeting shall we give? What shall we say? My own first impulse would be to send a cosmic SOS: PLANET IN DANGER . . . HELP NEEDED . . . WHAT SHALL WE DO? The problem with sending this message, of course, is that, across such distances, it would take over two hundred years to receive a reply. Their advice, enabling us at last to solve the problem of controlling aggression in order to survive, would, I am afraid, arrive here too late.

In Lewis Thomas's essay "Ceti," the title of which refers to a "relatively nearby star that sufficiently resembles our sun to make its solar system a plausible candidate for the existence of life," Thomas, the biologist, ponders the question of what news of ourselves we should transmit, and he concludes: "I would vote for Bach, all of Bach, streamed out into space, over and over again. We would be bragging, of course, but it is surely excusable for us to put the best possible face on at the beginning of such an acquaintance."*

Although I would like to add some Purcell, Handel, Haydn, and Mozart to augment Bach, I approve of Thomas's strategy. The message implied by our best music, howsoever the story of humankind continues or concludes, would be that we are or were capable of great pleasure, and, furthermore, we were capable of sharing that pleasure, getting outside ourselves, even (should this imagining turn true) reaching beyond the delicate membrane of our sky to other life among the stars.

If we take music to be the language of feeling—the composer's feelings, yes, but feeling that exists only by virtue of the creation of musical form—then listening to music is an act of virtually pure empathy. For a time, we, the listeners, feel only what the composer felt. We get outside ourselves into his or her being. For a time, it does not matter who we are, what we are like, or what we believe. We could be inhabitants on a planet in which sorrow and the excruciating awareness of mortality have been entirely transformed into impersonal pleasure.

The transformation of individual pain and distress into pleasure which can be empathetically shared is, it seems to me, the essential function of all art. Just so, Mozart describes the essence of his own artistic intent in a letter to his father: "Passions, whether violent or not, must never be expressed in such a way as to excite disgust, and music, even in the most

*Lewis Thomas, *The Lives of a Cell* (New York: Viking, 1974), 45.

terrible situations, must never offend the ear, but must please the hearer, or in other words must never cease to be *music*."

Unlike music, however, literature is an "impure" art in that, through words, it necessarily refers to the world outside its own form. The substance of literature includes ideas with which the reader will agree or disagree, and, inevitably, we are tempted to prefer those literary works that confirm our own beliefs. Yet it is not philosophical or political concurrence that matters most to those who value what literature has to offer the human spirit; rather, what the venturesome reader seeks is the empathetic experience of feeling what someone else has felt, living, as it were, in someone else's mind and body under circumstances other than one's own, in other places, in other historical times. Getting outside oneself—that is the ecstasy provided by the literary imagination. When, for example, Gerard Manley Hopkins cries out to God, "Send my roots rain!" the readers identify with his anguish whether or not they, too, believe in a god to whom one can pray; and when Thomas Hardy asks "Or are we live remains / Of Godhead dying downwards, brain and eye now gone?" we can equally identify with his pain of feeling abandoned in a world where a deity no longer abides to whom he can turn for meaning and consolation. Soon enough, we will put down our books and return to our own theology, our own politics, but we will feel less alone within the boundary of our own lives when we do so.

In attempting to describe the essential difference between literature and music—music does not have to overcome the resistance of personal belief in the listener—I used examples that emphasize the experience of pain or suffering. As readers, we ask, rightfully so, that the literary artist confront his or her version of reality, its threats and stresses, even though, finally, we expect that the literary work will offer us pleasure. The crucial difference between literature and fantasy is that literature must attempt to return us to the circumstances of the actual world. The source of pleasure, then, is not likely to lie in what is depicted because, even despite the physical beauty of much of the natural world, the news of humankind usually is bad. The pleasure offered by a literary work must reside, rather, in its formal aspects—those qualities of structure, design, pattern, that most resemble music. We recognize the beauty of the language itself in Shakespeare's *King Lear*, its expressiveness, its energy, its vividness, its ennobling elevation, even as we are horrified by Shakespeare's vision of human cruelty and waste. And yet, surely, there is a paradox in the additional pleasure we receive from the play in its ability to evoke our emotions of caring and sympathy—emotions we enjoy having enhanced within our hearts. Wordsworth declared in "Elegiac Stanzas," his poem about his brother's death by drowning: "A deep distress hath humanised my soul." And in "A Dialogue of Self and Soul," Yeats's poem of self-affirmation and self-transcendence, he declaims:

> When such as I cast out remorse
> So great a sweetness flows into the breast
> We must laugh and we must sing,
> We are blest by everything,
> Everything we look upon is blest.

Yeats's shift from speaking as "I" to speaking as "We," identifying himself outside himself, represents the ecstatic moment of transformation through artistic will that leads finally to the experience of musical blessedness. By such testimony we may be assured that the great gifts of literary art are its ability to evoke our powers of empathetic identification and the abstract beauty of order and form—like the elliptical orbits of the planets around our sun.

I agree wholeheartedly with Lewis Thomas that we should beam Bach out into the unknown vastness of space, searching for company in the universe, an audience, perhaps, for what we have accomplished. But should a reply come back saying

PLEASE SEND MORE, we might try some poems. I would suggest that we start with sonnets, our most musical form, and my preference would be Hopkins's poem "Henry Purcell," in which, beside himself with delight, Hopkins ends with his ecstatic description of Purcell's music whose "meaning motion fans fresh our wits with wonder." The first gift of our friends from outer space when they arrived on Earth to greet us in person, I am sure, would be a collection of sonnets that they themselves had composed in heavenly gratitude.

On Fire

THE ABILITY to employ fire for light, warmth, and protection may well mark the technology that began the evolution of human civilization. There is evidence that goes back a million years to the caves of southeastern France of hearths that functioned as the central gathering place to give ritual enhancement to the sense of human community. The earliest indication of artificial fire making is with iron-pyrite balls that are only about fifteen thousand years old. Intuitively, we understand the significance of the end of Aeschylus's play when Prometheus claims that he bestowed upon mankind a great gift: "I gave them fire."

One might speculate that although the precursor forms for human art were bodily adornments and cherished objects to accompany the dead in burial, art itself first appeared some forty thousand years ago with cave paintings that could only have been made by firelight. And since natural "elements," like fire and water, which are so precious to human survival, become invested with human feeling, inevitably they appear in our art as symbols as well as objects. So fire has come to represent energy and power, an emblem of procreative passion and artistic inspiration: "O! for a Muse of fire, that would ascend / The brightest heaven of invention" Shakespeare declaims in the prologue to *The Life of King Henry the Fifth.*

But wherever there is energy and power, the need to control them becomes an issue. Fire, like passion, can destroy as well as create. In *Civilization and Its Discontents,** Freud includes a notorious footnote that speaks to the need to control fire with the equally primal element of water. In his mythic imagining, Freud speculates: "It is as though primal man had the habit, when he came in contact with fire, of satisfying an infantile desire connected with it, by putting it out with a stream of urine." After identifying this infantile desire as a form of eroticism, Freud asserts that the control of desire is the very bedrock of civilization and culture: "By damping down the fire of his own sexual excitation, he [primal man] had tamed the natural force of life. This great cultural conquest was thus the reward for his renunciation of instinct."

Freud cites an example from Swift's *Gulliver's Travels* in which the primitive fantasy of extinguishing fire with urine is illustrated in a scene from chapter five during Gulliver's sojourn among the minute Lilliputians. Gulliver begins his account of the fire by informing his reader that he had been "intreated to come immediately to the Palace, where her Imperial Majesty's Apartment was on fire, by the Carelessness of a maid of Honour, who feel asleep while she was reading a Romance." There is a delectable irony in the suggestion that the maid's passion for the fantasy of romance has caused the destructive fire; the honor of the maid does not go as deep as her erotic wishes. Gulliver, who has been drinking wine, confronts the emergency and he rises to the challenge with a strategy that he describes as a form of inspiration: "This magnificent Palace would have infallibly been burnt down to the Ground, if, by a Presence of Mind, unusual to

*Sigmund Freud, *Civilization and Its Discontents,* ed. and trans. James Strachey (New York: Norton, 1961), 41.

me, I had not suddenly thought of an Expedient." Since, luckily, Gulliver had not yet "discharged" himself, the fire was able to produce in Gulliver its counterforce in water. Gulliver tells us: "The Heat I had contracted by coming very near the Flames, and by my labouring to quench them, made the Wine begin to operate by Urine." And thus mind and body in Gulliver conjoin to inspire Gulliver's "heroic" rescue: "I voided in such a Quantity, and applied so well to the proper places, that in three Minutes the Fire was wholly extinguished; and the rest of the noble Pile, which had cost so many Ages in erecting, preserved from Destruction."

Gulliver's goal is the preservation of art and societal structure, represented by the "magnificent Palace," yet the means by which he performs this service, Gulliver himself recognizes, may be antithetical to the achieved end:

> although I had done a very eminent Piece of Service yet I could not tell how his Majesty might resent the Manner by which I had performed it: For, by the fundamental Laws of the Realm, it is Capital in any Person, of what Quality soever, to make water within the Precincts of the Palace.

Gulliver's rumination implies that there is something potentially destructive in the attempt to control fire, just as there is in fire itself and the passions that fire represents. Making water, in this passage, then, represents a counterpassion associated with the wish to control energy, but it, too, is fraught with danger because it releases further bodily energies. The generation of counterpassion, and thus subsequent potential destructiveness, can be seen in the empress's reaction to Gulliver's urination, his attempt to employ bodily forces for constructive social purposes:

> the Empress conceiving the greatest Abhorence of what I had done, removed to the most distant Side of the Court, firmly resolved that those Buildings should never be repaired for her Use; and, in the Presence of her chief Confidents, could not forbear vowing, Revenge.

We recognize the familiar role of the empress's chief confidents, which is to disclose the confidential words of the empress's vow of revenge, though it is only implied here that Gulliver shares her disgust at the excremental functions of the human body. That disgust becomes manifest at the end of the book after Gulliver returns home and cannot abide the smell of his own family: "During the first Year I could not endure my Wife and Children in my Presence, the very Smell of them was intolerable; much less could I suffer them to eat in the same room." This disgust, however, is the source of Swift's parody, since ultimately Swift is even more deeply disgusted with the human pride that turns a man against his own body or his own species. We gradually learn that Gulliver himself is indeed such a man—a man blind to his own pride. Although Gulliver tells us that he pauses "to behold my Figure often in a Glass," he does not comprehend that the pride he despises is to be found also in himself: "But, when I behold a Lump of Deformity, and Diseased both in Body and in Mind, smitten with *Pride*, it immediately breaks all the Measures of my Patience; neither shall I be ever able to comprehend how such an Animal and such a Vice could tally together."

The image of the disease of body and mind—the fire of bodily passion and the bodily water that seeks to control this primal force—expresses the duality of human ambivalence that characterizes both our psychology and our art. Fire and water are equally basic parts of the body of the physical world and of the human imagination. The work of the artist reminds us that mind is an extension of body, that we are grounded in our creaturehood: we eat, we piss, we suffer, we enjoy sexual desire, we age, and we die back into the elements out of which we came. Yet something within us seeks to rise, like Shakespeare's muse of fire, above our bodily conditions, something perhaps that also is quintessential to art itself. Even as the imaginative mind ascends, however, we feel a kind of betrayal of the cry of the mortal flesh, and, again, we know ourselves as divided creatures—as creatures of inescapable conflict. This, I believe, is what Yeats sees in Swift when, referring to the martyr-hero, Parnell, he says in "Parnell's Funeral," "Through Jonathan Swift's dark grove he passed, and there / Plucked bitter wisdom that enriched his blood."

Swift's "bitter wisdom," which accounts for the conflicted power of his art, is succinctly embodied in the words of Yeats's antithetical self, Crazy Jane, when she cries "Fair and foul are near of kin, / And fair needs foul," and concludes:

> 'A woman can be proud and stiff
> When on love intent;
> But Love has pitched his mansion in
> The place of excrement;
> For nothing can be sole or whole
> That has not been rent.'

Though one may aspire proudly toward spiritual love, one cannot escape bodily needs which require both expression and control. Sexual desire and the body's demand for excremental relief are juxtaposed even in the anatomical placement of the organs of their functioning. Language itself is characterized by a duality of high and low as Yeats ends his poem with three egregious puns on "sole"/"soul"; "whole"/ "hole"; and "rent" as in torn but also implying that the mansion of love is rented; we do not own our mortal bodies. The conception of love's ideal wholeness which would unite man and woman, body and soul, is born in the sexual "hole" of Crazy Jane's body.

Duality—the power of fire and the power we use to control it—describes the inescapable conflict of human self-awareness and suffering, and thus it is a central theme of human art. Yeats asks, "What's water but the generated soul?" and in section 7 of his poem, "Vacillation," which begins "Between extremities/Man runs his course," Yeats offers his reader an image of fire in its cleansing and purgatorial aspect, as if in some ultimate realm of unified nature—nature transformed into art—fire and water might be reconciled into a single element.

It is significant, of course, that this little poem within a poem, takes the dualistic form of a dialogue between the Soul and the Heart, and that its subject should be the origin and source of art:

> *The Soul.* Seek out reality, leave things that seem.
> *The Heart.* What, be a singer born and lack a theme?
> *The Soul.* Isaiah's coal, what more can man desire?
> *The Heart.* Struck dumb in the simplicity of fire!
> *The Soul.* Look on that fire, salvation walks within.
> *The Heart.* What theme had Homer but original sin?

The Soul offers the Platonic argument that we seek transcendent knowledge beyond nature, to which the Heart replies that the primary themes of the human artist must be illusion and desire—both of which are forms of seeming. The Soul reminds the Heart of the purgatorial coal given by a seraphim to Isaiah to purge his lips of sin and proposes the coal's fire as an emblem of the antithetical desire to control and counteract carnal desire. The Heart recognizes the purgatorial fire of the coal as holding out a momentary hope for the relief from dualistic conflict, and thus the fire appears as an image of resolution and simplicity. And so the Soul urges the Heart to concentrate on this flaming image of resolved dualities which symbolizes the idea of salvation. But the Heart, struck dumb for only a moment, regains its speech and asserts that its role as a "singer born" is not to escape the torment of duality, of a fallen nature of unfulfilled desires, but to make that very condition, "original sin," the theme of its art, as poets, like Homer, have done from the beginning.

When Adam and Eve, as a result of original sin, are driven from the Garden of Eden into the fallen world of nature—duality, lies, and seeming—they, as Milton tells us, look back at "Paradise, so late their happy seat, / waved over by that flaming brand." In the words of the Bible, they see "a flaming sword which turned every way, to keep the way of the tree of life." Their vision of fire reveals the energy they will employ in their struggle to survive, and the equally inherent destructiveness of that energy which they must learn to control. Burning desire contending with desire, contending with itself, will remain the theme of their troubled but consoling art even as they sit, warming themselves beside the hearth.

On Empathy

A<small>N</small> E<small>NGLISH</small> <small>MAJOR</small> at Middlebury College, where I teach, was struggling during the oral examination that comes after a month of intensive review of the major works he had studied for the past three years. His three examiners were unable to evoke from him any clear recollection of the texts, and, even more discouraging, he seemed untouched by the books he supposedly had perused. He had chosen, who knows why, to discuss the theme of time and flux, so one of his examiners asked him to comment on Keats's lines describing the young lovers portrayed on the Grecian urn.

> Bold Lover, never, never canst thou kiss,
> Though winning near the goal—yet, do not grieve;
> She cannot fade, though thou hast not thy bliss,
> For ever wilt thou love, and she be fair!

The slumped young man suddenly sat upright in his chair: "Wow!" he exclaimed, "I can identify with that. He's in one hell of a situation!"

Although the student had missed the point—that Keats was trying to express the difficulty of imagining eternity, time without change—still I could identify with *his* situation. The power of identification for Keats, however, does not mean projecting oneself onto others. Rather, the strength of the writer's imagination resides in his ability for "filling some other body." *Other* is the key word, I believe, in Keats's phrase. The function of the poetic imagination, then, is not the defense or assertion of one's cherished self and one's own philosophical or political beliefs, but the expansion of self through identification and empathy into otherness. Keats gives a clear example of what he means when he says, "if a Sparrow come before my Window I take part in its existence and pick about the Gravel." The sparrow is not a trope for Keats's ideas; it is a presence in the world beyond Keats's own body, to be seized as such by his imagination, to be valued because it exists and is there to be contemplated. Unlike a belief, it cannot be refuted or become obsolete. It is there; forever, it will have been there.

The power of empathy does not, and need not, take an exclusively objective form in which observers view something or someone outside themselves as totally other. A sense of self is not always lost or denied when the imagination projects itself into another being to achieve identification, although, perhaps, in impassioned cases of romantic love, self vanishes into other and seems to be annihilated, as in Wagner's opera when Tristan says to Isolde, "Ich bin Isolde," and Isolde replies, "Ich bin Tristan."

In Hamlet's elusive speech to Horatio, midway in the play, Hamlet apprehends a quality in Horatio that Hamlet himself does not possess but with which he can identify. At the same time Hamlet is in part inventing Horatio by projecting onto him what he himself desires to feel, but cannot feel, at this point in the play.

> ... for thou hast been
> As one, in suffering all, that suffers nothing,
> A man that fortune's buffets and rewards
> Hast ta'en with equal thanks; and bless'd are those

> Whose blood and judgment are so well co-mingled
> That they are not a pipe for fortune's finger
> To sound what stop she please. Give me that man
> That is not passion's slave, and I will wear him
> In my heart's core, ay, in my heart of heart,
> As I do thee. (II.2.65–74)

Hamlet sees in Horatio a capacity for reason, a balance between passion and intellect, that allows one to choose and thus, in some sense, determine one's own fate. The play will reveal that Hamlet is partially accurate in his depiction of Horatio. When Hamlet broods obsessively about death and decay beside Yorick's grave, Horatio admonishes him by saying, " 'Twere to consider too curiously, to consider so." But when Horatio sees that Hamlet is dying of poison, and Hamlet asks Horatio to "report me and my cause aright / To the unsatisfied," Horatio, with passionate abandon, snatches the cup of poison from Hamlet to follow him in death. Identifying with Hamlet, and thus not wishing to survive him, Horatio says, "Here's yet some liquor left." Hamlet then wrests the cup from Horatio and gives him the reason why he must reject the "felicity" of death and survive: "If thou did'st ever hold me in thy heart, / Absent thee from felicity awhile, / And in this harsh world draw thy breath in pain / To tell my story." Horatio will be true to the bond in which each, through empathetic identification, holds the other in his "heart's core."

The story must be told, and it must fulfill Hamlet's elliptical prophecy, which is inherent in his projection of himself into Horatio "as one, in suffering all, that suffers nothing." In order to do so, Hamlet's capacity for identification with others must continue to expand, and indeed it does as when we later hear Hamlet tell Horatio that "I am sorry, good Horatio, / That to Laertes I forgot myself, / For by the image of my cause I see / The portraiture of his." In dying, Hamlet becomes the story of Hamlet, passing beyond his own suffering into the realm of artistic wonder and speculation. Yeats de-

scribed the transcendence of personal suffering into a visionary realm as "gaiety transfiguring all that dread," and Wordsworth alludes to artistic consciousness in "Immortality Ode"
as "Thoughts that do often lie too deep for tears." Hamlet
does not suggest a moral for his story—it is the story itself
that matters, and beyond the story there is only silence.
Hamlet's final words, "The rest is silence," take us to that
realm where human sorrow, human consciousness, and human identity pass back into the unspeaking matter of which
the universe is composed.

In James Joyce's great story "The Dead," Gabriel Conroy ar-
rives at the house of his aunts to attend their annual Christmas party. Gabriel is worried about how he appears to others,
and, trapped in his own self-conscious identity, he rehearses
to himself how he will deliver his ceremonial speech at the
dinner table. "He would only make himself ridiculous by
quoting poetry to them which they could not understand,"
the story's narrator tells us, depicting Gabriel's condescen-
sion. And later, though intending to praise his aunts lavishly
in public, unsympathetically he thinks to himself, "What did
he care that his aunts were only two ignorant old women?"

On the way back to the hotel after the party, taking his
wife's hand as they get out of the carriage, Gabriel feels a
"keen pang of lust" for Greta, which seems to renew his first
ardor for her. In the hotel room, however, Greta seems "ab-
stracted," and though Gabriel is now in a "fever of rage and
desire," he thinks to himself that "to take her as she was
would be brutal." At this moment, though Gabriel is caught
up in his own passion, Greta, surprisingly, says to him: "You
are a very generous person, Gabriel." Gabriel misreads the
meaning of her comment, and thinks that she, too, is in a
state of desire for him, but it soon is revealed that Greta is
thinking about a young man of frail health, Michael Furey,
who long ago stood under her window in the rain and subsequently died. While Greta is telling Gabriel about Michael,
Gabriel thinks that he is being compared unfavorably to the

youth, and the narrator tells us that "a shameful consciousness of his own person assailed him." Gabriel asks if Michael
died of "consumption," and Greta replies, "I think he died for
me." Gabriel realizes that it is Michael, not he, who is at that
moment in Greta's heart, and Gabriel is sure that his own
physical desire cannot compete with the power of Michael's
sacrificial gesture of love. In an instant of "vague terror,"
Gabriel feels that some "vindictive" fate has separated him
from his wife, though he continues to caress her hand.

Then a kind of Christian miracle occurs in which Gabriel
embodies the meaning of his own name which, as Joyce well
knew, comes from the Hebrew *gabher*, man, and *El*, God—or
man of God. Gabriel, for the first time in the story, identifies
himself with another's feelings, and he releases Greta's hand,
"shy of intruding on her grief." He looks at her "unresent-
fully," even though he realizes that she is still grieving for
Michael's premature death. Gabriel's self-consciousness begins to fall away as "a strange, friendly pity for her entered
his soul." Thus Greta's prophetic remark, which earlier had
seemed inappropriate, that Gabriel was a "generous" man, as
if she has seen into Gabriel's soul, is proven true when the
narrator tells us: "generous tears filled Gabriel's eyes. He had
never felt like that himself toward any woman, but he knew
that such a feeling must be love." In this instant, Gabriel is
also able to identify with Michael because he empathizes
with Michael's sacrificial love. But what he has not consciously realized is that he has made an equivalent sacrificial
gesture of his own toward his wife in accepting her separate-
ness, her own sorrowful passion. Paradoxically, Gabriel has
found love not in possession, but in generosity.

Joyce's narrator depicts the psychological and spiritual process of Gabriel's moving outside himself into otherness when
he says that Gabriel's "own identity was fading out into a
grey impalpable world." The mysterious last sentence of the
story suggests Gabriel's identification with the universe at
large that the reader, likewise, is invited to make: "His soul

swooned slowly as he heard the snow falling faintly through the universe and faintly falling, like the descent of their last end, upon all the living and the dead." Through the power of Joyce's narrative art, we are summoned to move beyond *our* identification with Gabriel, beyond the stories his life has touched, to an identification with the physical world of mutability and flux in the image of the snow that is now envisioned as falling everywhere in the universe.

Cells die continuously in the human body—red blood cells live about three months, white blood cells, about two weeks, yet the body survives through change. We do not grieve for the death of a cell. It may be that we need to think of the Earth as a single organism, in which every change and every death contributes to the ongoing life of the planet, and further still, perhaps we need to think of the universe as such a single organism, created out of the originating unity of the Big Bang. The artistic imagination invites us to move outward, beyond our lives, our place, our time, as in Joyce's vision of the snow "faintly falling" or in Shakespeare's image of the descending dark when he summons us to "Now entertain conjecture of a time / When creeping murmur and the pouring dark / Fills the wide vessel of the universe." From the perspective of the fifteen-billion-year story of evolving matter—where nothing might have been—a story told alike by poetry and by science, perhaps our imaginations really can pass beyond sorrow if we can identify our singular lives with all the living and all the dead, empathize with existence itself—the transformations of energy, continuing infinitely beyond us.

ૐ

On Desire and Sublimation

THE ANTITHESIS between age and youth in most dramatic or mythical accounts takes the form of moral combat. The limitations of old age become reembodied as moral constraints imposed through social tradition upon youthful desire, and the war of the generations becomes a battle in which the parent generation attempts to control the expression of sexual desire in the young. From a parental point of view, the unwillingness to tolerate sexual restraint, to accept a sublimated substitute, is seen as a form of rebellion. Embodied through tradition in myth and story, the assertion of freedom becomes the distinguishing characteristic of rebellious heroism which, inevitably, is represented in art with ambivalence, since in their hearts the fabricating parents continue to identify with the passions of their children.

The most pervasive and powerful myth of the defiance of sexual restraint may be found in the story of Don Juan, and Mozart's opera, *Don Giovanni,* as Soren Kierkegaard rightly insisted, is its crowning example. Kierkegaard argues that the medium of music is particularly effective in the rendering of sensuous immediacy, and that "Don Juan appears as

the sensuous which opposes the spiritual to the death."[1] Don
Giovanni's sensuousness will accept no substitute, and it
reveals its basic instinctiveness by taking two related forms:
seduction and eating. The Don's ebullient credo is "Vivan le
femmine / Viva il buon vino! / Sostegno e gloria / D'uma-
nita!" (Long live the women! Love live good wine! May they
sustain and glorify humanity!). Don Giovanni's own songs
never are intended as art; they serve only in seduction. When
Don Giovanni enlists his court musicians to play, their performance is appreciated merely as an aid or an accompani-
ment to his amorous adventures, part of the action of pursuit,
not as a pause for an aesthetic experience valuable in itself.

In Peter Gay's essay on *Don Giovanni*, "The Father's Revenge," Gay's psychoanalytic reading emphasizes the element of the warring generations. The Don's leading antago-
nist is the father of Donna Anna, a lady whom Don Giovanni
has either raped or seduced (the text leaves this issue mysteriously unresolved). Seeking to protect his daughter's virtue,
the Commendatore apprehends Don Giovanni as he tries to
flee, and in the ensuing duel, the Don kills him. At the end
of the opera, the Commendatore, in the form of a stone
statue, having been invited by Don Giovanni to join him for a
meal, returns to exact revenge and to reestablish conventional order. Gay sees the Commendatore as a projection of
Mozart's own father, who had opposed Mozart's marriage and
sensual wishes, and Gay argues that the Commendatore's
return after death expresses Mozart's guilt, deriving from the
ambivalence of hostility and love that plagued him following
his father's death:

> [Mozart's] remorse must have become particularly acute dur-
> ing the spring and summer of 1787, when he was doing his
> work of mourning for a father he had intensely loved and hated.

[1] Soren Kierkegaard, *Either/Or* (New York: Doubleday, Anchor Books, 1944),
87.

His sense of supremacy must have been poisoned, not by the anguish of guilt alone, but by the fear of revenge.[2]

Surely, there is much truth in this Freudian reading both of the historical Mozart and of the thematic centrality of an oedipal struggle in the opera. Gay is on the mark when he asserts that "Don Giovanni's duel with the Commendatore seems remarkably like a symbolic parricide" (76), and Donna Anna's excessive attachment to her father's memory, which prevents her from marrying her devoted suitor, Don Ottavio, even after Don Giovanni has been killed, deepens the incestuous undertones of the erotic attachments and hostilities in the opera. Nor can the possibility be ignored that Donna Anna prefers the instinctual Don Giovanni to the proper and moralistic Don Ottavio, just as Donna Elvira, another of the Don's conquests, continues through the opera to be willing to forgive Don Giovanni anything if only he will return her love. At the opera's end she chooses to retire to a convent, although for her the convent represents not achieved virtue or purity of heart, but defeated sexuality. If she can't have Don Giovanni, there is no other acceptable substitute. Her longing for the unattainable Don is the mirror image of Don Giovanni's longing for all womankind. The moralizing of the surviving characters in the sextet that concludes the opera, "Questo e il fin di chi fa mal" (This is how all evildoers end), as Mozart's parodic music makes clear, is pathetically hollow.

A psychoanalytic interpretation of the opera, which emphasizes the oedipal conflict between father and son battling for the possession of a woman, can explain Don Giovanni's distinguishing characteristics—his insatiable lust for women and his wish to keep a list of his conquests. The Don's passion for seduction is seen as an aberration, itself a sublimation of a prior wish, made manifest as a neurotic obsession,

[2]Peter Gay, "The Father's Revenge," in *Don Giovanni: Myths of Seduction and Betrayal*, ed. Jonathan Miller (New York: Schocken Books, 1990), 74.

and such a displacement is indeed comprehensible in Freudian terms. In his essay "A Special Type of Object Choice,"
Freud describes the effect the fixed love for the mother, established in infancy, may have on her grown son when it comes
time for him to choose a wife: "the pressing desire in the
unconscious for some irreplaceable thing [the mother] often
resolves itself into an endless series in actuality—endless for
the very reason that the satisfaction longed for is in spite of
all never found in any surrogate."[3] This description fits Don
Giovanni perfectly; it accounts for why he never can remain
content with a single woman, and it illuminates his need for
the great list which Leporello keeps for him, since the list
suggests the totality of womankind whose sum of love alone
could equal the infinity of love that the infant child feels for
his mother. When the Don says to Leporello, "Chi a una sola
e fedele verso l'altra e crudele" (He who is faithful only to one
woman betrays all the others), he is not being cynical but
psychologically sincere, for the aggregate of the others, in a
dreamlike reversal, represents the lost mother, and any single woman, then, represents an inadequate surrogate for a
love that originally was experienced without limits. Understood in this way, Don Giovanni must be seen as a desperate
character, incapable of satisfaction, longing for release in
self-destruction, for whom sexuality itself is a form of sublimation, a doomed substitution for a love that he is incapable of recapturing or even recognizing. Don Giovanni's defiance of morality, then, is fundamentally hypocritical, for it
does not represent a genuine alternative to sublimation but is
itself a symptom of his own inner repression, and the death
he suffers at the hand of the revenging father figure, the
Commendatore, is the death of social compliance and interiorized guilt.

Though this reading has a strong claim to an essential

[3] Sigmund Freud, *Collected Papers*, vol. 4 (New York: Basic Books, 1959),
197.

truth, it misses, I believe, the basically joyous spirit of the opera, and, even worse, assumes a moralizing posture much like the one Mozart exposes and parodies. This reading says, in effect, that Don Giovanni is punished by his own psychology, by being who he is, by his unacknowledged identification with a persecuting parent, symbolized by the vindictive Commendatore. What the psychoanalytic or any more obvious moralistic reading of the opera fails to apprehend is the energy that radiates from Don Giovanni. Gay does not miss this point when he rightfully dismisses an equally undercutting interpretation of Don Giovanni's apparent obsessiveness, which hypothesizes that the Don is driven by the denial of, and overcompensation for, repressed homosexual longings: "Don Giovanni's exuberance sounds unforced; his bravery, though extraordinary, is too secure, too relaxed, to be a mere cloak for repressed doubts" (76).

Anyone who listens without interpretative preconceptions to Don Giovanni's outpourings when he is wooing Zerlina, or to his champagne aria at the party, or even when he is in the cemetery inviting the statue of the Commendatore to dinner knows that the Don is having fun; he is enjoying himself, free of moral compunction. One can disapprove of him for his total lack of empathy as the other characters in the opera (and we in the audience) certainly do, but one cannot find comfort in thinking that deep in his psyche Don Giovanni is in pain or that he disapproves of himself. Don Giovanni's sensuality is the life-giving and life-destroying energy of nature, unburdened by self-consciousness.

To comprehend Don Giovanni's instinctive pleasure in sensuality, a Darwinian, as well as a psychoanalytic, model is needed, and beyond that, a comic model for sublimation—a model that shifts sublimation from being most dynamic at the unconscious level to one that emphasizes the willed aspect of sublimation, thus raising it from the realm of compensatory determinism to the realm of detached laughter. Taking a Darwinian approach, one can think of Don Giovanni as a singing sperm following genetic instructions. The biologist Richard Dawkins wittily describes the human body as a "survival machine," constructed by our genes "for their continued existence."[4] The goal of our genes is to replicate themselves, and our bodies, supporting our sexual organs, are the means by which genes fulfill their ongoing destiny.

Dawkins explains that there is only one fundamental feature that distinguishes male from female in both animals and plants: "The sex cells or 'gametes' of males are much smaller and more numerous than the gametes of females." The consequences of this are enormous, for the female egg, produced in limited numbers because of its size, contributes to the feeding of the embryo, while the sperm contributes nothing at all except for the passing on of its genes. Dawkins concludes that there is a "limit on the number of children a female can have, but the number of children a male can have is virtually unlimited. Female exploitation begins here" (153). The optimal strategy of the male gene is to program its body, its "survival machine," to copulate as widely as opportunity permits and thus to replicate itself, if possible, virtually to infinity. If one can imagine a sperm as having the voice of a bass baritone, one might hear him singing, like Don Giovanni, "Vivan le femmine!"

In his comprehensive book, *The Evolution of Human Sexuality*, Donald Symons illustrates the incentive of males to disperse their seed as widely as possible by recounting how a stud animal, apparently satiated, will copulate with a succession of females with renewed vigor if they become available. It is as if the genes, inspiring his sexuality, are whispering in his ear, "Keep replicating!" Symons tells us that the "phenomenon of male rearousal by a new female is called the Coolidge Effect," according to the following anecdotal account:

[4]Richard Dawkins, *The Selfish Gene* (New York: Oxford University Press, 1976), 21.

One day the President and Mrs. Coolidge were visiting a government farm. Soon after their arrival they were taken off on separate tours. When Mrs. Coolidge passed the chicken pens she paused to ask the man in charge if the rooster copulates more than once a day. "Dozens of times" was the reply. "Please tell that to the President," Mrs. Coolidge requested. When the President passed the pens and was told about the rooster, he asked, "Same hen every time?" "Oh no, Mr. President, a different one each time." The President nodded slowly, then said, "Tell that to Mrs. Coolidge."[5]

The serially copulating animal is not sublimating; rather, he is in complete harmony with his genetic programming, and let's call this harmony, when experienced on the human level, happiness. Then let us acknowledge that such happiness for human beings is a fiction, for no longer is it natural for us to behave simply according to our nature. Too much culture has flowed under the bridge. To know this well and to accept it, despite our fantasies of natural spontaneity and sexual omnipotence, are the gifts of Mozart's comic art. Don Giovanni represents the healthy power of sensuality, and so we cheer him on, yet, also, he reveals the limits of sensuality's power when it passes over into the denial of psychological and moral limits. This revelation of limits, however, symbolically represented by Don Giovanni's damnation, is not to be experienced unequivocally as tragic; Mozart calls his work a *Dramma giocoso,* a jocular drama, for Don Giovanni's defeat and punishment—despite the fact that no one at heart wants the Don to repent, which, heroically he does not—is subsumed by the opera, the happiness of the work of art itself.

I believe that the key (excuse the musical pun) to viewing the opera as ultimately being about the sensuality of its own form is to be found first in the list Leporello keeps of Don

[5]Donald Symons, *The Evolution of Human Sexuality* (New York: Oxford University Press, 1979), 211.

Giovanni's conquests. The list makes permanent what in the flesh is fleeting and defuses whatever is neurotic and obsessive in the Don's psychology, frees it from compulsive sublimation, and releases it as conscious laughter. But the extreme example of the shift from what may begin as genetic determinism or compulsive sensuality to comic detachment may be found in the scene when Don Giovanni is gormandizing while waiting for the Commendatore's statue to arrive at his house. The attending musicians strike a familiar tune, and then they play a brief passage from Mozart's earlier opera, *The Marriage of Figaro*. Leporello comments "Questa poi la conosco pur troppo!" (That's a piece I already know too well). With this insider's joke, the controlling presence of Mozart unmistakably becomes manifest, for Mozart is not merely representing his genetic nature, or his unconscious and unresolved sexual desires, or his guilty ambivalence toward his father, in sublimated form; rather, through the consciousness of his craft, he is asserting his dominance over his materials. This dominance is the transcendence of unconscious sublimation, the triumph of the laughter of Mozart's deliberated art.

On Nothing

In the beginning God created the heaven and the earth. And the
earth was without form, and void; and darkness was upon the
face of the deep. And the spirit of God moved on the face of the
waters. And God said, Let there be light: and there was light.

THE BIBLICAL account of creation in which God creates
the universe out of a "void" in an instant of illumination has
a remarkable resemblance to contemporary Big Bang theory,
which propounds a spontaneous creation out of nothing.
Edward Tryon speculated in 1973, reasoning that the total
energy of the universe can be calculated as zero since there is
a balance between positive and negative energy, "our universe could have appeared from nowhere without violating
any conservation laws."* In a more anecdotal mood, Tryon
stated: "Our universe is simply one of those things which
happen from time to time" (256). In the same spirit of cosmic

*Quoted in Marcia Bartusiak, *Thursday's Universe: A Report from the
Frontier on the Origin, Nature, and Destiny of the Universe* (Redmond,
Wash.: Tempus Books, 1988), 257. Further page citations to this work are
given in the text.

playfulness, Alan Guth remarked that "the universe may be the ultimate free lunch" (246).

We know that at the quantum level, where nature functions according to probabilities, not by mechanical causal laws, "within one billionth of a trillionth of a second, an electron and its antimatter mate, the positron, can emerge out of nothingness without warning, come back together again, and then vanish" (259). Nothingness is a necessary idea against which the idea of existence can be better understood and defined. The opposite of creation may be thought of as destruction, but perhaps it is even more meaningful to conceive of nothingness as the opposite of creation. Both the biblical account of God's creation of the world out of a void and the Big Bang theory of the universe's origin can serve as metaphorical models for artistic creation, as in Shakespeare's description of the poetic imagination which makes "out of airy nothing a local habitation and a name," or, as Emily Dickinson says: "Nothing is the force / That animates the world."

In Andrew Marvell's poem "The Garden," the mind is depicted in its double capacity to create and uncreate:

> The Mind, that Ocean where each kind
> Does streight its own resemblance find;
> Yet it creates, transcending these,
> Far other Worlds, and other Seas;
> Annihilating all that's made
> To a green Thought in a green Shade.

Like the ocean out of which life originally emerged, the mind can generate further creation by finding resemblances between itself and other minds or even physical objects. Yet beyond the extending of itself through resemblance and identification, the mind also is able to create imaginary structures, "other worlds, and other seas"; its power to do so, however, depends on its ability to negate mentally the world of nature, of "all that's made." The power of transcendent creation, therefore, derives from the power of thought to annihilate both the world and itself, attuning itself to original nothingness. Surprisingly, Marvell describes that nothingness, the result of imaginative annihilation, as fertile: "a green Thought in a green Shade." Nothingness, for Marvell, when apprehended by the poetic imagination, possesses the color of nature itself, the green of generation. In holding creation and annihilation simultaneously in his mind and uniting them, Marvell anticipates the moment in Wallace Stevens's "The Auroras of Autumn" when, looking at the northern lights, trying to hold both their immediate presence and their imminent vanishing in his mind at once, the aged speaker declares:

> This is nothing until in a single man contained,
> Nothing until this named thing nameless is
> And is destroyed.

Poetic creation, naming the world, and the poet's mental annihilation of the named world, which renders it nameless again, are in Stevens, too, twin aspects of a single power. This imaginative power sees forms, possessed in their naming, collapsing back into loss, and sees loss generating new forms in an ongoing process of poetic naming and unnaming in which absence becomes presence, and presence, absence.

If nothingness is regarded, paradoxically, as the presence of absence, this concept can serve to objectify feelings associated with the experience of loss, which can be embodied in the metaphorical structure of a poem. In his poem "The Snow Man," the image of the snow man represents the failure of the human mind when it responds to the physical landscape without projecting anything of itself onto the landscape. The poet must hear "misery in the sound of the wind," as if the wind were not only a physical fact but also a symbolic entity that implied a corresponding human emotion such as misery.

In arguing for the inseparability of physical fact and of

human perception's affecting that fact, Stevens is following Heisenberg's principle of indeterminacy, which claims that at the quantum level any light that we use to enable us to see a particle affects the movement of that particle, so the very act of observation changes the thing observed. This powerful idea applies also to the imagining of nothingness, which, in Stevens's poem, represents the diminished reality of a physical world if there is no human consciousness to contemplate it. Imagining absence, we project ourselves onto that absence and thus create a new entity in the physical world. Hence, nothingness possesses a potential fertility out of which a poem, or even a universe, may be born. Stevens ends his poem by imagining a snow man who is "nothing himself" without Stevens's imagining of him, thus making a distinction between well imagined and poorly imagined nothingness: "nothing that is not there and the nothing that is." The nothing that IS THERE is, indeed, the womb out of which the poem emerges, and, for the human mind to begin to fathom itself, the mind must contemplate its inner nothingness. As Stevens says in "The Plain Sense of Things," "Yet the absence of the imagination had itself to be imagined."

In his late poem, "Long-Legged Fly," Yeats depicts Caesar preparing for a battle that, from his point of view, must be fought to preserve civilization. His maps are spread out before him in his tent so he can concentrate on conceiving a successful military strategy, and yet Yeats tells us: "His eyes [are] fixed upon nothing." In this visionary instant, the world itself and all its concerns have been reduced to nothing, and the nothing, then, that Caesar contemplates becomes the divine nothing out of which all future creation will emerge. The poem's narrator tells us that Caesar's "mind moves upon silence"; this silence resembles that of God brooding upon the face of the deep before the creation of the world. Yeats summons this God of silence and nothingness in his poem "A Prayer for My Son" when he says: "Though You can fashion everything / From nothing every day, and teach / The morning stars to sing." And when he contemplates the revealed truth of God's creation—the spectacle of human history in which each civilization is born out of the death of the previous civilization—Yeats acknowledges the mysterious source of his vision: "Out of nothing it came." Yeats recognizes the silence of nothingness as the medium in which he can glimpse eternity, "heaven blazing into the head."

Antithetical to the idea of nothingness as a fruitful womb, as a divine or existential source of creation, is nothingness perceived as the absence of meaning or moral values. A version of nothingness seen in its totally negative aspect can be found in a passage of Shakespeare's play *The Winter's Tale*, when the paranoid king, Leontes, is bitterly expressing suspicion and jealousy toward his faithful wife, Hermione:

> Is whispering nothing?
> Is leaning cheek to cheek? is meeting noses?
> Kissing with inside lip? stopping the career
> Of laughter with a sigh?—a note infallible
> Of breaking honesty,—horsing foot on foot?
> Skulking in corners? wishing clocks more swift?
> Hours, minutes? noon, midnight? and all eyes
> Blind with the pin and web but theirs, theirs only,
> That would unseen be wicked? is this nothing?
> Why, then the world and all that's in't is nothing;
> The covering sky is nothing; Bohemia nothing;
> My wife is nothing; nor nothing have these nothings,
> If this be nothing. [I.2.284–96]

In this speech, Shakespeare portrays the opposite of trusting love as negating doubt. And since love is a human invention, an idea that transfigures animal desire into a passion that seeks to serve, as well as to receive gratification, then the doubting of this conception of love, born of the imagination, throws the world back into being a place without meaning, a place of moral chaos. In an emotional sense, Leontes has deconceived his own marriage, and, in doing so, he has given birth to a nothingness that he cannot imagine is capable of breeding anything but further nothingness. And so, in this passage, the word "nothing" begets more of "nothing" until even sense and comprehensibility are emptied from Leontes' mind.

Twenty years later, at the end of the play, thinking that his wife has long been dead, and now deeply repentant and still longing for forgiveness, Leontes accepts an invitation to the house of his friend Paulina to see a statue of Queen Hermione. Paulina says: "prepare / To see the life as lively mock'd as ever / Still sleep mock'd death." Astounded by the statue's likeness to his wife, Leontes responds by observing: "The fixture of her eyes has motion in't / As we are mocked by art." If earlier, only nothing could come of nothing, here, to the contrary, satiric mockery—the painful reminder that a statue of stone, no matter how accurate the resemblance, cannot replace his wife—is transformed into the mockery of art, artistic imitation. This artistic imitation is so compelling to Leontes that, despite his skepticism, he moves toward the statue to kiss it: "What fine chisel / Could ever yet cut breath? Let no man mock me, / For I will kiss her."

Beyond Leontes' uttermost belief, but not beyond his secret hope, Hermione, however, truly is alive, though to the eyes of Leontes she has been miraculously reborn out of stone. In reality, this is a psychological miracle, love reborn out of long absence and contrition, that has been made possible by a restoration of faith on Leontes' part. Paulina expresses this deepest of Shakespeare's beliefs in the power of faith and forgiveness in her line: "It is required / You do awake your faith." Embracing her at last, her love restored from stone, from death, from nothingness, Leontes cries: "O! she's warm. / If this be magic, let it be an art / Lawful as eating." And thus art as creation out of nothing, as mockery, as imitation, as magic, is returned to the realm of reality, to the realm of eating and ordinary bodily survival.

The affirmation of inventing artistic form must be renewed in every generation if the human spirit is to endure. "When in doubt there is always form for us to go on with," said Robert Frost in expressing his faith in what the artist, the poet, contributes to our collective effort to survive. Yet, he goes on to add, "it is everybody's sanity to feel it and live by it." The existential void, the inescapable condition within which artistic form must be created, is always the same; this is what Frost implies when he says that "Whatever progress may be taken to mean, it can't mean making the world an easier place in which to save your soul." Frost's description of that void makes it clear, however, that chaos is to be taken as a fruitful challenge:

> The background is hugeness and confusion shading away from where we stand into black and utter chaos. . . . To me any little form I assert upon it is velvet, as the saying is, and to be considered for how much more it is than nothing. *

If the universe is, indeed, something that happens from time to time, old zero's gift, we must care for it as if we had chosen it, as if we had created it ourselves at the very beginning.

HUMMINGBIRD

From nothingness, by chance,
according to all conservation laws,
   BIG BANG occurred, and on a hunch,
     "The universe may be,"
said Alan Guth, "the ultimate free lunch."

     "And you can chew on that!"
I chastise my voracious self,
which hungers for some purpose from blue air
   whose whitened radiance replies
     reflecting on your hair

as you, composed within the window frame,
   stand staring at a hummingbird.
Her wings seem manifest as liquid light,
     as if they will dissolve
     this whirring instant in your sight

---

* Robert Frost, *Selected Prose*, ed. Hyde Cox (New York: Collier Books, 1968), 107.

into the nothingness from which they came,
    from which all laws emerged
    some fifteen billion years ago.
But now she sips the secret dew that lies
    within the petals' purple glow,

the hanging basket of impatiens her small beak
    will visit daily at this hour
    until broad summer ends,
until you are no longer there to watch,
    and mirrored nothingness commends

    my absent-minded thoughts
for thinking absence is so palpable
    that I can taste it on my lips.
I see you in the room you've left; I see
    the hummingbird just as she sips

the succulent, sweet nectar, though
    she is no longer there,
    held absolutely still in place
    by wings that beat so fast
that they create an opening in space

    from which she can come forth
or disappear—as if chance can be willed,
    like my stilled thoughts of you
    composed within the window frame
where blue returns to white and white to blue.

    As long as I think, *nothingness,*
absence is in the room for me to fill,
    and I feel blessed merely to stand,
watching, as you watch our home hummingbird,
    a sandwich in my hand.

PART THREE

꙳

The Long View:
Darwin and the Book of Job

I

T HE MOST INCREDIBLE aspect of Darwin's *On the Origin of Species*, from a psychological perspective, is that it does not culminate in despair and pessimism. What Darwin calls the "Struggle for Existence" is inevitable and unrelenting, leading inexorably to the replacement of one species by another as conditions change. Unlike the imagining of a Christian God who loves every hair on each human head, Darwin's nature is not concerned with the failure or suffering of individuals:

> As more individuals are produced than can possibly survive, there must in every case be a struggle for existence, either one individual with another of the same species, or with the individuals of distinct species, or with the physical conditions of life.[1]

[1]Charles Darwin, *The Origin of Species*, abridged by Philip Appleman (New York: W. W. Norton, 1979), 27. Further citations to this edition are given in the text.

At no point does Darwin speculate on the possibility of nature itself as being revealed as sympathetic to human wishes and human needs. Yet, astonishingly, Darwin sees beauty in the very process of change, the absolute interdependence of creation and destruction:

> I can see no limit to the amount of change, to the beauty and complexity of the coadaptations between all organic beings, one with another and with their physical conditions of life, which may have been affected in the long course of time through nature's power of selection, that is by the survival of the fittest. (61)

Darwin's description of how evolution works, however, is not simply factual and objective; it is also evaluative. In order to regard nature as "beautiful," Darwin must take the long view; he must think of time not on the human scale of generational love extending to children and to grandchildren, but on the scale of millions of years in which individual identity and achievement are imperceptible. Darwin ecstatically expresses this view in his final paragraph:

> Thus, from the war of nature, from famine and death, the most exalted object which we are capable of conceiving, namely, the production of the higher animals, directly follows. There is grandeur in this view of life, with its several powers, having been originally breathed by the Creator into a few forms or into one; and that, whilst this planet has gone cycling on according to the fixed law of gravity, from so simple a beginning endless forms most beautiful and most wonderful have been, and are being evolved. (123)

In the rapture of his meditation, Darwin moves beyond the themes of the war of nature, famine, and death—as if they should not be dwelt upon for long. He speculates about the endlessness of creation and the emergence of new forms without mourning for what has been superseded. His theory of evolution does not negate the idea of God, but it does change the image of God from that of a compassionate intercessor to that of a profligate but potent creator. God, according to Darwin, in the beginning created life from only a few "prototypes" or perhaps from only one. "I believe," says Darwin, "that animals are descended from at most only four or five progenitors, and plants from an equal or lesser number." Darwin's mind is liberated from thinking about his own particular fate, or the fate of his generation, or even the fate of humankind, and what he contemplates fills him with the sense of beauty and wonder: the spectacle—as if seen through the eyes of God the creator—of evolution endlessly unfolding its productions. Darwin shifts the emphasis of his concern from God to his creation, and further, he shifts the emphasis on the creation of people to the ongoingness of creation itself. Creation does not culminate in the emergence of human beings. The detachment from human involvement that characterizes Darwin's vision is both terrifying and magnificent; it can serve as a source of comfort for personal despair and as a corrective for a view of nature that regards the species *Homo sapiens* as its crowning achievement. But this detachment carries with it a growing human need to express and offer sympathy precisely because such sympathy cannot be found in nature or in the God who created nature. I consider Darwin's visionary detachment, combined with his emphasis on the development of human sympathy, the capacity to offer comfort that does not deny nature's indifference, to be the modern culmination of a philosophy of existence whose exemplary poetic precedent is to be found in the Book of Job. Further, I consider such visionary detachment, what I am calling the long view, to be a model for all poets to consider and, perhaps, to emulate.

II

There are two moralities in the Book of Job: God's morality of creation and humankind's morality of justice. God takes pride in power and plenitude, the bounty and energy of living

forms, while humans concern themselves with punishment
and reward, with pain and happiness, demanding from God
that there be a connection between one's behavior and one's
fate. These two moralities are in fundamental conflict because they are mutually exclusive. The confrontation between God's manifestation of his power and man's cry for
justice is the dramatic heart of the Book of Job.

Unpredictability and randomness are represented in the
prologue by the casualness with which the discussion between the Lord and the Accusing Angel is introduced. No
necessity elicits this encounter; it simply happens:

> One year, on the day when the angels came to testify before the
> Lord, the Accusing Angel came too.
>   The Lord said to the Accuser, "Where have you come from?"
>   The Accuser answered, "From walking here and there on the
> earth, and looking around."
>   The Lord said, "Did you notice my servant Job? There is no
> one on earth like him: a man of perfect integrity, who fears God
> and avoids evil."[2]

The Accuser's reply—"Doesn't Job have a good reason for
being so good?"—provides the preliminary insight into the
need for humans to imagine God in reference to themselves.
We expect to be rewarded for being virtuous; thus, the virtue
of loving virtue for itself escapes us. In confronting the Lord
with this knowledge, the Accuser, in effect, forces the Lord to
reveal a flaw in his own creation when irrationally, and un-
justly, he gives the Accuser power to abuse Job without cause.

When Job's possessions are taken away or destroyed and his
body is afflicted with boils, Job continues to cling to his
beliefs. He says to his disenchanted wife: "We have accepted
good fortune from God; surely we can accept bad fortune
too." When his three friends come to comfort him, assuming

[2] *The Book of Job,* trans. Stephen Mitchell (San Francisco: North Point Press,
1987), 6. All quotes from Job are from this translation. Citations are given in
the text.

that Job's affliction is the result of some unspeakable guilt, Job's acceptance of the will of the Lord collapses. What finally breaks him, what he finds unacceptable and insupportable, is the misjudgment of his friends. Beyond the loss of his wealth and the agony of his body, the failure of human sympathy and understanding defeats Job's spirit and destroys his optimism. He sinks into despair and turns against his creator, cursing him.

Job's curse represents the satanic spirit of absolute negativity—*non serviam*—for it is directed against creation itself, including his own creation, and thus Job sets himself against the will of God, which is the will of creation:

> God damn the day I was born
>   and the night that forced me from the womb.
> On that day—let there be darkness;
>   let it never have been created;
> Let it sink back into the void. (13)

God's original "Let there be light" is reversed in Job's "let there be darkness," and even the past, time itself, is rejected by Job as if memory, too, can be obliterated. Job wishes for the nothingness, the void, that preceded God's creation. Job must recover from this nihilism in the course of this epic poem; his spiritual journey leads him to confront his friends, himself, and, finally, through revelation, his God.

Caught up in his curse of creation, and thus doubly cursed, Job desires to be relieved of his sorrow through death. His very consciousness is a form of unjust punishment to him:

> Why is there light for the wretched,
>   life for the bitter-hearted,
> who long for death, who seek it
>   as if it were buried treasure,
> who smile when they reach the graveyard
>   and laugh as their pit is dug? (14)

At the conclusion of his curse, Job makes a desperate acknowledgment: he realizes that he has always known that he would come to this confrontation between him and God's creation when he says, "My worst fears have happened; / my nightmares have come to life." Throughout the days of his well-being, Job had repressed his inner knowledge, but although he is now at the nadir of his suffering, his ability to express "his worst fears" begins the process of his transformation and redemption.

Job's friends intend to give useful advice and true comfort to Job. While they do offer conventional wisdom, their reasoning can be reduced to a basic premise: a good God would not allow a good man to suffer. From this premise, Job's suffering and misfortunes are irrefutable evidence of the presence of evil in his deeds or thoughts. Thus Eliphaz, the first of the comforters, rhetorically asks Job:

> Can an innocent man be punished?
>   Can a good man die in distress?
> I have seen the powers of evil
>   reaping the crimes they sowed.
> One breath from God and they shrivel up;
>   one blast of his rage and they burn. (17)

In projecting this image of a just God onto the universe—a God who can be comprehended through moral reasoning— Eliphaz in effect represents the human need for consolation in the face of forces that seem cruel and indifferent to human desires and wishes. Indeed, the comforters express the point of view with which Job rationalized his previous wealth and happiness as divinely merited.

Job's complaint continues as he responds to Eliphaz, "God has ringed me with terrors," and he continues to seek death— "If only he made an end to me"—yet a new assertiveness begins to well up in Job. He wants his suffering to be recognized for what it is, not reasoned away, and so he resists Eliphaz's implication that he confess to a crime that he has not committed:

> Do you want to disprove my passion
>   or argue away my despair?

> Look me straight in the eye:
>   is this how a liar would face you?
> Can't I tell right from wrong?
>   If I sinned, wouldn't I know it? (22)

Job insists on holding to the truth of his own moral intelligence which conflicts with the belief that God's justice can be found in the world or in human affairs. Job's identity, then, resides in his testimony to this terrible truth; Job has become the voice of his suffering: "I refuse to be quiet; / I will cry out my bitter despair."

Job's second comforter, Bildad, is more vociferous in his criticism of Job, as if Job's claim of innocence has somehow threatened him. In defense of his own moral system, Bildad reveals his anger against Job's blasphemous truth, going as far as to attack Job's children for their misfortune as well:

> How long will you go on ranting,
>   filling our ears with trash?
> Does God make straightness crooked
>   or turn truth upside down?
> Your children must have been evil:
>   he punished them for their crimes. (25)

Bildad insists on the connection between behavior and reward, for without such a belief God's power would be too mysterious and too terrifying for him to contemplate: "God never betrays the innocent / or takes the hand of the wicked."

In his reply, Job rejects this rational account of God, and although he is dismayed by God's exercise of his power, Job, nevertheless, expresses his widening sense of bewilderment and awe:

> His workings are vast and fathomless,
>   his wonders beyond my grasp.
> If he passed me, I would not see him;
>   if he went by, I would not know. (27)

Insisting upon his innocence, Job offers to testify before God in his own behalf. He has not yet relinquished the idea of a just God, though he denies that God's justice can be seen in the vagaries of human fortune. Still, Job imagines that in God's court he would be acquitted:

> If I testify, will he answer?
> Is he listening to my plea?
> He has punished me for a trifle;
> for no reason he gashes my flesh. (28)

Then a great change occurs in Job's imagining of his relationship with God. Having been accused and punished, yet having proclaimed himself guiltless, Job reverses his relationship with God by becoming God's accuser, and in effect putting God on trial:

> I am guiltless, but his mouth condemns me;
> blameless, but his words convict me.
> He does not care; so I say
> he murders both the pure and the wicked.
> When the plague brings sudden death,
> he laughs at the anguish of the innocent.
> He hands the earth to the wicked
> and blindfolds its judges' eyes.
> Who does it, if not he? (28)

With utter blasphemy, Job holds God accountable for his power to bring about or to prevent death and suffering. From here on, the motif of man in God's court, and God in man's court, informs the poem.

The argument of the third comforter, Zophar, is more subtle than those of Eliphaz and Bildad, though its premise that God can be understood through moral reasoning is the same. Zophar realizes that Job has not committed a crime against God's law, so he assumes that Job has sinned in his heart and has concealed that sin even from himself. Sustaining Job's image of himself as a man on trial, Zophar says:

> But if God were to cross-examine you
> and turned up your hidden motives

> and presented his case against you
>   and told you why he has punished you—
> you would know that your guilt is great. (31)

Zophar's arrogance is twofold: first, he presumes to understand Job's inner motivation better than Job, and, second, he
presumes to understand the ways of God. Thus, it is ironic
when Zophar says, "How can you understand God / or fathom
his endless wisdom?" since he has acted as if his understanding of God were complete.

This irony deepens as we remember that the comforters are
Job's friends who want to help him through his ordeal, but
who are repressing their own motives of self-vindication.
Job's suffering becomes the means by which they justify
themselves, and their guilts about their own motivations are
hence projected onto Job. To avoid confronting his own soul,
Zophar says to Job:

> Come now, repent of your sins;
>   open your heart to God.
> Wash your hands of their wickedness;
>   banish crime from your door. (32)

The failure of his friends' empathy is as painful to Job as the
abyss of inscrutability between Job and his God.

Job is aware of the irony of Zophar's arrogance, as his
sardonic response reveals:

> You, it seems, know everything;
>   perfect wisdom is yours.
> But I am not an idiot:
>   who does not know such things? (33)

Job does not lack humility before God's wisdom, and he fully
understands that "power belongs to him only," but Job will
not be cowed into denying that he is innocent. He will not
sentimentalize the idea of guilt by assuming that he is guilty
merely because he is human, for real distinctions must be
made between human goodness and human evil. Thus, Job

insists on having his day in court, on being heard by God: "But I want to speak before God, / to present my case in God's court."

If Job is to be tried by God, he wants his friends to testify in his behalf, not to perjure themselves as his accusers in order to win God's approval. As Job has combined his roles as defendant and accuser of God, so, too, he becomes the accuser of the comforters when he says:

> Will you lie to vindicate God?
>   Will you perjure yourselves for him?
> Will you blindly stand on his side,
>   pleading his case alone? (34)

In his courage to stand alone before God and man, Job has found strength that supersedes his earlier nihilism. In defiance, holding to the truth as he knows it, Job has advanced in what Stephen Mitchell calls his "spiritual transformation." Job declares:

> He may kill me, but I won't stop;
>   I will speak the truth to his face.
> Listen now to my words;
>   pay attention to what I say.
> For I have prepared my defense,
>   and I know that I am right. (35)

The pain of isolation will not deter Job from holding to his last possession—his integrity. Nothing can ameliorate this isolation since Job views death for humankind as absolute, unlike nature's cycles of renewal:

> Even if it is cut down,
>   a tree can return to life.
> Though its roots decay in the ground
>   and its stump grows old and rotten,
> it will bud at the scent of water
>   and bloom as if it were young.
> But man is cut down forever;
>   he dies, and where is he then? (36)

The debate between Job and his comforters is elaborated
with the comforters' accusations about Job's blasphemy,
"You are undermining religion / and crippling faith in God,"
and Job's counteraccusations about the comforters' hypocrisy: "I am sick of your consolations / How long will you pelt
me with insults? / Will your malice never relent?" Tech-
nically, the comforters are correct in accusing Job of blasphemy and in claiming that he is undermining religious
faith, but, in the deeper sense, they fail to see that Job is
justified, even heroic, in challenging God. And Job is right
also in attacking the comforters' malice (though they are
unconscious of their own motivations), particularly since
Job wants to receive compassion and empathy from his
friends, to have them acknowledge their common human
predicament:

> My breath sickens my wife;
>   my stench disgusts my brothers.
> Even young children fear me;
>   when they see me, they run away.
> My dearest friends despise me;
>   I have lost everyone I love.
> Have pity on me, my friends,
>   for God's fist has struck me.
> Why must you hunt me as God does? (49)

Job asks his friends to ally themselves with him according to
their human bond, not add to his torment by condemning
him as if they were God's punishing judges.

Throughout his ordeal Job, claiming innocence, continues
to wish for a fair trial in God's court:

> If only I knew where to meet him
>   and could find my way to his court.
> I would argue my case before him;
>   words would flow from my mouth.
> I would counter all his arguments
>   and disprove his accusations. (59)

But in this invocation to justice, Job still is caught in a structure of rational thought, as are the comforters. Although Job
has realized that the logic which argues that God rewards the
virtuous and punishes the wicked does not pertain to human
affairs, Job has not yet relinquished his belief that God can be
comprehended in moral and rational terms: "Surely he would
listen to reason," Job declares. In his journey of spiritual
transformation, Job has not yet accepted God's "morality" as
something completely different from human morality. Job
has not yet understood that God's commandments, his laws,
apply only to human behavior. Although Job knows that "I
have kept all his commandments, / treasuring his words in
my heart," he knows, too, that God, in his infinite power,
permits evil to thrive in the world:

> In the city the dying groan
>   and the wounded cry out for help;
> but God sees nothing wrong.
>   At twilight the killer appears,
> stalking his helpless victim.
>   The rapist waits for evening
> and roams through the darkened streets.
>   The thief crawls from the shadows
> with a hood over his face. (60–61)

In Zophar's final speech, before Job's summary response to
them all, Zophar asks: "What can the sinner hope for / when
God demands his life?" But Job perceives himself as having
been convicted of a crime that has not been proven. The
comforters' sole "evidence" of Job's "guilt" is that misfortune
has befallen him. The question of hope that Zophar raises,
however, is the appropriate one because only hope remains
to Job. Until Job is confronted by the voice of God from
the whirlwind, Job continues to hope that he will be fairly
judged; his faith persists that God will reveal himself in
ethical terms. In contrast to Job's passionate adherence to the
truth of his own moral innocence and his refusal to submit to

a logic that would force him to lie ("I will hold tight to my innocence; / my mind will never submit"), Zophar's imagination is morbidly inspired by the vision of punishment for the sinner he considers Job to be:

> Waves of terror flood over him;
>   panic sweeps him away.
> The east wind flings itself on him,
>   whirls him out of his bed,
> claps its hands around him
>   and whistles him off in the dark. (65)

In his summation to the comforters, as if in a court of law, Job pleads his case on the basis of his history of upright behavior:

> For I rescued the poor, the desperate,
>   those who had nowhere to turn.
> I brought relief to the beggar
>   and joy to the widow's heart.
> Righteousness was my clothing,
>   justice my robe and turban.
> I served as eyes for the blind,
>   hands and feet for the crippled.
> To the destitute I was a father;
>   I fought for the stranger's rights. (70)

There is every reason to believe—though the comforters do not—that Job is giving an accurate account of his life, and the only fault that one might find in Job, from a moral perspective, is that he has behaved well for the sake of reward, rather than for the sake of virtue:

> And I thought, "I will live many years,
>   growing as old as the palm tree.
> My roots will be spread for water,
>   and the dew will rest in my boughs." (70)

Job has not been made to suffer because God has found fault with him. Indeed, Job is prepared to answer any charges against him. His agony resides in the appalling fact that no charges have been made; there is only silence on God's part.

Job's losses, his physical suffering, and the alienation of his friends torment Job, but his anguish comes also from the violation of his moral imagination. The concept, based on the evidence of his own life, that God is not just becomes Job's obsession: "Yet instead of good came evil, / and instead of light there was darkness." Job feels himself to be an outcast—as remote from God as the wild animals; he is a part of nature but not one with nature because his consciousness separates him from the animals, who follow the laws of their instincts:

> I despair and can find no comfort;
>   I stand up and cry for help.
> I am brother to the wild jackal,
>   friend to the desert owl.
> My flesh blackens and peels;
>   all my bones are on fire.
> And my harp is tuned to mourning,
>   my flute to the sound of tears. (72–73)

So Job is driven to the final blasphemy: he sees God as his ethical inferior, a vast power not in control of his own designs: "Can't he tell right from wrong, / or keep his accounts in order?"

Yet Job still cannot relinquish his need for justice, his need to be heard, his supreme demand of the cosmos—that it respond to him:

> Oh if only God would hear me,
>   state his case against me,
> let me read his indictment.
>   I would carry it on my shoulder
> or wear it on my head like a crown.
>   I would justify the least of my actions;
>   I would stand before him like a prince. (75)

Eventually God does respond to Job, but not in the ethical terms on which Job has insisted. God presents himself only as the designer of the universe. Where Job has challenged God in the name of justice, God replies in the amoral terms of the joy of creation:

> Where were you when I planned the earth?
>   Tell me, if you are so wise.
> Do you know who took its dimensions,
>   measuring its length with a cord?
> What were its pillars built on?
>   Who laid down its cornerstone,
> while the morning stars burst out singing
>   and the angels shouted for joy? (79)

God does not even talk about the creation of humankind; rather, he evokes existence itself, physical matter, elements such as snow, hail, wind, and rain, the "patterns of heaven," thunderclouds, and the storm that turns "dust to mud."

Most prominently, God presents Job with a catalog of the animals he has set upon the earth, and he describes their characteristic behavior, making no distinctions among them according to virtues. They are all equally beautiful in God's eyes: the lioness "who finds her prey at nightfall"; the wild ass who "ranges the open prairie"; the wild ox who must be forced to "harrow the fields"; the ostrich who "treats her children cruelly, / as if they were not her own"; the horse who "laughs at the sight of danger"; the vulture who "makes his home on the mountaintop, / on the unapproachable crag. / He sits and scans for prey; / from far off his eyes can spot it; / his little ones drink its blood" (81–84). God makes no excuse for the cruelty and death that is depicted here. Only God's ecstatic pride in the plenitude of his creation is expressed. Even though he has not answered Job's accusation that he has been unjust, God challenges Job, "Has God's accuser resigned? / Has my critic swallowed his tongue," and Job, dumbfounded, replies, "I am speechless: what can I answer? / I put my hand on my mouth" (84).

God's next challenge to Job contains the essential paradox

of the poem. God questions: "Do you dare to deny my judgment? / Am I wrong because you are right?" (84) Stephen
Mitchell's rendering of the more literal version of the King
James Bible—"Wilt thou also disannul my judgment? Wilt
thou condemn me, that thou mayest be righteous?" (Job
40.8)—makes explicit dramatically that God assumed that
Job's righteousness does not exclude or negate the larger
goodness of God's design. In both versions, God reveals that
he cannot be comprehended by reason; he cannot be circumscribed by moral categories. God is wholly other; what is
right for humans does not apply to God. God's medium is
power and creation; man's medium is morality and social
law. Man does not have the power to save himself through his
own government, his own ethical systems. God ironically
reminds Job that only he possesses that power:

> Unleash your savage justice.
>   Cut down the rich and the mighty.
> Make the proud man grovel.
>   Pluck the wicked from their perch.
> Push them into the grave.
>   Throw them, screaming, to hell.
> Then will I admit
>   that your own strength can save you. (85)

God's concluding revelation of himself to Job comes
through his description of his two primal creatures, the Beast
and the Serpent. The style of their evocation differs from
God's earlier catalog of the animals because the Beast and the
Serpent are depicted both as they occur in nature and as
symbols of universal forces. The Beast is an emblem of procreative power, the source of God's fundamental delight in
creating creatures that also have the power to create. In this
sense, the Beast represents the ongoing creativity of nature
itself:

> Look now: the Beast that I made:
> he eats grass like a bull.

> Look: the power in his thighs,
>   the pulsing sinews of his belly.
> His penis stiffens like a pine;
>   his testicles bulge with vigor.
> His ribs are bars of bronze,
>   his bones iron beams.
> He is first of the works of God,
>   created to be my plaything. (85)

The awesome Serpent is presented as a model of nature's destructiveness. Although it embodies what Mitchell calls "the forces of chaos," chaos and destructiveness are evoked as essential aspects of ongoing creation. The Serpent represents the elements of nature that cannot be tamed or rationalized by man into any moral system based on compassion or justice. A symbol for those natural forces which surpass all human powers, the Serpent is a kindred aspect for the whirlwind itself out of which God speaks to Job:

> Who would dare to arouse him?
>   Who would stand in his way?
> Who under all the heavens
>   could fight him and live?
> Who could pierce his armor
>   or shatter his coat of mail?
> Who could pry open his jaws,
>   with their horrible arched teeth?
> He sneezes and lightnings flash;
>   his eyes glow like the dawn. (86)

There is no doubt about the significance of God's description of the Serpent: God delights in his creation, in his abiding power. God makes no apologies to Job for the dominance of the destructive Serpent:

> No one on earth is his equal—
>   a creature without fear.
> He looks down on the highest.
>   He is king over all the proud beasts. (87)

Job's culminating realization of his relationship to God has
nothing to do with the question of justice: he does not stand
before God in a court of morality or law. Job's revelation is of
God's power, his incomprehensible vastness. Before God's
bewildering magnitude, Job humbles himself: "I have spoken
of the unspeakable and tried to grasp the infinite."

Job's humility, however, is neither self-despising nor self-
castigating, but rather detached and objective. As Mitchell
says, "Anyone who acts with genuine humility will be as far
from humiliation as from arrogance" (xxvi). Job's abstract
concept of justice, connecting virtue with reward, has collapsed in the face of experience itself, but Job, unlike his
friends, has had the courage and integrity to acknowledge the
indifference of reality to human desires. God's appearance to
Job is synonymous with the clarity of Job's perception of
reality:

> I have heard of you with my ears;
>   but now my eyes have seen you.
> Therefore I will be quiet,
>   comforted that I am dust. (88)

Job's resignation to silence acknowledges that he is God's
creation out of the dust; it acknowledges his finitude, against
which he no longer rebels. Like everything in nature, he,
too, is subject to extinction. His comfort finally comes from
his acceptance of this ineluctable fact. Unlike Job's opening
curse in which he sought death as an escape from existence,
he now has only to accept the mortal condition, the condition of his humanity. Through all his agony, Job does not
renounce or relinquish his human understanding, his morality, his otherness from God; rather, he accepts it within a
larger context of power and the magnitude of existence. As
Darwin also saw, man cannot be understood as having been
created in God's image:

> Astronomers might formerly have said that God ordered each
> planet to move in its particular destiny. In the same manner
> God ordered each animal created with a certain form in a

certain country, but how much more simple & sublime [to
imagine God's] power let attraction act according to certain
laws [so that as an] inevitable consequence the animals [would]
be created. (Notebook B)[3]

To contemplate the diversity and plenitude of God's nature is
to free one's thoughts from one's own life, one's own fate,
even the fate of one's own species into a larger sublimity. For
Darwin, an enlarged sense of grandeur is inherent in viewing
creation as ongoing and dynamic, as a process of endless
evolution, rather than as static and complete, even though
moral law is removed from God's creative intent just as it was
removed for Job.

> [In time] instincts alter, reason is formed, & the world is peo-
> pled with myriads of distinct forms from a period short of
> eternity to the present time to the future. How far grander [is
> this idea] than the idea from a cramped imagination that God
> created . . . the Rhinoceros of Java & Sumatra, that since the
> time of the Silurian, he has made a long succession of vile
> Moluscous animals. How beneath the dignity of him, who is
> supposed to have said, "Let there be light & there was light."
> (Notebook D, 343)

Though God has refused to respond to Job's accusation that
he has been punished despite his innocence, that the world of
God's creation is unjust, God does express his anger to the
comforters for having borne false witness: "I am very angry at
you and your two friends, because you have not spoken the
truth about me, as my servant Job has" (91). Here, God makes
it explicit that human beings must adhere to the tenets of
morality; they must pursue justice, despite the fact that such
ethical restrictions do not pertain to God. Man and God
remain in different realms. Human caring and compassion
are compensation, however, for God's otherness and nature's
indifference, and so, finally, Job is blessed with the com-

---

[3] *Charles Darwin's Notebooks, 1836–1844*, ed. David Kohn. (Ithaca, N.Y.:
Cornell University Press, 1987), 195. Further citations are given within the
text.

miseration of his relatives and friends: "All his relatives and everyone who had known him came to his house to celebrate. They commiserated with him over all the suffering that the Lord had inflicted on him" (91).

Ultimately, when God's otherness is understood and accepted, his creation, physical existence itself, can be seen in the fullness of its beauty. This acceptance is represented in the spirit of fable by God's restoration of Job's sons and daughters: "He also had seven sons and three daughters: the eldest he named Dove, the second Cinnamon, and the third Eye-Shadow. And in all the world there were no women as beautiful as Job's daughters" (91). Mitchell emphasizes the importance of this naming of Job's daughters: "The names themselves—Dove, Cinnamon, and Eye-Shadow—symbolize peace, abundance, and a specifically female kind of grace. The story's center of gravity has shifted from righteousness to beauty" (xxx). This shift completes the poem's transformation from Job's curse to his blessing in which natural death is experienced as benign: Job "lived to see his grandchildren and his great-grandchildren. And he died at a very great age" (91). Man's visionary imagination cannot sustain itself to dwell on the long view, the vastness of time—on Darwin's spectacle of evolution into an indefinite and undisclosed future—but must return to the scale of more immediate concerns, to human justice and the search for human happiness. And so Job, having been rewarded with the ecstasy of God's revelation from the whirlwind of ongoing and endless creation, is relieved of that intensity which his mind can only briefly contain, and he is allowed to die comfortably within the finite scope of family love.

III

Darwin was aware that his theory of evolution would be seen as blasphemous by the pious, just as Job's utterances questioning God's justice were condemned by his comforters.

Stephen Jay Gould points out in his essay "Darwin's Delay" that Darwin "gave vent to his beliefs, only when he could hide them no longer, in the *Descent of Man* (1871) and the *Expression of the Emotions in Man and Animals* (1872)." Further, Gould quotes Darwin's letter to Karl Marx in which Darwin writes:

> It seems to me (rightly or wrongly) that direct argument against Christianity and Theism hardly have any effect on the public; and that freedom of thought will best be promoted by that gradual enlightening of human understanding which follows the progress of science.[4]

At the end of *The Descent of Man*, Darwin acknowledges his iconoclasm when he says: "I am aware that the conclusion arrived at in this work will be denounced by some as highly irreligious" and then he goes on to argue that if we can accept natural childbirth as part of a divine plan, we should be able to accept evolution also as within the parameters of religious belief. Thus, for Darwin, it is not

> more irreligious to explain the origin of man as a distinct species by descent from some lower form, through the laws of variation and natural selection, than to explain the birth of the individual through the laws of ordinary reproduction.[5]

Indeed, understanding Darwin's Jobian mentality in which a belief in God is preserved, even though God cannot be comprehended as having created the human race in his own image, or in having a purpose that corresponds to the human longing for justice, seems crucial to me. Darwin's key statement regarding this issue reads: "The birth both of the species and of the individual are equally parts of that grand

---

[4] Stephen Jay Gould, *Ever Since Darwin: Reflections in Natural History* (New York: W. W. Norton, 1977), 26–27.
[5] Charles Darwin, *The Descent of Man in Darwin*, ed. Philip Appleman (New York: W. W. Norton, 1979), 202. Further citations are given within the text.

sequence of events, which our minds refuse to accept as the result of blind chance" (202–3).

This statement, however, is not entirely unambiguous. It might be interpreted to mean that even though our minds refuse to accept evolution—that grand sequence of events— as the result of blind chance, nevertheless, that is precisely what we must learn to accept. Or the statement might imply—as I think is the case—that our minds are right to refuse to accept evolutionary theory as the result of blind chance. If such refusal is justified for reasons that go beyond scientific inquiry, that refusal must necessarily imply the existence of a God of creation, but a creation that takes all time as its medium. Evolution, then, must be seen as the law that describes the infinitude of a creation that remains ongoing and is thus never completed. Darwin emphasizes his rejection of evolution as the result of blind chance by emphasizing that our "understanding revolts at such a conclusion" (203).

Although Darwin places his faith in that "gradual enlightening of human understanding which follows the progress of science," his writing is replete with phrases that reveal both his aesthetic and his moral sense. He refers, for example, to the "dignity of mankind" or to the "wonderful advancement" that has come from the development of "articulate language." Above all, Darwin focuses on the appearance of the human capacity for sympathy. He speaks, for example, of the "acquirement of the higher mental qualities, such as sympathy and the love of his fellows" (175), whose foundation lies in social instincts and family ties. The "distinct emotion of sympathy" and the "moral sense" are related by Darwin to the "high activity of man's mental faculties." When Darwin writes of an "advance of morality" or a "considerable advance in man's reason" (202), he is not using such words as "higher," "qualities," or "advance" only to indicate man's power of adaptation to his environment; rather, he makes an evaluation that is spiritual, as well as pragmatic. His concept of human advancement is not bound exclusively to his concept of the survival of the fittest.

Darwin says that the conclusion he has come to in *The Descent of Man* will be offensive: "that man is descended from some lowly organized form, will, I regret to think, be highly distasteful to many," and from our vantage point, we must include him in that "many." Darwin's repugnance for the behavior of our human ancestors is unmistakable in his description of the savage "who delights to torture his enemies, offers up bloody sacrifices, practices infanticide without remorse, treats his wives like slaves, knows no decency, and is haunted by the grossest superstitions" (208). Darwin is optimistic, however, that humankind may improve its collective behavior and cast off its superstitions, but that hope is not based on an appeal to divinity, only on the evolutionary "fact of his having thus risen, instead of having been aboriginally placed there." Thus Darwin's "hope for a still higher destiny in the distant future" resides entirely in the human capacity for "sympathy which feels for the most debased, with benevolence which extends not only to other men but to the humblest living creature" (208).

Darwin, like Job, turns back to the plenitude of creation, to the animals, and takes his comfort both from the spectacle of existence and in man's "god-like intellect" that provides the sympathy which nature itself, and perhaps the God of nature as well, is lacking. Darwin ends his book, however, with a note of warning, reminding us of our human history which we must be vigilant to remember: "Man still bears in his bodily frame the indelible stamp of his lowly origin" (208). Without the humility of such remembrance, we are doomed to remain what we have been for so long.

Those who suffer, as Darwin believes some individuals must, from "the war of nature, from famine and death" and those who are washed away, or crushed, or scorched, or blasted by flood, earthquake, fire, or whirlwind are not likely, in the agony of their unmerited fates, to sing praises to the designer of the universe. A human being, who possesses reason and language with which to cry out, will be tempted, rather, to appeal to a merciful God who empathizes with his or her suffering, a comprehensible God who offers comfort. The universe, however, has never offered such comfort. If comfort is to be offered at all, it is only within the capacity of other human beings to do so. Although the beauty of the universe, the wonder at physical existence itself, has always been a primal source of poetic inspiration, the magnificence of the created world will not appear to be sufficient compensation for the unwarranted pain of a random death, either at the hands of other humans or as a result of worldly conditions, unless one can embrace Job's or Darwin's long view. Should one choose protest, rather than acceptance and praise, one's adversarial cry against nature would not reach even the nearest stars. One's human cry would be too small, too fleeting, too personal. Other cries of other voices are waiting their turns to live and die.

GRANDEUR

Thus, from the war of nature, from famine and death, the most exalted object which we are capable of conceiving, namely, the production of the higher animals, directly follows. There is grandeur in this view of life . . . whilst this planet has gone cycling according to the fixed law of gravity, from so simple a beginning endless forms most beautiful and most wonderful have been, and are being evolved.

Charles Darwin, *The Origin of Species*

You've made it clear, Charles Darwin, why
    famine and war and failure
are inevitable—thus our highest cause
    must be to contemplate
the twisting rabbit in the fox's jaws

       as evolution's art,
as if our species' brains had been designed
   for awe: to witness a parade
of stalking creatures softly passing through.
     Contrived to be unmade

by the same law, as fixed as gravity,
   that made them from a single cell
     in what, we can surmise,
had been the simplest of beginnings, they
     have learned to use their eyes

to find their prey, avoid detection—anything
   to keep themselves alive
   another second in the sun—
while we, on high above the higher animals,
   are free to stand apart for one

     stunned blink of cosmic time
in which we flourish, to observe our fate.
   I watch my life unfold
as if it were the story of a distant friend;
     although he has grown old,

his daily correspondence keeps me young
   as his observer, permanent
     in speculation. No,
   I am not fooled; I don't believe him
when he says, while pausing in the swirling snow

     as he is splitting wood,
or standing in his garden with an eggplant
   like a planet in his palm,
that fifteen million years of human life can be
   held still in a containing calm;

     not so, the letters tremble
where he signs his name, and I can hear
   his moaning smothered in his sleep.

And yet his sorrow still seems beautiful
   from the calm distance that I keep—

      the distance thought allows,
   the highest view that you can take
in seeing grandeur as new forms replace
   their predecessors with no end
in sight. Your wonder helps me see my face

   in both the rabbit and the fox,
      and when I feel exalted,
I conceive a species someday will evolve
   whose sense of grandeur is
   so absolute that they will solve

the ultimate enigma of regret—
   grieving for loss that life
can't thrive without—by celebrating everything
   merely for being what it is:
      both here and vanishing—

forever gone, forever having been,
   forever unrepeatable.
And now the lumbering brontosaur browses past,
   and now the mastodon,
   and now, Charles Darwin, you at last—

yourself a radical mutation, so
      extreme that human thought
never shall be the same again.
      And now my turn is come
   to watch my friend fade out, as when

      one wave, rampaging in,
merges with backflow surging from the shore;
   or when the dissipating dew
dissolves into a mist, and with low, morning wind
      the white mist filters through

the valley, pausing in the marsh
among stiff cattails and bright jewelweed,
    then ambles on—although
some rebel grandeur in my heart resists
    my willingness to let him go.

೭ಾ

Comfort and Comforters:
Job and His Inheritors

T HE BOOK OF JOB established permanently for the religious imagination the threatening and challenging idea that
divine justice or mercy cannot be found in nature or in human fate. Nature provides us with the spectacle of destruction equal to creation, of indiscriminate suffering and profligate death; and in human affairs, there is no relationship
between virtue and reward, malefaction and punishment.
Nature can be seen as wonderful, awesome, and beautiful, as
the voice of God from the whirlwind boasts and proclaims to
the dumbfounded Job—

> Where were you when I planned the earth?
>   Tell me, if you are so wise.
> Do you know who took its dimensions,
>   measuring its length with a cord?
> What were its pillars built on?
>   Who laid down its cornerstone,

> while the morning stars burst out singing
>   and the angels shouted for joy! (79)*

—but nature cannot be seen as kind or as moral; it is not in accord with the deepest human needs and wishes for meaning and for comfort. Only human beings can offer each other sympathy and comfort, and on the human level—not man facing God or nature, but man facing man—the collapse of a common assumption about the existence of justice, a collapse that results in the breakdown of empathy, becomes the poem's central concern. Thus Job's most excruciating suffering is caused by isolation, by being cut off and spiritually abandoned by his friends; most cruelly, this breach takes place in the name of God, so that Job cries out to his would-be comforters:

> Will you lie to vindicate God?
>   Will you perjure yourselves for him?
> Will you blindly stand on his side,
>   pleading his case alone? (34)

And then again, with the most bitter irony, Job confronts them:

> How have I sinned against you?
> Why do you hide your face
>   as if I were your enemy? (35)

In the grimly realistic depiction of the world in the Book of Job, nature can be enjoyed and marveled at when one is not suffering directly from its random cruelty, but when one is smitten, when one is grieving and in pain, then one needs human commiseration. To be blamed for his misery by his friends is for Job the most grotesque form of injustice. Unlike the indifferent cruelty of nature that cannot be controlled

---

* All quotes from Job are from *The Book of Job,* trans. Stephen Mitchell (San Francisco: North Point Press, 1987) and page citations are given within the text.

and remains part of the mystery of God's creation, the pain humans cause one another, so it would seem, is within the realm of their own choosing and can be avoided.

The Book of Job is framed by a prologue and an epilogue; these sections provide a fairy-talelike contrast to the main body of the poem, which focuses with realistic detail on Job's unmerited suffering and his confrontation with an unscrutable God of creation who, like nature itself, absolutely refuses to respond to Job's ethical questioning. God's wagering with Satan in the prologue is no more believable than the happy ending in the epilogue when he "returned all Job's possessions and gave him twice as much as he had before," and, in compensation, replaced Job's dead children with seven new sons and three new daughters.

In fact, there are two distinctly different endings to the Book of Job. The first ending, when God speaks to Job out of the whirlwind, leaves us with the painful certainty that God will not respond to Job's questioning about the absence of justice in the world and that God's concerns and the concerns of humankind cannot be reconciled. Men and women can find magnificent beauty in nature, in God's creation of the universe, but that very beauty is inseparable from nature's indifference and wanton destructiveness. Man can accept that he is merely another creature, a blink of time, a speck of matter among a multitude of stars, and in this acceptance of his finitude, he can find a measure of comfort, as indeed Job does when he says: "Therefore I will be quiet, / Comforted that I am dust." Let us call this the comfort of honesty; it is essentially tragic, and, in human terms, it does confer a kind of heroic dignity—the dignity of confronting unflinchingly the truth of a pitiless universe.

The second ending comes as a relief from the first—even as comic relief—with its blatantly absurd assertion of redeemed losses and unmitigated happiness. Perhaps we would be right in perceiving deep irony in the poem's radical shift into the mode of the fairy tale, as if the poem had to acknowledge that we cannot bear to confront the truth of an indifferent universe of which we are such a minute part. Let us call this the comfort of the illusion of reward or rescue. Such comfort anticipates, I believe, the Christian version of history in which, through miracle, through the direct intervention of God, human beings are delivered from nature and thus from death: in a reversal, mankind is reborn out of nature, and the cruelty of death loses its sting. The happy ending of the Book of Job—so touching as an acknowledgment of human wishfulness, so tender in its granting us a respite from the reality of injustice and natural destructiveness—nevertheless reveals our vulnerability as a species burdened by consciousness, unable to face the reality of our utter finitude which is the inescapable Jobian conclusion of conscious thought.

From the dawn of human history, when our species first began to bury our beloved dead, the knowledge of death and the denial of death have contended in our minds and split our psyches in two. This split is the manifestation of an uncured obsession that has dominated human thinking throughout recorded history, and in the rest of this essay, I will examine this wound of consciousness as the manifest influence of the Book of Job on four poets: Blake, Hopkins, Frost, and Stevens. I will try to show how they attempt to resolve the conflict of the Book of Job's two endings—nature and God seen as indifferent or as redemptive—either by reconciling them, or by subsuming one into the other, or, paradoxically, by finding comfort in the ability to reject the wish for comfort.

II

The speaker in William Blake's poem "The Tyger" is a Jobian figure contending with God, although Blake has interiorized this conflict in the speaker's mind. In trying to define God by contemplating the creatures he has created, the speaker attempts to assuage his fears about the destructiveness inher-

ent in the physical world; thus the issue of the poem becomes the speaker's psychic health, which depends upon his
ability to imagine God's intent. God's creation of the "fearful
symmetry" of the natural world is countered by the symmetry of the poem itself, as if the poem were an attempt to
contain the very dread—God's creative power—that is the
poem's subject.

In the Book of the Prophet Jeremiah, God asks: "Is not my
word like a fire? and like a hammer that breaketh the rock in
pieces?" This image of a flaming God of destructive power
informs Blake's image of the "burning" tiger, who appears
remote and mysterious "In the forests of the night." Blake
depicts his speaker as imagining God embodied in the tiger's
power, and not as a human figure capable of pity and compassion. Although in "Auguries of Innocence" Blake says, "God
does a human form display / To those that dwell in realms of
day," the speaker in this poem dwells in the realm of night in
a fearful symmetry framed by darkness. God is depicted, not
as a face, but as a "hand or eye," thus emphasizing his physical rather than his spiritual aspect and making him seem
even more threatening and unapproachable. God can control,
or "frame," the design of his creation, but the speaker of the
poem, like Job before the whirlwind, is awestruck in the
presence of God's tiger.

The theme of God's remoteness is developed in the second
stanza when the speaker, who thinks in the mode of conjecture, wonders whether God dwells in hell or in heaven, the
"distant deeps or skies," and then alludes to Icarus and Prometheus, who were defeated by God for having dared to
approach him. When Icarus made wings so he could ascend
into the sky, the sun melted them, and Icarus fell into the sea.
And when Prometheus seized Zeus' fire to give to humankind, he was chained to a rock as punishment. In both allusions, God and man are seen as adversaries: man is the victim
of God's power.

The inquisitorial voice, in gasping phrases of terror, con-

tinues as the speaker's contemplation of God's creative power
unfolds in details emphasizing his physicality, his "shoulder," and the brute force of his ability to "twist the sinews" of
the heart of the tiger into existence. Only the word *art* in
the third stanza suggests the possibility of some motivation
other than the manifestation of God's power. With the creation of the breathing heart of the tiger, God's terrifying power
is transformed into his creation. The hand and the feet of the
tiger are virtually identical with the hand and feet of God;
thus, the intimidated speaker cannot distinguish his fear of
God from his fear of the natural world. Nature, as Robert
Frost will express a century and a half later, appears as a
"design of darkness to appall."

The speaker's feeling of dread is blurted out in short, abrupt
phrases as the imagery of creation focuses on the means of
creation, not on its intent or purpose. The images of the
hammer, the chain, the furnace, and the anvil all suggest the
forging of a piece of machinery, rather than the creation of
human consciousness that might be kindred to God's own
intelligence. Only a God of the creation of "deadly terrors" is
invoked by the speaker's dark incantation.

"When the stars threw down their spears, / And water'd
heaven with their tears" evokes the scene of battle in Milton's *Paradise Lost* (Bk. 6, ll. 824–52) in which God sends his
son to vanquish the rebellious angels, who become fallen
stars, along with their leader, Lucifer: the son of God "into
terror changed / His count'nance too severe to be beheld /
And full of wrath bent on his enemies." Attacking his adversaries, spears against spears, "in his right hand / Grasping ten
thousand thunders," God defeats the rebels: "they astonished all resistance lost / All courage; down their idle weap-
ons dropped." The speaker of Blake's poem then imagines
God's satisfaction, even his gloating, at his victory: "Did he
smile his work to see?" Just as it is ambiguous as to whether
the rebellious angels "water'd heaven with their tears" because of their defeat, or, possibly, because they regretted their

betrayal of God, so, too, God's "smile" can be interpreted as God's response to their capacity for remorse. In his terrified state, identifying with the opposing angels, as he had earlier with Icarus and Prometheus, the speaker can only respond to the wrathful aspect of God, the predatory aspect of nature. This response, however, proves not to be definitive, as the next line of the poem reveals.

Suddenly, it enters the speaker's head—as if this possibility had been lurking in his mind all along—that the God of creation has an alternative aspect to the apparent wrathfulness inherent in the aesthetic symmetry of the tiger. The poem must be read with a great intake of breath before the line, "Did he who made the lamb make thee?" for at this moment the reader becomes aware that the poem's speaker (in Blakean terms) is capable of a larger imagining of his deity than was previously apparent. The reader now perceives that the speaker can conceive of a God of compassion, as well as a God of fearful wrath. Further, if he can imagine a merciful and a sacrificial God, then he can also imagine a God who takes a "human form," as in the figure of Jesus Christ.

In this poem, however, the speaker does not realize his imaginative capability; he remains baffled by his own question, "Did he who made the lamb make thee?" and does not attempt to answer it. He fails to pursue his conjecture about a single God who can both destroy and create, whose beauty is both fearful and benign, both powerful like the tiger and meek like the lamb. The speaker retreats in the spirit of uncertainty and confusion, according to the defeated wisdom of Blake's lines from "The Marriage of Heaven and Hell": "The roaring of lions, the howling of wolves, the raging of the stormy sea, and the destructive sword, are portions of eternity too great for the eye of man."

But it is a strategic retreat. The speaker, in the guise of the adversary poet who both mocks and seeks to emulate God, completes his own creation, the poem, by repeating the first stanza and thus asserting his own symmetry as his final attempt to counter the fear that God has provoked in him. Thus, the poem turns into a confrontation of symmetry versus symmetry, God versus man. The speaker's contending motive becomes apparent in the single word change in the last stanza that represents the speaker's will to break God's symmetry and replace it with his own poetic art. The first stanza, referring to God's creation of the tiger, ends with the lines, "What immortal hand or eye / Could frame thy fearful symmetry?" In the last stanza, *Could* is changed to *Dare*, and with this deliberate word choice there is a powerful shift of implication: the daring becomes that of the speaker-poet in opposition, still contending with God, attempting to frame and thus defy God's fiery symmetry with a Promethean symmetry of his own.

If, however, one looks at Blake's engraving *The Tyger* after reading the poem, one is astonished to find an anxiety-ridden tiger with a puzzled expression and without prominent musculature—as if it had not hunted anything, certainly not a poet, for a long time. This depiction of the tiger—more like a lamb in the guise of a tiger—suggests that the fearfulness of the tiger is the parodied speaker's projection of his own subjective fear onto the tiger. Through such parody, Blake distinguishes his own poetic vision from that of the poem's speaker. Blake's revisionary interpretation of the Book of Job, as seen in Blake's engravings that illustrate the book, begins with Blake's implied identification of the tiger with the Beast and the Serpent, but culminates in Blake's demystification of the tiger and the exorcising of man's dread of nature. Unlike the Job of the poem's first ending, in which God presents himself and his creation as unaccountable in ethical terms, Blake rejects the otherness of God and nature and insists on the humanity of the godhead. Blake's final engraving of the Book of Job, based on the epilogue, shows Job and his family performing on their chosen instruments; man and the God of creation are thus seen reconciled and in harmony. But this consoling image, taken from the second ending, is antitheti-

cal to Job's culminating vision of God's inscrutability when
God confronts him from the whirlwind and declares his remoteness from claims for justice or moral purpose as understood by human beings. Blake, in his mocking parody of his
rebellious yet terrified speaker, finds comfort, after all, in his
rejection of what he considers to be a fallen vision: nature
seen as fearful, and the God of nature depicted as remote,
alien, and obscure. In effect, Job is reconciled with his comforters, not on his own terms of skepticism in the face of
God, but on their terms, which require the rationalization of
God's ways.

III

In his poem "Carrion Comfort," Gerard Manley Hopkins
directly identifies himself with Job in his affliction. His lines,
spoken to God as his tormentor, "But ah, but O thou terrible,
why wouldst thou . . . lay a lion limb against me? . . . and fan, /
O in turns of tempest, me heaped there; me frantic to avoid
thee and flee?" directly echo the lines from the Book for Job:
"For he breaketh me with a tempest" and "Thou huntest me
as a fierce lion." The bitter comfort of being dead flesh,
merely carrion, is reminiscent of Job's opening curse in its
negation of existence itself when Job says: "Let the day perish
wherein I was born, and the night in which it was said, There
is a man child conceived." The poem begins with the word
"Not" and ends with "God"—the opposing principles of nonbeing and being through which the poem makes its spiritual
journey. Hopkins depicts himself as being tied up in the *knot*
of his own individual suffering, and there appears to be no
escape from his despair since it is built into his very creaturehood, his bodily nature. When he tries, in a desperate gesture
of almost blind hopelessness, to negate his own passion of
negation, "not choose not to be," he is immediately confronted by his terrifying God who torments him for no apparent reason. There is no ostensible crime that has caused the

"wring-world right foot rock" response of God as a form of just punishment. And so, humanly enough, the frantic Hopkins attempts to flee his tormentor.

In turning away from God, however, Hopkins has to question himself, "Why?" and confront his own motivation: "That my chaff might fly; my grain lie, sheer and clear." He realizes that he is seeking to reap the bounty of his own mortal life, as if, in doing so, he could harvest his own soul even in spite of God. But his self-confrontation turns again, and now he asks himself if in this battle between himself and God he knows whose victory he is rooting for: "Cheer whom though? the hero whose heaven-handling flung me, foot trod / Me? or me that fought him?" The two, God and man, who seemed opposite and distinct, now merge in his mind: "O which one? is it each one?" In the blurring of their separate identities, God shares man's suffering, and, likewise, man partakes of God's victory.

In the breakdown of what appeared to be an unbridgeable antithesis between the "not" of man's mortality and God's eternality (as in the figure of Jesus Christ who is both mortal and divine), Hopkins has a revelation of the continuity and the simultaneity of all time, as if he experienced time from God's perspective. In his concluding sentence, "That night, that year / Of now done darkness I wretch lay wrestling with (my God!) my God," what took place in the past, "that night" of his Jobian despair, was extended in psychological time into "that year," and now, in retrospect, appears to be over as "now done darkness." Hopkins's "wrestling" with God, however, continues in his mind as an ongoing and thus permanent awareness of the abiding presence of God. The "wretch" who "lay wrestling" with God is also the Jobian figure— now transformed to the Jacob who wrestled with the angel and won God's blessing—who exclaims "(my God!)" in the awareness that suffering must be continuously experienced, not as the absence of God, but as God's presence. "Wrestling" becomes Hopkins's extreme image of a passionate embrace, and blessing, thus, is not to be found in simple peace or comfort, but in the ability to find God in adversity, for only in adversity can one, ecstatically, rise out of oneself. Hence, Hopkins solves for himself the dilemma of Jobian suffering by turning suffering into an opportunity to affirm God for reasons that are not self-serving, or, in terms of the imagery of this poem, not self-harvesting. Human lives, human souls, must be harvested by God, or they will be lost, and one, somehow, must find a way to wish for such restoration, not merely because it is good for one, but because in the larger scheme of God's creation, it is good.

The Jobian theme of man's contending with God is given even more direct treatment in Hopkins's sonnet that begins with Hopkins's translation from Jeremiah (12:1), "Thou art indeed just, Lord, if I contend / With thee." Like Job, Hopkins confronts God with the worldly evidence that there is no correlation between one's deeds and one's rewards, and that, inscrutably, even "sinners' ways prosper." Hopkins is not as defiant and blasphemous as Job, and his opening gambit rings with deferential insincerity in calling God "just" when he really wishes to make the point that God is unjust. The best Hopkins can do is ask for a hearing for his own human point of view: "sir, so what I plead is just." The tone of address in calling God, "sir," sets God at a distance and creates the feeling of God's authority as alien and fearful. Yet Hopkins perseveres and even allows himself to ask why his own "endeavors" to approach God, to serve him, meet with rebuff.

The anger beneath the controlled surface of Hopkins's speech momentarily bursts forth in his accusatory conjecture, "Wert thou my enemy," but immediately Hopkins catches himself up and corrects himself with the perfunctory and not very convincing, "O thou my friend," only to continue with his complaint that God, for no reason Hopkins can comprehend, has defeated and thwarted him. And Hopkins goes further still in the specificity of his complaint, God's rewarding of lust rather than love, when he cries: "Oh, the sots and thralls of lust / Do in spare hours more thrive than I that spend / Sir, life upon thy cause." Still intimidated into respectfulness, Hopkins again addresses God as "Sir," but the emotional distance between them, between Hopkins's cry for justice and the facts of who wins and who loses in this world, seemingly remains unbridgeable.

Then, a great shift in mood occurs. Despair is transformed into inspiration as Hopkins abruptly ceases questioning God about the issues of justice, which had dominated his thoughts. Suddenly, Hopkins says to himself, as if at God's command, "See, banks and brakes / Now, leaved how thick! laced they are again / With fretty chervil," and with this injunction to *see*, rather than to reason or dispute, the poem undergoes a radical change. Instead of trying to comprehend God's purposes within the human category of morality and justice, Hopkins now simply responds with newly awakened eyes to the reality of God's creation in lush imagery of natural growth. The command, "see," is reinforced with the similar command, "look, and fresh wind shakes / Them," and what remains, then, in Hopkins's mind is not concerns with abstract concepts like justice or moral categories like sinfulness, but only the idea of creation. Now, in response to the idea of ongoing creation, Hopkins's thoughts return painfully to himself: "birds build—but not I build; no, but strain, / Time's eunuch, and not breed one work that wakes." In comparing himself to a bird, however, Hopkins is not separating himself from, but numbering himself among, God's creatures for whom "Be fruitful, and multiply" is the first of God's commandments. He, too, is part of God's creation, and thus his role is to extend God's creation through imaginative imitation.

In replacing his demand that God reveal himself in terms of reward for moral behavior by the more direct revelation of the plenitude of nature, Hopkins, like Job, is able to approach God and receive a response. The formal term of address, "sir," falls away, and is superseded by the possessive and intimate

word, "Mine." God is not invoked as his judge, but as his
creator: "Mine, O thou lord of life" declares Hopkins in his
most personal voice. And with this change of voice, with God
now not distant but nearby, Hopkins is able for the first time
in the poem to pray. With four emphatically stressed syllables, "send my roots rain," Hopkins asks for fruitfulness of
his own—fruitfulness which will be its own reward—so that
he will be a part of the continuity of time, not "time's eunuch," and again he identifies himself with God's creation in
comparing his own spiritual roots to the earthly roots of a
plant. Miraculously, in the very act of being able to pray, in
the prayer itself, the prayer is answered in the completion of
the poem: the mental nest that Hopkins has built for himself. Like Job, Hopkins has contended with God in ethical
terms, but has received no answer; and also, like Job, he has
found his measure of comfort in the fact that he is part of
creation, blown by the "fresh wind" of God's breath, the
peaceful version of a God who can also appear in the angry
form of a tempest or a whirlwind. Only by renouncing his
demand that God reveal himself as just, by repressing the
bifurcation between morality and creativity, is Hopkins able
to heal the split in his own mind.

IV

Like Blake and Hopkins, Robert Frost is profoundly influenced by the Book of Job, and in his narrative poem, "A
Masque of Reason," Frost creates witty dialogue between
God and Job about the relationship between justice and power, behavior and reward. By keeping these issues at the level
of intellectual debate, however, Frost creates a comic work
that is deliberately devoid of the terror and bafflement of the
main body of the Book of Job. If Blake, through satire, offers
comfort because he rejects the validity of the vision of those
who dread the wrath of God and the cruelty of nature, Frost
offers comfort through punning wit and playful banter. God's
first words to Job in Frost's poem are casual and jaunty:

> Oh, I remember well: you're Job, my Patient.
> How are you now? I trust you're quite recovered,
> And feel no ill effects from what I gave you.

Job's reply is appropriately sassy as he continues the repartee
with the assumption that they are intellectual equals:

> Gave me in truth: I like the frank admission.
> I am a name for being put upon.
> But, yes, I'm fine, except for now and then
> A reminiscent twinge of rheumatism.
> The letup's heavenly. You perhaps will tell us
> If that is all there is to be of Heaven,
> Escape from so great pains of life on earth
> It gives a sense of letup calculated
> To last a fellow to Eternity.

Here, Job's ironic reply to God, particularly in reference to his
rheumatic "twinge," is at the other end of the emotional
spectrum from Job's curse of God in the biblical account.

Although God's rejoinder to Job maintains the mood of
jocularity, it has a serious undercurrent: it does address the
great theme of the separation between man and God in the
biblical poem in which God's otherness cannot be spanned
by human reason:

> I've had you on my mind a thousand years
> To thank you someday for the way you helped me
> Establish once for all the principle
> There's no connection man can reason out
> Between his just deserts and what he gets.

Frost's God gives Job his due, just as God in the Bible
acknowledges that Job has "spoken the truth" about him, but
the whirlwind in God's voice has been diminished into philosophical argument—the reasonable "principle" that human
reason has its limits: "My thanks are to you [Job] for releasing
me / From moral bondage to the human race." On the con-
ceptual level, these words by God enhance the import of the
Book of Job, but, with the dread of God removed from the

confrontation between God and Job, the glibly comforting effect of these lines is antithetical to the toughness of God's speech from the whirlwind.

In his more visionary poems, however, Frost rejects the impulse to offer himself or his readers such comfort. "Design" exemplifies the essential Jobian spirit in which terror and awe are combined. This poem is divided into two stanzas; the first is written in a style dependent upon similes that attempt to offer consolation by presenting images of destruction in aesthetic terms, while the second stanza rejects the illusion that nature is benign because the poet can control how he describes nature. Thus, the central rhetorical term of the first stanza, "like"—a word implying poetic control—is replaced in the second stanza with the repetition of "what," which evokes bafflement and lack of control.

Frost's spider is introduced to the reader as being "dimpled"—hardly a word that evokes fear, since it connotes cherubic cuteness. The description of the spider as "fat and white" augments the first impression that this chubby spider is not dangerous; it is an innocent creature going about its morning business. The image of the spider sitting on a "white heal-all" further evokes an atmosphere of enchantment, of benign innocence. The heal-all, normally a blue flower, becomes part of the apparent design of whiteness the poet perceives in the scene, so its name, suggesting curative powers, is concordant with its color. Although the spider is "holding up a moth," an ominous image, the poet compares this moth to a "white piece of rigid satin cloth," as if to insist that this image, too, can be viewed as part of a pattern of whiteness. The awareness of the moth as a dead creature is almost negated by the simile of "satin cloth," and the effect of the line is thus one of aesthetic loveliness. "Rigid," however, undermines the poet-speaker's attempt to render the scene in comforting terms because it functions as a breakthrough of the poet's repressed awareness of the moth's rigor mortis.

The poet's denial continues in the next two lines through tonal means. Although "Assorted characters of death and blight / Mixed ready to begin the morning right" appears to confront the spectacle of death, the lines are facetiously mocking, culminating in the pun on "right," suggesting rite. The poet, creating a ritual of linguistic display, is in control, and so he is able to offer the reader (and himself) another simile, "Like the ingredients of a witches' broth." Since the poet knows that we no longer believe in witches, his line serves as a parody of the possibility of malevolent forces at work. (The spider and the white heal-all are not replacements for the equivocating witches in Shakespeare's *Macbeth*.) The poet resolves the stanza by returning to a decorative image, the "snow-drop spider." The heal-all, too, is portrayed in a pretty simile; it is "like a froth." And if we could gloss over the word "dead" in the last line of the stanza, the wings of the moth would seem like a light-hearted image suggesting a child's game. The simile, "like a paper kite," reveals the poet's attempt to master nature and impose upon nature's design the willfully cheerful design of his own poetic description. The speaker-poet's power of language momentarily seems to make him sovereign over the circumstances of the physical world.

But the reality of "death and blight" that the poet has struggled to repress in the first stanza asserts its power in the second. The poet's tone changes from playful to grim. Because the poet realizes that he cannot control the design of nature through consoling similes, he is left only with the unguarded honesty to ask questions. The poet now admits that the extraordinary whiteness of the scene need not imply nature's innocence, or that the attribution of innocence to the spider or the flower can have curative power for a mind searching for meaning in the physical world. Since he can provide no answer to his own question, "What had the flower to do with being white, / The wayside blue and innocent heal-all?" he can only pose more questions that acknowledge his previously repressed terror. With the following line, "What brought the kindred spider to that height," the presence of a controlling force in the universe with its own design or intent is made by implication, and, horrifyingly, this power may be "kindred" to the spider. This is as close as Frost comes to Jobian blasphemy; the designer of nature, God, is predatory like his creation, the spider.

The suggestion of the presence of an omnipotent controlling force in nature becomes even more explicit in "Then steered the white moth thither in the night." "Steered" emphasizes the designer's deliberate intent: this force has chosen the white moth as victim as it has chosen the spider as agent. Everything—so the awestruck poet now speculates—seems to have been determined according to a plan whose purpose, however, remains unknown. With the repetition of the third "What," the poet ventures his dreadful guess: "What but design of darkness to appall?" The images of whiteness, which in the first stanza had appeared to symbolize innocence, now appear to have been a deception, a disguise for the "design of darkness." The only discernible purpose of this design is to terrify those human beings who are capable of perceiving it because they have the courage to reject their need to be comforted. In Frost's earlier version of the poem, this line read: "What but design of darkness and of night?" Frost's revision and his choice of the stunning word "appall" express the personal aspect of his cosmic dread. In this moment of speculative revelation, the blood drains from the poet's face, so he is left with a deadly pallor, as if he envisions himself on his own pall; literally, he has turned white. His is not the whiteness of some redeeming innocence, but the whiteness of dread that has come from the contemplation of the universe and its design. This is the terror of Job as he stands dumbfounded before his God who speaks of the grandeur of creation from a whirlwind.

The concluding speculation, "If design govern in a thing so small," throws the poem back on itself because of the uncertain reference of the word "thing." Surely, it alludes to the spider in its action of catching the moth, but also it refers to the poem's speaker, who has designed his sonnet with the intent to appall his readers with his own dark revelation. Trapped in the intricate web of the poem by the poet—who can then also be seen as "kindred" to the spider—the reader, too, becomes a victim in the larger design of a spider-like deity. Such an encompassing design—in which creatures imitate both the creative and the destructive aspects of their creator (the making of webs and the making of poems)—is awesome. The beauty of nature, humanized in poetic similes, and nature's terror and vileness, apprehended in the breaking down of these protecting similes, are Jobian in the sublimity of their juxtaposition. Frost's courage, like Job's, is to look directly at nature, the spider, to be appalled, and not to flinch. His comfort comes from his ability to reject any innocent but untenable form of consolation. Nature—and the God of nature if he exists—are both beautiful and terrible. Like Job, the main virtue of the poem's speaker lies in his integrity, his willingness to bear witness to the universe, not as he wishes God to have made it, but according to the testimony of his own senses as Frost claims in his poem "The Strong Are Saying Nothing":

> Wind goes from farm to farm in wave on wave,
> But carries no cry of what is hoped to be.
> There may be little or much beyond the grave,
> But the strong are saying nothing until they see.

V

The case for reading Wallace Stevens's late masterpiece "The Auroras of Autumn" as a poem influenced by the Book of Job is less definitive than for Blake, Hopkins, and Frost because there are no direct references to Job. The entire poem, however, is suffused with Jobian themes and echoes. We do know that Gustav Wolf sent Stevens a copy of the Book of Job, illustrated with his own wood engravings, and that Stevens wrote back to thank him for the gift: "I have looked at the JOB a number of times, but haven't yet carefully studied it." My argument here is that with Stevens—as with so many poets—the way he studies or absorbs an influence is by re-creating it in an imaginative structure of his own.

"The Auroras of Autumn" is a meditation, in ten cantos, of an old man as he watches the night sky and contemplates the minuteness of his own existence against this cosmic back-drop, aware that time has already washed away most of his life. This is a poem of flux in which the only absolute is change itself. Thought, too, is part of this flux as ideas are transformed into images and images into ideas, and even the sense of self seems to vanish in the very instant of its appre-hending. The poem opens as the speaker looks at the stars and, in effect, "sees" an idea—the idea of knowledge—and this idea takes the form of a traditional image, the "serpent," thus suggesting that there is something fatal about knowl-edge, or, as Keats expressed it: "Where but to think is to be full of sorrow."

The idea of the serpent is first described as "bodiless" as if it were a Platonic absolute, but Stevens undercuts this for-mulation by asking if even this positing of an absolute is merely another variation of a human theme: "Another image at the end of the cave." Stevens asserts that ideas are part of the structure of reality; knowledge and the knowledge of knowledge are as real as physical nature, so he locates his serpent-idea in the actual landscape of the poem:

> This is where the serpent lives. This is his nest,
> These fields, these hills, these tinted distances,
> And the pines above and along and beside the sea.

Like the beast and the serpent in the Book of Job that rep-resent the inseparability of God's creativity and destruc-tiveness, Stevens's serpent represents the knowledge that nothing remains permanent and unchanged. When Stevens tries again to imagine an absolute, a Platonic serpent beyond change, "In another nest, the master of the maze / Of body and air and forms and images," thought itself breaks down into self-contradiction as he describes the serpent as "Relentlessly in possession of happiness." Relentlessness and possessed happiness are mutually exclusive; thus, Stevens is forced to acknowledge that there is no mastery of time and flux in which we can believe. The serpent of knowledge is, in truth, the serpent of the inadequacy of knowledge to conceive of a happiness that we can possess and in which we can believe: "This is his poison: that we should disbelieve / Even that."

The "plot" of the poem is made explicit in the second canto when the speaker observes himself as "The man who is walking" along a deserted beach and who stops to look up at the northern lights, saying "farewell" to the ideas that have brought him comfort and consolation in the past. Indeed, this is a poem of farewells, and in this canto, the first refrain, "Farewell to an idea," refers to the idea of innocence. What Stevens means by innocence is that reality exists apart from our ideas about reality, even though we only can know reality through our ideas; furthermore, reality carries no meaning inherent in it before what we make of it, since there is no God who was the purposeful inventor of this world. In his earlier poem "Notes toward a Supreme Fiction," Stevens asserted: "Never suppose an inventing mind as source / Of this idea nor for that mind compose / A voluminous master folded in his fire"; it is to this theme that Stevens now returns. This innocence—which for Stevens had betokened the possibility of human beings' creating meaning and purpose for themselves—is symbolically represented by the traditional color of innocence, white, but this "white" has now taken on an appalling effect, as in Frost's poem "Design." Stevens's innocence is also analogous to Job's paradoxical innocence—paradoxical because Job has lost his innocent belief that innocence from wrongdoing can prevent misfortune.

Stevens continues to depict the literal scene of the deserted

beach in which the old man walks—it is equally the landscape of his mind—in shaded variations on the theme of
whiteness, in order to evoke the old man's deep sense of loss:

> A cabin stands,
> Deserted, on a beach. It is white,
> As by a custom or according to
>
> An ancestral theme or as a consequence
> Of an infinite course. The flowers against the wall
> Are white, a little dried, a kind of mark
>
> Reminding, trying to remind, of a white
> That was different, something else, last year
> Or before, not the white of an aging afternoon, . . .

Stevens cannot bring back that earlier sense of innocent
whiteness, "a white / That was different," for it has been
replaced with a white that now symbolizes absence and emptiness: "Here, being visible is being white, / Is being of the
solid of white." Ironically, the sense of absence becomes so
strong that absence appears palpable and solid, and Stevens's
past poetic efforts to find value in the world through his
fictive responses to physical reality now seem to amount to
nothing; they are no more than the "accomplishment / Of an
extremist in an exercise." Yet even this change, this sense of
the loss of innocence, is not final; Stevens tells us that the
man walking on the deserted beach "observes how the north
is always enlarging the change." Thus, what he confronts is a
display of lights which is frightening in its cold indifference
to human need and feeling, but which, nevertheless, is magnificent as an endlessly unfolding spectacle. The awesome
power of this display is the emotional equivalent of God's
challenge to Job: "Where wast thou when I laid the foundation of the earth?"

In Canto 3 Stevens tries to find consolation for the loss that
seems to epitomize all losses, the comfort associated with his
youthful mother, and he declares that the "purpose of the

poem" is to bring back his "mother's face" through a flight of memory. For a moment, he is successful; his mother's presence "fills the room," and past intimacy seems to be restored. In the exquisite line, "She makes that gentler that can gentle be," spoken in the present tense, it is indeed as if his mother were with him at that very instant. But that consoling illusion immediately collapses, and Stevens must confront the truth that she is no longer with him: "she too is dissolved, she is destroyed." In another heart-rending image, "The necklace is a carving not a kiss," Stevens negates the association of his mother's necklace with the warmth of her body by turning the necklace into a carving, like the letters on a tombstone.

For one more moment, however, the consoling image of the past returns as if it were truly renewed in the present, as if the mind could create its own reality: "They are at ease in a shelter of the mind / And the house is of the mind and they and time, / Together, all together," but the dominant fact of inevitable flux and physical change, represented by the "Boreal night," will wipe away the sweet constructs of the mind and, so it seems, defeat the purpose of the poem. The final image of the mother in this canto is of her falling asleep, but sleep has already become death in the section that is a "farewell" to her. Stevens says that "Upstairs / The windows will be lighted, not the rooms," because, in fact, the lights in the house of his past, where he was warmed by his mother, have all gone out, and now only the lights from the northern sky remain to reflect on the windows. The "cold wind" of unrelenting change that chilled the beach in Canto 2 is now acknowledged as the force that prevails over Stevens's effort to console himself through memory: "The wind will command them with invincible sound."

The figure of the father to whom Stevens says "farewell" in Canto 4 is modeled on the Old Testament God who "sits / In space, wherever he sits," a god who can be everywhere at once and thus can contain all contradictions. He is the master of both assertion and creation since he can say "no to no and yes to yes," but when he "says yes / To no," he loses control of negation; thus, time and flux become a force beyond his mastery. In saying "yes" to "no," the father-god is saying "farewell" to the idea of mastery, to the very idea of omnipotence and, thus, of divinity. And so Stevens ends the canto with extravagant mockery, invoking a God who is not there, in whom he does not believe: "Master O master seated by the fire / And yet in space and motionless and yet / Of motion." Stevens rejects as nonsense such physical contradictions of being in two places at once or of being simultaneously motionless and still, and thus when he declaims, "Look at this present throne," he shows us the old image of the throne of God, but reveals to us that it is now vacant.

In Stevens's essay, "Two or Three Ideas," he had said:

> To see the gods dispelled in mid-air and dissolve like clouds is one of the great human experiences. It is not as if they had gone over the horizon to disappear for a time; nor as if they had been overcome by other gods of greater power and profounder knowledge. It is simply that they came to nothing. . . . It was left for [man] to resolve life and the world in his own terms.*

God's refusal to answer Job's questions about justice and morality had left Job in exactly the same situation, and Stevens, like Job, will not be able to find his own resolution until, also like Job, he confronts the indifferent magnificence and grandeur of physical reality, of existence as spectacle.

In Canto 5, the parody of a creator father-god continues, growing wilder almost to an extreme of madness, and Stevens now likens him to a Prospero gone berserk: "The father fetches pageants out of air, / Scenes of the theatre." But no order comes of this, and Stevens declares, "We stand in the tumult of a festival. / What festival?" Before Stevens can find any order within this whirlwind of images, he must consider

---

*Wallace Stevens, *Opus Posthumous* (New York: Alfred A. Knopf, 1957), 206–7.

cosmic creation itself as the theater to be contemplated, and that, indeed, is what he sets out to do in the next canto.

Still staring at the display of northern lights, Stevens now regards them as a theatrical spectacle in which the drama is change itself. Even the clouds seem to him as if they were rocks and mountains that had been transformed, and everything, no matter how solid, appears fluid and in motion. The seasons are seen as if they take delight in their capacity for endless transformation.

> It is a theatre floating through the clouds,
> Itself a cloud, although of misted rock
> And mountains running like water, wave on wave,
>
> Through wave of light. It is of cloud transformed
> To cloud transformed again, idly, the way
> A season changes color to no end,
>
> Except the lavishing of itself in change,
> As light changes yellow into gold and gold
> To its opal elements and fire's delight,
>
> Splashed wide-wise because it likes magnificence
> And the solemn pleasures of magnificent space.

As in the Book of Job, there is no human, no moral component in the magnificence of nature. Nature's only "end" is in the "lavishing of itself in change," and thus its end, paradoxically, is to have no end. Since change is an absolute, all structures of thought, as well as all structures in the physical world, will always be "emerging," and they must always suffer "collapse."

The culmination of this canto comes when Stevens tells us that these twin ideas of order and of chaos must be held simultaneously by the mind; they must appear to the imagination as absolutely inseparable—as in the single image of the northern lights. This effulgent image, however, in which order and chaos are one, "is nothing until in a single man contained, / Nothing until this named thing nameless is / And is destroyed." Stevens's point is that we do not see anything in the world accurately through our description of it, our naming of it, until we see the thing in its annihilation as well, which renders it nameless. Likewise, to apprehend itself, the imagination must also apprehend its own destruction, and with this awareness Stevens, like Job, experiences what we can call cosmic dread, the intensified sense of his finitude within the scheme of ongoing creation and destruction:

> He opens the door of his house
>
> On flames. The scholar of one candle sees
> An Arctic effulgence flaring on the frame
> Of everything he is. And he feels afraid.

This mixture of terror and beauty is a perfect example of the experience of the sublime, as in Wordsworth's vision of eternity when, crossing the Simplon Pass, the poet beholds "the immeasureable height / Of woods decaying, never to be decayed." Stevens's similar vision will be the source, in Canto 8, of his ability to recapture his lost sense of innocence.

In Canto 7, however, Stevens tries once more to conceive of a divine imagination that can encompass such contradictions as being both grimly judgmental and benevolently merciful, a God who, like Job's God, is just and unjust simultaneously:

> Is there an imagination that sits enthroned
> As grim as it is benevolent, the just
> And the unjust, which in the midst of summer stops
>
> To imagine winter?

A god for whom all time is omnipresent, for whom summer and winter exist, not in their unfolding but in a stasis of omniscient knowledge, leaves no room for change and spontaneity in the universe, and so Stevens tells us that such a figure "dare not leap by chance in its own dark." Ironically, this god's seeming omnipotence is revealed as a lesser thing than a chanceful and changeful reality that has no authorship. Such an imagining of a god who cannot encompass

chance, such "mournful making," as Stevens calls it, must be
rejected, and a revitalized act of imagination must "move to
find / What must unmake it and, at last, what can."

Out of this "unmaking," Stevens begins a new meditation
on the theme of innocence in which he asserts that human
ideas—including the idea of innocence—have a status in
reality that is equal to the concreteness of material objects
that exist in the dimensions of time and space: "existing in
the idea of it alone, / In the sense against calamity, it [inno-
cence] is not / Less real." The very need for such an idea—
since it would be calamitous to the human spirit to live
without it—grounds the idea of innocence in human emotion and thus in reality. But the converse is equally true, for
when Stevens declares that innocence is "Like a book at
evening beautiful but untrue, / Like a book on rising beautiful and true," he is arguing that ideas enter reality as fictions
but then truly become part of reality, part of nature. And if
this is indeed so, then whatever meanings life may yield are
not given by God or inherent in nature before one discovers
them, but are imposed by human beings through the creation
of their own ideas. This ability to invent reality within the
confines of mortality and the natural law of entropy is, I
believe, exactly what Stevens means by innocence as it is
redefined at this point in the poem.

As Stevens continues to look up at the northern lights, it
now follows that he sees them as devoid of any preassigned
meanings. The spectacle is not a revelation of God, and the
destructive transformations of nature, therefore, do not represent any judgment of human beings or malice toward people on God's part:

> So, then, these lights are not a spell of light,
> A saying out of a cloud, but innocence.
> An innocence of the earth and no false sign
>
> Or symbol of malice.

The fact that there are no inherent meanings in nature is
what makes the earth innocent, and if this is indeed so, the

"white of an aging afternoon," the empty innocence of Canto 2, can be redeemed by a new act of imaginative consolation. The holiness of the earth does not derive from God's creation, but from the potential of our own ability to create holiness in a world that innocently allows this imposition of a human idea upon physical reality to take place. In this spirit, even death can be accepted as a holy aspect of life, just as we accept sleep as the completion of a day, and we can "Lie down like children in this holiness." Knowing that such consolation is his own improvisation, which exists as an idea against calamity, Stevens can again conjure up the primary consoling image of his mother who, as his muse, "the purpose of the poem," represents the human power to augment reality with human inventions—as in the music the mother plays on the accordion:

> As if the innocent mother sang in the dark
> Of the room and on an accordion, half-heard,
> Created the time and place in which we breathed . . .

Just as Job, in his cry against divine injustice, holds to the integrity of his innocence as his most precious human possession, so, too, does Stevens in the cry of his poem, "in the idiom / Of the work, in the idiom of an innocent earth," reject original or inherent sinfulness as his human inheritance. The essential mystery is that of human possibility, not the "enigma of the guilty dream." This return to an idea of innocence in which Stevens can believe seems momentarily to resolve the poem, and yet the awareness of change and death, according to Stevens's inescapable logic, will not allow any final resolution. And so again the image of the invincible wind of ephemerality reappears as a reminder of inevitable personal disaster:

> Shall we be found hanging in the trees next spring?
> Of what disaster is this the imminence:
> Bare limbs, bare trees and a wind as sharp as salt?

Nevertheless, since death is no longer associated with guilt or punishment, Stevens now is able to accept its coming—as Job accepts his return to dust—with easeful and gentle equanimity: "Almost as part of innocence, almost, / Almost as the tenderest and the truest part."

The word *almost* should not be glossed over in this lyrically affirmative passage, since for Stevens no resolutions are final even though we experience some moments of satisfaction as complete unto themselves. And so the final canto begins with Stevens, now projecting himself in the role of a rabbi, as he examines the dialectic of self and world, trying to see where he can locate the source of human happiness. In addition to being a scholar of the Old Testament, the rabbi is significant in that he is a man in social contact with others who "Read[s] to the congregation." Just as Job had suffered from alienation from his friends and had felt cut off, so, too, Stevens's image of himself as an old man walking alone on a beach represented his own sense of isolation. But now, in the role of the rabbi-poet, Stevens can feel that he is in touch with his audience, his congregation. In a late letter, Stevens wrote: "The figure of the rabbi has always been an extremely attractive one to me because it is the figure of a man devoted in the extreme to scholarship and at the same time to making some use of it for human purposes."* Stevens's depiction of himself in Canto 6 as the isolated "scholar of one candle" has now been replaced by the image of himself as a rabbi, a man among men.

Concomitant with this change from isolation to communal connectedness is a radical change of tone: the poem takes on a comic aspect. With the kind of skewed logic that is typical of Jewish humor, the rabbi rejects the formulation that we are "An unhappy people in an unhappy world" for the pragmatic reason that such an idea is likely to mire us in unhappiness. Stevens casts out this idea with casual irony:

* *Letters of Wallace Stevens* (New York: Alfred A. Knopf, 1966), 786.

"Here are too many mirrors for misery." The shift in tone that comes with Stevens's assertion of the possibility of human happiness is analogous to the shift into what I have called the second ending of the Book of Job, where losses are restored and reconciliations occur. Furthermore, the exact equivalent of God's saying to Job's comforters that "ye have not spoken of me the thing that is right, as my servant Job hath" is to be found throughout Stevens's poem in his rejection of divinity as a false idea, an untenable consolation, while maintaining both a sense of the magnificence of physical reality and a sense of the holy.

Dismissing the idea that we can be happy if we think of ourselves as living in an "unhappy world" because the conditions of change and mortality are a poisonous form of knowledge, Stevens, the rabbi-poet, declares that in a poetry of despair "There's nothing there to roll / On the expressive tongue, the finding fang." The serpent's poison of disbelief in Canto 1 has now been replaced by the "finding fang" of our human ability to determine freely our own fate—an ability which, paradoxically, lies only in the *attitude* we take toward the necessities of change and death. This freedom-creating ability is made incarnate in this very poem, which, finally, celebrates itself for being a poem. In this spirit of celebration, as his mind rejoices in itself, Stevens cries out with comic exuberance: "Buffo! A ball, an opera, a bar." Just as we live in a theater of cosmic dimensions, so, too, do we live in an operatic theater of our own creation.

In Canto 2, Stevens had ridiculed the usefulness of his own poetry by describing himself as "an extremist in an exercise," but now he affirms his own poem, calling it "this extremity, / This contrivance of the spectre of the spheres, / Contriving balance to contrive a whole." The serpent of fatal knowledge that he had imagined as he observed the northern lights at the beginning of the poem, he realizes now, can represent any knowledge that he chooses it to represent. He himself is the contriver of such knowledge, and the "balance" he determines to create is between seeing change and death as necessities and seeing human creativity as free to make of these necessities whatever we will. Within the limits of physical reality, there are, nevertheless, infinite human possibilities for creating structures of meaning. The "whole" that Stevens seeks to contrive includes the innocence of physical reality and the human need to create a sense of the holy. Stevens's phrase "The full of fortune and the full of fate" refers to what we make of our lives, our "fortune," and what nature exacts of us, our "fate." In bringing these two together, Stevens no longer experiences death as an assault, as if he were the victim of nature, but, rather, as a spur to his own imagination which enables him to empathize with the lives of others: "As if he lived all lives, that he might know." This expanded knowledge frees him from the two destructive alternatives of repressing the idea of death, denying it through a fantasy of another life in heaven, or of rebelling against death as if the laws of nature can be overthrown.

In Canto 6 Stevens had said that his vision of the northern lights as a theater of change was "nothing until in a single man contained, / Nothing until this named thing nameless is / And is destroyed." And in Canto 7 Stevens had asked if there were an imagination "which in the midst of summer stops / To imagine winter?" In the last stanza of the poem Stevens tries to meet these challenges to the imagination with a final affirmation of the necessity of speech, since we do not live in a "hushful paradise," but in an ongoing dialogue with nature, "a haggling of wind and weather." The whirlwind out of which God addressed Job has, in Stevens, become, simply, the physical conditions of the world, the awesome, indifferent, and inescapable reality that our imaginations must contrive to humanize as we attempt to "choir it with the naked wind." The final image of the poem completes Stevens's meditation of the cosmic theater of the sky, "these lights," and provides him, in the nick of time before the onset of winter and death, with a vision, "a blaze of summer straw," that he can indeed contain in his own single mind—a vision of a conflagration of the harvested hay, occurring there in place and time, yet vanishing in the same instant. With summer and winter in his mind at once, and with his poem both naming what he sees in the northern sky and unnaming the same images as they change even as his meditation seizes them, Stevens resolves his poem with a deliberate gesture of irresolution. Everything remains open. The meditation will have to begin again in another poem, or in another hopeful poet, forever contending with the wind and weather of the world, who, nevertheless, would find the world itself to be enough.

Stevens's poem differs from the Book of Job in that its primary emphasis is not placed on the ethical issue of whether goodness is rewarded and evil punished in the scheme of the universe, and yet, I believe that in its insistence on the indifferent grandeur and magnificence of physical reality and on the human capacity to "contain" the knowledge of this indifference, to see it as innocence, it is closer to the Book of Job in spirit than the directly influenced poems by Blake, Hopkins, and Frost. In this respect, Stevens's poem puts forth exactly the same argument as God does when he speaks to Job out of the whirlwind: Behold the vast theater of My creation; it is for you to make of its terrible beauty, of flux and death, what consolation you can, but do not expect to find inherent within it human meaning or human purpose.

IT WOULD HAVE BEEN ENOUGH

If only daffodils had caught the light,
      that would have been enough;
   and if to add variety,
      just crocuses and tulips
  splashed their colors in the dawn,
      that, too, would have sufficed;
and if just sparrows, common sparrows,

not white-throated, dusky-evening, golden-crowned,
    had tilted on a limber bough
amid the silver smooth and silver rough
    and twined their whistlings in the leaves,
        that would have been enough.
To add variety, it would have been enough
        if only chickadees,
    the plain gray junco, and the nuthatch
also frequented the maple tree and played
        upon a puff of wind,
and, certainly, it would have been sufficient
    if, beside the steady maple,
for the sake of contrast in the hazy rain,
    a clump of gleaming birches swayed.
It would have been sufficient for variety
        without the tamaracks,
    without the pines, without the firs,
without the hemlocks harboring the wind;
        it would have been enough
to have the chipmunk pausing on his log
        without the browsing deer
who, one by one by one, their white tails flashing,
    leap across the minnow stream.
        We didn't need that much
    to want to make ourselves at home
        and building our dwellings here—
just light upon the lake would have sufficed to see,
        just changing light at evening
on a birch clump or a single maple tree.
    For us to make ourselves at home,
        it would have been enough
if only we had said, "This is enough,"
        and for variety,
it would have been sufficient if we said,
        "This surely will suffice,"

and when dawn brushed its shadows in the apple tree,
        if we had only said
how bountiful those shaded circles are,
        how silently they pull
    themselves together toward the stem,
that bounty would have seemed more bountiful.
        And even now, if I should say,
"How bountiful," then just one daffodil,
    a single daffodil unfolding
        in a yellow vase
upon a maple table in the breeding sun,
        would be enough
    and seem abundant far beyond
what was sufficient to desire, except
        for one brown, ordinary sparrow
        on my windowsill,
which I cannot resist including in this light,
    and maybe one wide row of cedars,
winding up the valley to the misted hill.

William Blake

THE TYGER

Tyger, Tyger, burning bright
In the forests of the night,
What immortal hand or eye
Could frame thy fearful symmetry?

In what distant deeps or skies
Burnt the fire of thine eyes?

On what wings dare he aspire?
What the hand dare seize the fire?

And what shoulder, & what art
Could twist the sinews of thy heart?
And when thy heart began to beat,
What dread hand? & what dread feet?

What the hammer? what the chain,
In what furnace was thy brain?
What the anvil? what dread grasp
Dare its deadly terrors clasp?

When the stars threw down their spears,
And water'd heaven with their tears,
Did he smile his work to see?
Did he who made the Lamb make thee?

Tyger, Tyger, burning bright
In the forests of the night,
What immortal hand or eye
Dare frame thy fearful symmetry?

Gerard Manley Hopkins

(CARRION COMFORT)

Not, I'll not, carrion comfort, Despair, not feast on thee;
Not untwist—slack they may be—these last strands of man
In me or, most weary, cry *I can no more.* I can;
Can something, hope, wish day come, not choose not to be.
But ah, but O thou terrible, why wouldst thou rude on me
Thy wring-world right foot rock? lay a lionlimb against me?
    scan
With darksome devouring eyes my bruised bones? and fan,
O in turns of tempest, me heaped there; me frantic to avoid
    thee and flee?
  Why? That my chaff might fly; my grain lie, sheer and clear.
Nay in all that toil, that coil, since (seems) I kissed the rod,

Hand rather, my heart lo! lapped strength, stole joy, would
    laugh, cheer.
Cheer whom, though? the hero whose heaven-handling flung
    me, foot trod
Me? or me that fought him? O which one? is it each one? That
    night, that year
Of now done darkness I wretch lay wrestling with (my God!)
    my God.

Thou art indeed just, Lord, if I contend
With thee; but, sir, so what I plead is just.
Why do sinners' ways prosper? and why must
Disappointment all I endeavour end?
    Wert thou my enemy, O thou my friend,
How wouldst thou worse, I wonder, than thou dost
Defeat, thwart me? Oh, the sots and thralls of lust
Do in spare hours more thrive than I that spend,
Sir, life upon thy cause. See, banks and brakes
Now, leavèd how thick! lacèd they are again
With fretty chervil, look, and fresh wind shakes
Them; birds build—but not I build; no, but strain,
Time's eunuch, and not breed one work that wakes.
Mine, O thou lord of life, send my roots rain.

Robert Frost

DESIGN

I found a dimpled spider, fat and white,
On a white heal-all, holding up a moth
Like a white piece of rigid satin cloth—
Assorted characters of death and blight
Mixed ready to begin the morning right,
Like the ingredients of a witches' broth—
A snow-drop spider, a flower like a froth,
And dead wings carried like a paper kite.

What had that flower to do with being white,
The wayside blue and innocent heal-all?
What brought the kindred spider to that height,
Then steered the white moth thither in the night?
What but design of darkness to appall?—
If design govern in a thing so small.

Wallace Stevens

THE AURORAS OF AUTUMN

I

This is where the serpent lives, the bodiless.
His head is air. Beneath his tip at night
Eyes open and fix on us in every sky.

Or is this another wriggling out of the egg,
Another image at the end of the cave,
Another bodiless for the body's slough?

This is where the serpent lives. This is his nest,
These fields, these hills, these tinted distances,
And the pines above and along and beside the sea.

This is form gulping after formlessness,
Skin flashing to wished-for disappearances
And the serpent body flashing without the skin.

This is the height emerging and its base.
These lights may finally attain a pole
In the midmost midnight and find the serpent there,

In another nest, the master of the maze
Of body and air and forms and images,
Relentlessly in possession of happiness.

This is his poison: that we should disbelieve
Even that. His meditations in the ferns,
When he moved so slightly to make sure of sun,

Made us no less as sure. We saw in his head,
Black beaded on the rock, the flecked animal,
The moving grass, the Indian in his glade.

II

Farewell to an idea . . . A cabin stands,
Deserted, on a beach. It is white,
As by a custom or according to

An ancestral theme or as a consequence
Of an infinite course. The flowers against the wall
Are white, a little dried, a kind of mark

Reminding, trying to remind, of a white
That was different, something else, last year
Or before, not the white of an aging afternoon,

Whether fresher or duller, whether of winter cloud
Or of winter sky, from horizon to horizon.
The wind is blowing the sand across the floor.

Here, being visible is being white,
Is being of the solid of white, the accomplishment
Of an extremist in an exercise . . .

The season changes. A cold wind chills the beach.
The long lines of it grow longer, emptier,
A darkness gathers though it does not fall

And the whiteness grows less vivid on the wall.
The man who is walking turns blankly on the sand.
He observes how the north is always enlarging the change,

With its frigid brilliances, its blue-red sweeps
And gusts of great enkindlings, its polar green,
The color of ice and fire and solitude.

III

Farewell to an idea . . . The mother's face,
The purpose of the poem, fills the room.
They are together, here, and it is warm,

With none of the prescience of oncoming dreams,
It is evening. The house is evening, half dissolved.
Only the half they can never possess remains,

Still-starred. It is the mother they possess,
Who gives transparence to their present peace.
She makes that gentler that can gentle be.

And yet she too is dissolved, she is destroyed.
She gives transparence. But she has grown old.
The necklace is a carving not a kiss.

The soft hands are a motion not a touch.
The house will crumble and the books will burn.
They are at ease in a shelter of the mind

And the house is of the mind and they and time,
Together, all together. Boreal night
Will look like frost as it approaches them

And to the mother as she falls asleep
And as they say good-night, good-night. Upstairs
The windows will be lighted, not the rooms.

A wind will spread its windy grandeurs round
And knock like a rifle-butt against the door.
The wind will command them with invincible sound.

IV

Farewell to an idea . . . The cancellings,
The negations are never final. The father sits
In space, wherever he sits, of bleak regard,

As one that is strong in the bushes of his eyes.
He says no to no and yes to yes. He says yes
To no; and in saying yes he says farewell.

He measures the velocities of change.
He leaps from heaven to heaven more rapidly
Than bad angels leap from heaven to hell in flames.

But now he sits in quiet and green-a-day.
He assumes the great speeds of space and flutters them
From cloud to cloudless, cloudless to keen clear

In flights of eye and ear, the highest eye
And the lowest ear, the deep ear that discerns,
At evening, things that attend it until it hears

The supernatural preludes of its own,
At the moment when the angelic eye defines
Its actors approaching, in company, in their masks.

Master O master seated by the fire
And yet in space and motionless and yet
Of motion the ever-brightening origin,

Profound, and yet the king and yet the crown,
Look at this present throne. What company,
In masks, can choir it with the naked wind?

V

The mother invites humanity to her house
And table. The father fetches tellers of tales
And musicians who mute much, muse much, on the tales.

The father fetches negresses to dance,
Among the children, like curious ripenesses
Of pattern in the dance's ripening.

For these the musicians make insidious tones,
Clawing the sing-song of their instruments.
The children laugh and jangle a tinny time.

The father fetches pageants out of air,
Scenes of the theatre, vistas and blocks of woods
And curtains like a naive pretence of sleep.

Among these the musicians strike the instinctive poem.
The father fetches his unherded herds,
Of barbarous tongue, slavered and panting halves

Of breath, obedient to his trumpet's touch.
This then is Chatillon or as you please.
We stand in the tumult of a festival.

What festival? This loud, disordered mooch?
These hospitaliers? These brute-like guests?
These musicians dubbing at a tragedy,

A-dub, a-dub, which is made up of this:
That there are no lines to speak? There is no play.
Or, the persons act one merely by being here.

VI

It is a theatre floating through the clouds,
Itself a cloud, although of misted rock
And mountains running like water, wave on wave,

Through waves of light. It is of cloud transformed
To cloud transformed again, idly, the way
A season changes color to no end,

Except the lavishing of itself in change,
As light changes yellow into gold and gold
To its opal elements and fire's delight,

Splashed wide-wise because it likes magnificence
And the solemn pleasures of magnificent space.
The cloud drifts idly through half-thought-of forms.

The theatre is filled with flying birds,
Wild wedges, as of a volcano's smoke, palm-eyed
And vanishing, a web in a corridor

Or massive portico. A capitol,
It may be, is emerging or has just
Collapsed. The denouement has to be postponed . . .

This is nothing until in a single man contained,
Nothing until this named thing nameless is
And is destroyed. He opens the door of his house

On flames. The scholar of one candle sees
An Arctic effulgence flaring on the frame
Of everything he is. And he feels afraid.

VII

Is there an imagination that sits enthroned
As grim as it is benevolent, the just
And the unjust, which in the midst of summer stops

To imagine winter? When the leaves are dead,
Does it take its place in the north and enfold itself,
Goat-leaper, crystalled and luminous, sitting

In highest night? And do these heavens adorn
And proclaim it, the white creator of black, jetted
By extinguishings, even of planets as may be,

Even of earth, even of sight, in snow,
Except as needed by way of majesty,
In the sky, as crown and diamond cabala?

It leaps through us, through all our heavens leaps,
Extinguishing our planets, one by one,
Leaving, of where we were and looked, of where

We knew each other and of each other thought,
A shivering residue, chilled and foregone,
Except for that crown and mystical cabala.

But it dare not leap by chance in its own dark.
It must change from destiny to slight caprice.
And thus its jetted tragedy, its stele

And shape and mournful making move to find
What must unmake it and, at last, what can,
Say, a flippant communication under the moon.

VIII

There may be always a time of innocence.
There is never a place. Or if there is no time,
If it is not a thing of time, nor of place,

Existing in the idea of it, alone,
In the sense against calamity, it is not
Less real. For the oldest and coldest philosopher,

There is or may be a time of innocence
As pure principle. Its nature is its end,
That it should be, and yet not be, a thing

That pinches the pity of the pitiful man,
Like a book at evening beautiful but untrue,
Like a book on rising beautiful and true.

It is like a thing of ether that exists
Almost as predicate. But it exists,
It exists, it is visible, it is, it is.

So, then, these lights are not a spell of light,
A saying out of a cloud, but innocence.
An innocence of the earth and no false sign

Or symbol of malice. That we partake thereof,
Lie down like children in this holiness,
As if, awake, we lay in the quiet of sleep,

As if the innocent mother sang in the dark
Of the room and on an accordion, half-heard,
Created the time and place in which we breathed . . .

IX

And of each other thought—in the idiom
Of the work, in the idiom of an innocent earth,
Not of the enigma of the guilty dream.

We were as Danes in Denmark all day long
And knew each other well, hale-hearted landsmen,
For whom the outlandish was another day

Of the week, queerer than Sunday. We thought alike
And that made brothers of us in a home
In which we fed on being brothers, fed

And fattened as on a decorous honeycomb.
This drama that we live—We lay sticky with sleep.
This sense of the activity of fate—

The rendezvous, when she came alone,
By her coming became a freedom of the two,
An isolation which only the two could share.

Shall we be found hanging in the trees next spring?
Of what disaster is this the imminence:
Bare limbs, bare trees and a wind as sharp as salt?

The stars are putting on their glittering belts.
They throw around their shoulders cloaks that flash
Like a great shadow's last embellishment.

It may come tomorrow in the simplest word,
Almost as part of innocence, almost,
Almost as the tenderest and the truest part.

X

An unhappy people in a happy world—
Read, rabbi, the phases of this difference.
An unhappy people in an unhappy world—

Here are too many mirrors for misery.
A happy people in an unhappy world—
It cannot be. There's nothing there to roll

On the expressive tongue, the finding fang.
A happy people in a happy world—
Buffo! A ball, an opera, a bar.

Turn back to where we were when we began:
An unhappy people in a happy world.
Now, solemnize the secretive syllables.

Read to the congregation, for today
And for tomorrow, this extremity,
This contrivance of the spectre of the spheres,

Contriving balance to contrive a whole,
The vital, the never-failing genius,
Fulfilling his meditations, great and small.

In these unhappy he meditates a whole,
The full of fortune and the full of fate,
As if he lived all lives, that he might know,

In hall harridan, not hushful paradise,
To a haggling of wind and weather, by these lights
Like a blaze of summer straw, in winter's nick.

Betrayal and Nothingness:
The Book of Job and *King Lear*

I

Wʜᴇɴ Jᴏʙ, in his undeserved suffering, loses his faith in the justice of God and feels betrayed by God, he curses the fact of his human existence and wishes not merely to die, but never to have been born. In his despair, Job's way of trying to control the future is by denying time itself. Job tries to negate himself even from his own history:

> God damn the day I was born
>   and the night that forced me from the womb.
> On that day—let there be darkness;
>   let it never have been created;
> Let it sink back into the void. (13)*

God's initial act of creation—"Let there be light"—is replaced in Job's mind with the nothingness of original darkness. From then on, throughout the poem, nothingness re-

* All quotes from Job are from *The Book of Job*, trans. Stephen Mitchell (San Francisco: North Point Press, 1987). Page citations are given in the text.

mains an alternative to existence itself, since the universe seems to be devoid of moral meaning and of justice. It is not until the end that these intertwined themes of nothingness and justice finally are resolved in Job's attitude toward the randomness and indifference of nature. Job, confirmed in his knowledge that Bildad is wrong in his assertion that "God never betrays the innocent," nevertheless accepts his return to dust.

So, too, is the theme of nothingness central to Shakespeare's *King Lear*, and here, as well, it is inextricably bound to the theme of justice. When Lear asks Cordelia to proclaim publicly her love for him so that he can give her a share of his inheritance larger than what he gives his other two daughters, "What can you say to draw / A third more opulent than your sisters," the embarrassed Cordelia responds: "Nothing, my Lord." Lear questions, "Nothing?" and Cordelia repeats the ominous word, "Nothing," to which Lear's reply will echo throughout the play: "Nothing will come of nothing" (I.1.86–88). Spiritually, however, everything eventually will emerge out of nothing because Lear will be reduced to nothing before he is reborn out of the empty figure he had become when he gave away his kingdom and banished the one daughter and the true friend, Kent, who sincerely love him.

In the Book of Job the motif of nothingness, conceived as the human opposition to God's creation of human life, is made manifest in the imagery of dust, and Job's changing attitude in the way he views himself as dust most fully reveals his spiritual transformation. After Job's sons and daughters have been killed by a desert wind, but before Job's friends appear on the scene to comfort him, Job still holds onto his faith in God. Job's faith is expressed in a gesture of acceptance in which he lies down "with his face in the dust" (7). In effect, Job affirms that he was essentially nothing before God breathed life into the dust in order to create him and that he will return to the condition of nonbeing as a consequence of the inevitable rhythm of nature. And so Job, still without bitterness, is able to say: "Naked came I from my mother's womb, and naked I will return there. The Lord gave, and the Lord has taken; may the name of the Lord be blessed" (7). Even after Job's wife loses faith and, with extreme bitterness, urges Job to "Curse God, and die," Job remains grateful and true to the God who has created him, and he replies to his wife: "We have accepted good fortune from God; surely we can accept bad fortune too" (8). When Job's friends arrive to comfort him, they see how terribly he has changed, and they "cried out and tore their clothing, and sprinkled dust on their heads" (9). There seems to be something about their gesture—as if in beholding them as dust Job now truly sees himself also as dust—that breaks Job's mood of sublime acceptance of God's inscrutable will and causes Job to abandon his faith, curse his own existence, and challenge God.

Job's sense of himself as dust is a close variant of envisioning himself as being essentially naked; his attitude, as represented by these two words, *dust* and *naked,* includes feelings that range from self-contempt to complete vulnerability. So, too, King Lear comes to see the basic human condition as one of nakedness; in order to acknowledge this existential truth, Lear tears off his clothing and declaims: "Unaccommodated man is no more but such a poor, bare, forked animal as thou art. Off, off you lendings!" (III.4.105–7). His vision here is identical to Hamlet's when, in his disillusionment (which results, like Lear's, from suffering the betrayal of loved ones) Hamlet characterizes mankind as a "quintessence of dust." For both Job and Lear, man in his nakedness and human life seen as dust are versions of nothingness that appear to be beyond redemption and that cannot be accepted in any way by the reflections of consciousness. It appears brutally paradoxical that the only ways to contend with nothingness, so understood, are to escape consciousness through madness, in which the mind avoids the concept of the future, of ongoing time, or, suicidally, to seek the nothingness of death and become the very nothingness that one abhors.

Lear's denial of the future can be seen in the interrelated images of space and time when Lear, with the map of his kingdom before him, determines to appropriate his lands according to his manipulation of his daughters' professions of love as if in controlling their speech, their language, he can control their feelings as well. When Lear proclaims: "Know we have divided / In three our kingdom; and 'tis our fast intent / To shake all cares and business from our age, / Conferring them on younger strengths (while we / Unburthen'd crawl toward death)" (I.1.38–42), he is, in fact, fantasizing a condition of power so great, and therefore free of care, that it does not require further worldly power to sustain it. Imagining a human state without burdens is, in effect, a fundamental denial of the human condition; it is an illusion the aged Lear has as he faces his impending death. In the most terrible darkness of their psyches, all parents feel that they have been betrayed by their children when the children become separate and unique individuals, for in doing so, they leave their parents uncloned and thus mortal, not to be replicated into eternity. Lear's prototypical wish to control his children is psychically the same as his wish to determine the future, and both are manifestations of his unconscious refusal to accept his mortality, the ultimate condition of returning to dust.

Lear's presumptive will to control the lives of his children is made further explicit when he says: "We have this hour a constant will to publish / Our daughters' several dowers, that future strife / May be prevented now" (I.1.44–46). The irony of this statement is, of course, immense, since the effect of Lear's attempt to determine the future according to his conscious will (though it may well correspond to an unconscious desire to destroy a future without him by rending it back into chaos) is to precipitate strife between the daughters and their husbands. Out of the despair that comes from discovering that the consequence of abnegating worldly power is not a blissful state beyond care and without burdens—a despair that leads inevitably to madness as a defense against the impotent nothingness that he has brought upon himself— Lear will come to learn the equally powerful, but kinder, paradox of fertile nothingness.

After the fool has recited a nonsense poem, Kent comments, "This is nothing, fool," and the bantering fool, turning toward Lear, rejoins with "Then 'tis like the breath of an unfee'd lawyer. You gave me nothing for 't.—Can you make no use of nothing, nuncle?" (I.4.132–37). But Lear has not yet begun to discover, within the depths of his own darkness, this astonishing paradox of fertile nothingness, and, repeating his earlier remark to Cordelia, he dumbly responds to the fool's pointed question: "Why, no, boy, nothing can be made out of nothing." The fool continues to taunt Lear's conscience with elliptically penetrating remarks:

> I had rather be any kind o' thing than a fool; and yet I would not be thee, nuncle. Thou hast pared thy wit o' both sides, and left nothing in the middle. . . . Now thou art an O without a figure. I am better than thou art now. I am a fool, thou art nothing. (I.4.189–98)

Lear will begin to understand his own nothingness when, naked himself, he is able to empathize with other people's losses and deprivations, and he will then measure whatever is good in life against that nothingness. During the storm in Act 3, Lear instructs Kent and the fool to enter a hovel before he does; in his mind, they become emblems of human nakedness in the face of nature's indifferent cruelty, and in the following speech, Lear reaches outside the hollow "O" of his own figure:

> Poor naked wretches, whereso'er you are,
> That bide the pelting of this pitiless storm,
> How shall your houseless heads and unfed sides,
> Your loop'd and window'd raggedness, defend you
> From seasons such as these? O! I have ta'en
> Too little care of this. Take physic, pomp;

> Expose thyself to feel what wretches feel,
> That thou mayst shake the superflux to them,
> And show the heavens more just. (III.4.28–36)

For Lear "superflux" is the antithesis of nothing. In physical terms superflux is any commodity, like food or clothing, that protects mankind from its nakedness as a creature of bodily vulnerability; in moral terms superflux means human compassion. In Lear's world, where the cruelty and indifference of nature are synonymous with the absence of a merciful or a just god, only human caring and generosity have the power to counteract existential nothingness, to fill the empty space of absent divinity, and, thus, to "show the heavens more just."

Having been betrayed by his daughters, Lear's vision of his own past failure to care sufficiently for the suffering of others, the "wretches" of nature, elevates the capacity for empathy and compassion to a divine status. Lear's speech implies that if we would care for each other, that in itself would be a sufficient sign of heavenly justice on earth. In effect, the absence of God is virtually synonymous with the deliberate cruelty of human beings to one another so that there is no moral force to counteract the thoughtless indifference of nature. Lear's sense of having been betrayed by his daughters epitomizes betrayal as the inescapable law of family intimacy, just as Job's sense of having been betrayed by his inscrutable God is inseparable from his experience of being misunderstood and thus emotionally deserted by his friends:

> All my friends have forgotten me;
>   my neighbors have thrown me away.
> My relatives look through me
>   as though I didn't exist.
> My servants refuse to hear me;
>   they shun me like a leper. (48–49)

For Job, as for Lear, the appeal to an absent God is made as an appeal for pity and empathy between human beings. Lear looks into his own heart to find this resource, and Job directly asks his condemning comforters: "Have pity on me, my friends, / For God's fist has struck me" (49).

Betrayal becomes a morbid expectation in Lear, and when the destitute Edgar emerges with the fool from the hovel into the storm, the now half-mad Lear assumes that Edgar, too, must have been betrayed by daughters to have come to such a state; Lear exclaims: "What! has his daughters brought him to this pass? Could'st thou save nothing?" (III.4.61–62). Lear sees Edgar as reduced to "nothing," just as he has been, and, envisioning himself as the representation of the fundamental human condition of having been betrayed, Lear strips himself of his clothing: "Unaccommodated man is no more but such a poor, bare forked animal as thou art. Off, off, you lendings! Come; unbutton here" (III.4.104–7). "Unaccommodated man" is Lear's version of nothingness in the absence of the "superflux" of human kindness—a kindness that even here on the desolate heath is growing as a new capacity in Lear as the result of his increased understanding of nothingness.

In the overt structure of the play, Gloucester is ostensibly represented as a figure parallel to Lear in that he, too, is a father betrayed by one of his children. Both fathers are treated by their unpreferred offspring with extreme cruelty beyond any measure of deserving. Goneril is correct in saying to Regan that "He always loved our sister [Cordelia] most" (I.1.293–94). Gloucester's preference for Edgar over Edmund, whom he crudely humiliates in the first scene, is based on Edgar's legitimacy. These rivalries between brothers or between sisters are variants of the Cain and Abel story which in *Hamlet* results in one brother's murdering another and which Shakespeare calls the "primal eldest crime." But if Gloucester is Lear's parallel as father, Edgar is Lear's alter-image as son. The converse of Lear as the abandoner and the betrayer of his daughter is the betrayal of Edgar by both his brother and his father. Thus we, the audience, will witness Edgar, in his own deliberate way, undergo a regenerative pro-

cess of moral understanding that first requires a descent into
nothingness remarkably similar to Lear's.

Having been forced to flee his home and his father's intem-
perate and injudicious wrath, Edgar elects to disguise himself
as a beggar:

> To take the basest and most poorest shape
> That ever penury, in contempt of man,
> Brought near to beast. My face I'll grime with filth,
> Blanket my loins, elf all my hair in knots,
> And with presented nakedness outface
> The winds and persecutions of the sky. (II.3.7–12)

With uncanny exactness, Edgar's words and conjured images
anticipate Lear's subsequent rejoinder to Goneril when she
tells Lear to reduce the number of his followers, and Lear
replies, "O reason not the need. Our basest beggars / Are
in the poorest things superfluous" (II.4.265–66), and when
Lear strips himself naked on the heath to face the storm as
"unaccommodated man." Edgar concludes his speech with
the ringing words, "Edgar I nothing am," and thus he is
profoundly linked with Lear's descent into nothingness. Although Edgar means that he has lost his identity as Edgar,
Gloucester's son and inheritor, his words equally imply that
his true identity now in his banished and betrayed condition
is to be found in the vision of nothing, and this vision is
precisely the one that Lear will come to acknowledge and
embrace. What Lear will learn is that to be nothing, to be
naked, to be stripped of all superfluity, all necessities, is to
know what man cannot live without. "The art of our necessities is strange," Lear later says to Kent, "That can make vile
things seem precious" (III.2.70–71).

Edgar is betrayed by both his brother and his father; Lear is
betrayed by his daughters, and, as he comes to understand, by
himself as well. Likewise, Job is also twice betrayed: by God
and by his friends. Mysteriously, these two betrayals are inextricably linked to each other, and it seems as if Job could

endure being abandoned by God if it did not result in his
friends also turning against him. Their pity and understanding could have, to use Shakespeare's words, "shown the heavens more just." Job directly confronts Eliphaz, the first comforter, with the accusation: "You too have turned against me;
my wretchedness fills you with fear" (22). Job bitterly com-
prehends the irony that exacerbates the difficulty of human
beings showing compassion and empathy for each other because need itself, affliction and wretchedness, appears as a
form of ugliness, so that the greater the need for sympathy,
the more the potential sympathizer is repelled. Thus Bildad's
rebuke of Job can be seen as a psychological defense against
offering sympathy that manifests itself as theological dogma:
"God never betrays the innocent / or takes the hand of the
wicked" (26). With such rationalization in defiance of the
obvious truth of Job's victimization by a randomly hostile
God, Bildad's betrayal of Job becomes a direct extension of
God's betrayal of Job.

The model for proper moral behavior in Job's mind had
earlier been established in the way God had treated him after
his creation, and Job takes pains to remind God of his original
care and solicitude:

> Remember: you formed me from clay . . .
> clothed me in flesh and skin,
>   knit me with bones and sinews.
> You loved me, you gave me life,
>   you nursed and cared for my spirit. (30)

God had been both mother and father to Job, and it is precisely God's tender and sympathetic treatment of Job that—
as Job claims later in the poem—has shaped Job's own compassionate attitude toward his fellow man:

> Did I ever strike down a beggar
>   when he called to me in distress?
> Didn't I weep for the wretched?
>   Didn't I grieve for the poor? (72)

And so, in Job's mind, God's betrayal of him, God's undeserved and inscrutable withdrawal of mercy, pity, and protection, destroys the foundation of human connectedness. Without a divine or a human bond of empathy, Job feels himself
to be alone in nature, as Lear is on the heath, related only to
the indifferent elements and the animals who lack moral
consciousness:

> I despair and can find no comfort;
> I stand up and cry for help.
> I am brother to the wild jackal,
>   friend to the desert owl. (72)

And yet Job persists in his cry for help. No longer wishing to
die or never to have been born, as he did at the commence-
ment of the poem, Job chooses to endure so that he can
persevere in his demand that God answer his complaint and
make clear his purposes.

Like Job, Gloucester must overcome the temptation of
suicide and, like Job, Lear must summon his utmost powers
of will and determination to endure with patience. Lear,
however, differs from Job, whose primary cry for justice is
directed toward God, since Lear comes to expect no kindness
from the worldly manifestation of God's elements, only from
people, from family. If there is justice in Heaven, it will reveal
itself only through human behavior:

> Rumble thy bellyful! Spit fire! spout rain!
> Nor rain, wind, thunder, fire, are my daughters.
> I tax you not, you elements, with unkindness;
> I never gave you kingdom, call'd you children,
> You owe me no subscription. (III.2.14–18)

But this view, with its emphasis on human kindness in the
face of the indifference of nature and the random cruelty of
the elements, marks a radical change from Lear's earlier Job-
like invocation to a rescuing divinity when he had prayed:

> O Heavens,
> If you do love old men, if your sweet sway
> Allows obedience, if you yourselves are old,
> Make it your cause. Send down and take my part!
>
> (II.4.190–93)

All the heavens send down, however, is rain and wind; if there is any meaning in natural destructiveness and disaster, it only can be found in the human will to endure and to resist and in the occasion such suffering provides for human introspection and self-judgment. Thus, when Lear says: "No, I will be the pattern of all patience. / I will say nothing" (III.2.37–38), he is affirming in his despair the moral nothingness of a universe in which the heavens do not make human suffering their cause, a nothingness within which Lear will replace divine judgment with human judgment.

And so Lear's imagination, replacing the absent gods, takes as its own the perspective of a wrathfully judgmental but just divinity, and from this point of view Lear surveys the earth and sees sinfulness—whose only recourse is to cry for mercy—wherever he looks:

> Tremble, thou wretch,
> That hast within thee undivulged crimes
> Unwhipp'd of justice; hide thee, thou bloody hand,
> Thou perjur'd, and thou simular of virtue
> That art incestuous. Caitiff, to pieces shake,
> That under covert and convenient seeming
> Hast practiced on man's life. Close pent-up guilts,
> Rive your concealing continents, and cry
> These dreadful summoners grace. (III.2.51–59)

All the most fundamental violations of human morality, from incest, to hypocrisy, to the abuse of power, to murderousness are cataloged here. Finally, the judgmental Lear turns these accusations against himself and, in effect, confesses to them all and cries for grace, yet, astonishingly, declares that "I

am a man / More sinned against than sinning" (III.2.59–60).
What Lear has in mind, no doubt, is the treatment he has
received from Goneril and Regan, and yet his claim directs
itself also against the unanswering heavens that betray human faith by refusing to take up the cause of human suffering.
In claiming, without rationalization or sentimentality, that
he is "more sinned against than sinning," Lear places himself
squarely with Job, who had not claimed absolute and unreal
purity in confronting God: "Can't you forgive my sins / or
overlook my mistakes?" (24). Lear expresses the irrefutable
truth of his own experience: the suffering of human beings
does not exist in relation even to their admitted transgres-
sions; there is no morally justifiable connection between
one's behavior and one's fate.

The accusing and tormenting fool must be regarded as an
aspect of Lear's mind—his conscience that functions at the
border of madness—but also as a character who exists in his
own right with his own emotions and needs. It follows with
inevitable logic that when Lear allows himself to feel some
sympathy for himself, to acknowledge the measure of his
own innocence as one "more sinn'd against than sinning,"
then his empathy for the fool also should become manifest.
Lear says to him, "Come, your hovel, / Poor fool and knave, I
have one part in my heart / That's sorry yet for thee" (III.2.71–
73). The fool's song in response expresses Lear's own inner
knowledge, so recently come upon, that the elements, representative of absent divinity, constitute the Fortune of the
human world that often is cruel beyond an individual's deserving:

> He that has and a little tiny wit,
>   With hey, ho, the wind and the rain,
> Must make content with his fortunes fit,
>   For the rain it raineth every day. (III.2.74–77)

Lear's reply to the fool's song is simple, direct, and comprehensive, "True, my good boy," for it acknowledges that

Fortune and the moral nothingness of nature are what Lear must accept as absolutes.

Since Fortune is the immemorial and thus ongoing condition of nature, to understand it is to be able to see into the future, which is precisely what the fool does next when he says "I'll speak a prophecy before I go":

> When every case in law is right,
> No squire in debt, nor no poor knight;
> When slanders do not live in tongues;
> Nor cutpurses come not to throngs;
> When usurers tell their gold i' th' field,
> And bawds and whores do churches build:
> Then shall the realm of Albion
> Come to great confusion.
> Then comes the time, who lives to see't,
> That going shall be us'd with feet. (III.2.85–94)

The theme of the fool's prophecy is justice and virtue, and the rhetorical structure of the passage is to anticipate a time in the future when the vices of the world, represented by Albion, shall come to an end. What all this anticipation leads to, however, is not revelation, but "confusion," for the prophecy ends with a mighty non sequitur, a crashing anticlimax: in the new age people will walk on their feet. The point of this anticlimax is that nothing has been revealed and that nothing will change: we have witnessed a revelation of non-revelation.

The fool's comment about his own prophecy, which concludes the scene, is an amazing anachronism: "This prophecy Merlin shall make, for I live before his time" (III.2.95). This is truly a mystical moment in the play. Living in "Prehistoric Britain," the fool nevertheless can see into the future of King Arthur's court where Merlin the king's magician served, and this future, for Shakespeare's audience, is, of course, the deep historical past. All time seems to be collapsed in the fool's mind, to exist in a single moment of insight, and that is because what the fool envisions, the emptiness and nothingness of human existence, the failure of both human and divine justice, are unchanging and unchangeable conditions. The fool's anachronism is a parody of Jesus' remark, "Before Abraham was, I am" (John 8.58), since it replaces the abiding presence of divinity throughout time, transcending chronology, with an abiding absence: we have a prophecy of a prophecy that prophesizes nothing.

II

The Book of Job and *King Lear* are profoundly alike in their basic themes. Both Job and Lear lose their children and property, suffer betrayals, endure great physical hardships, and confront the elements, which represent ambiguously answering or unresponding divinity: Job encounters the whirlwind and Lear contends with the storm. Both the Book of Job and *King Lear* are filled with trial scenes and allusions to trials. Eliphaz says to Job: "If I were you, I would pray; / I would put my case before God" (19). Job replies as if the trial already had taken place: "Man's life is a prison; he is sentenced to pain and grief" (23). And after Bildad, assuming that Job's claim of innocence is both blasphemous and false, excoriates him with the presumed certainty that "Such is the fate of the impious, / the empty hope of the sinner" (25), Job replies with rhetorical irony:

> How can I prove my innocence?
>   Do I have to beg him for mercy?
> If I testify, will he answer?
>   Is he listening to my plea? (28)

Although deep in his heart, where his faith was once grounded, Job still hopes that God will intervene and explain himself, Job now knows with certainty—a certainty that has replaced his earlier belief in a just God—that "He has punished me for a trifle; / for no reason he gashes my flesh" (28).

But Job goes further; he becomes God's accuser, putting God on trial in the courtroom of his own imagination as he recites the horrendous indictment: God "hands the earth to the wicked / and blindfolds its judges' eyes" (28). Beyond this indictment of God's deeds, Job goes further by impugning God's motive, castigating him for hypocrisy:

> For you keep pursuing a sin,
>   trying to dig up a crime,
> though you *know* that I am innocent. (29)

Zophar tries to turn Job's questioning of God's justice and God's motives back onto Job, again placing Job in a courtroom where he is being cross-examined for a crime he is presumed to have committed:

> But if God were to cross-examine you
>   and turned up your hidden motives
> and presented his case against you
>   and told you why he has punished you—
> you would know that your guilt is great. (31)

Job responds by linking Zophar in a conspiracy with God against him: "Will you lie to vindicate God? / Will you perjure yourselves for him?" (34). In such a courtroom, as Job knows to his despair, he cannot receive justice or mercy at the hands of either God or man. In utter isolation, then, Job ends his speech with a desperate plea to God to restore their former relationship when God treated Job as a loving father: "you would come to me and rejoice, / delighting in my smallest step / like a father watching his child" (37). But having betrayed Job by abandoning him, God also has "destroy[ed] man's hope," and Job is left, cut off both from God and from man, trapped entirely in his own pain, without consolation or compassion, doomed therefore to mourn for himself and, still worse, to realize that, trapped in the labyrinth of his own grief, his inward mourning must breed upon itself: "Only his own flesh hurts him, / and he mourns for himself alone" (37).

Like Job, Lear is accused of a crime that seems both absurd and without justification. Regan says to him, "O, sir, you are old," and tells him that he owes Goneril an apology: "Say, you have wrong'd her." Appalled by the false accusation and Regan's attempt to intimidate him into making a hypocritical confession, Lear replies, "Ask her [Goneril's] forgiveness?" and then, with even more bitter irony, Lear acknowledges his supposed crime: "Dear daughter, I confess that I am old. Age is unnecessary" (II.4.152–55). This absurdity would seem to destroy any meaningfulness in the concepts of guilt and forgiveness and supersede Lear's actual wronging of Cordelia, but Lear, though innocent of Regan's charges, will have to acknowledge his need to ask for Cordelia's forgiveness even though, in the balance of the scale of justice, he is now "more sinn'd against than sinning" (III.2.10). So, too, Job, though innocent of any specific legal or moral crime, nevertheless is guilty of insisting that God make himself understood in human terms: "I have spoken of the unspeakable / and tried to grasp the infinite." This presumption of being able to fathom divine mystery is the violation to which Job ultimately will repent.

There are two scenes in the play in which Lear in his madness fantasizes that he is presiding at a trial. In the first, Edgar is pretending that he has been possessed by the devil— "the foul fiend bites my back"—and, by virtue of this reverse qualification, Lear selects him to be the judge at the trial of Goneril and Regan: "Thou robed man of justice, take thy place" (III.6.36). Lear instructs the fool to take his place on the bench beside Edgar as "his yoke-fellow of equity." Lear orders the trial to begin, "Arraign her first," and then assumes the stand as the first witness against Goneril for the prosecution: " 'Tis Goneril, I here take my oath before this honorable assembly, kicked the poor king her father" (III.6.46–48). As if any worse assault by a daughter against a father were unimaginable, between bitter irony and denial, Lear exhausts his testimony, except to add, "She cannot deny it," and the fool completes the parody of the legal issues of clemency versus justice by declaiming to the imagined Goneril, "Cry you mercy, I took you for a joint-stool." Lear then turns to the imagined figure of Regan, "And here's another, whose warp'd looks proclaim / What store her heart is made on," but immediately the trial comes to an end as Regan avoids conviction because of "corruption" in the court, and Lear says to Edgar in his role of judge: "False justicer, why hast thou let her 'scape?" (III.6.55). Lear's thwarted longing for justice, for the exposure of true guilt, and for the meting out of meaningful punishment is perverted in his imagination, making him mad. So, too, the world comes to seem mad to Job without a court of appeal in which to be heard by God: "If only I knew where to meet him / and could find my way to his court" (59). Under such conditions, Job's testimony, like Lear's, becomes a convoluted perversion and a vain blasphemy: "I swear by God, who has wronged me / and filled my cup with despair" (64).

In the second trial scene the mad Lear meets the blinded Gloucester near the cliffs of Dover. Gloucester recognizes Lear by his voice, "Is't not the king?" and Lear responds by interpreting the main function of a king to be that of a judge. In this trial scene, however, Lear no longer plays the role of accuser, but the radically different role of pardoner: "I pardon that man's life. What was thy cause? Adultery? Thou shalt not die" (IV.6.110–11). In pardoning the anonymous figure in the above passage, Lear also is pardoning himself, for, unconsciously, his daughters' betrayal of him carries the connotation of adultery; this accounts for his identification with the man on trial whose life Lear spares in his fantasy. The following speech about forbidden "copulation," ending with Lear's identification of the female genitals as "hell," testifies both to Lear's sense of his own guilt and to his inner awareness of the need for pardon and forgiveness. Nevertheless, Lear, again like Job, despairs that justice cannot be counted on and must fail: "And the strong lance of justice hurtless breaks; /

Arm it in rags, a pigmy's straw does pierce it" (IV.6.161–62).
Job differs from Lear, however, in that he continues to turn to
God in his desperate wish for vindication—"Oh if only God
would hear me, / state his case against me, / let me read his
indictment" (75)—while Lear begins to take it upon himself
to declare everyone, including himself, in the final balancing
of the scales, to be innocent: "None does offend, none, I say
none" (IV.6.164). Thus, in Lear's mind, the trial comes to an
end, but what still remains to be resolved is Lear's forgiveness of himself which cannot occur until forgiveness has
been offered to him by Cordelia.

After Lear is rescued by Cordelia, we find him in a deep
sleep in the French camp. Cordelia prays over his body, "O
you kind gods, / Cure this great breach in his abused nature," and the attending doctor says that "in the heaviness of
sleep, / We put fresh garments on him" (IV.7.14–15). The
symbolism of dressing Lear anew suggests his return from
spiritual and literal nakedness in the earlier scene when Lear,
"Contending with the fretful elements" (III.1.4), had been
reduced to nothing. As described by the gentleman, Lear
"Tears his white hair, / Which the impetuous blasts, with
eyeless rage, / Catch in their fury and make nothing of"
(III.1.7–9). At the curative hands of Cordelia and the doctor
who truly "shake the superflux" of their love and concern
upon him, Lear, the "unaccommodated man," begins to become accommodated. It is deeply symbolic that Lear wakes
from a heavy sleep, as if being reborn, so that he thinks that
he has come back from death when he first sees Cordelia
leaning over him: "You do me wrong to take me out of the
grave" (IV.7.44). Lear does not yet feel sufficiently worthy of
being treated with such solicitude, and, filled with guilt for
having betrayed Cordelia by rejecting her, he says to her:

> If you have poison for me, I will drink it.
> I know you do not love me, for your sisters
> Have (as I do remember) done me wrong.
> You have some cause, they do not. (IV.7.71–74)

Cordelia's spontaneous response, "No cause, no cause," is the human equivalent of creation out of nothingness since the ordinary connections to be found in nature between cause and effect are replaced by a kind of magical leap. Cordelia offers her love to Lear beyond cause, not as reward or in the fulfillment of duty, but as a gift that generates its own goodness and satisfaction. Her gift has a healing effect on Lear, and the doctor says: "Be comforted, good madam. The great rage, / You see, is cur'd in him" (IV.7.77–78). The immediate result of this cure is that Lear is released from the grip of his guilt and can now implore Cordelia to "forget and forgive," thus completing the movement from rage and the wish for vengeance toward tolerance and self-acceptance that began when Lear claimed that he was "a man more sinn'd against than sinning." Lear's new innocence, his ability to "forgive" and to receive forgiveness (since forgiveness implies that the past can be changed or redeemed) works as if by miracle. This restorative power, when love seemed lost, refutes Lear's opening statement that "Nothing will come of nothing" and begins to mitigate the betrayal both of himself and of his daughter.

Earlier, the powerless Lear, whose identity had depended on his image of himself as king, had asked: "Who is it that can tell me who I am?" (I.4.235). After Lear has been reunited with his daughter, the question of his identity returns, but in the most fundamental terms of the human condition. The whole reunion scene is suffused with echoes and variants on the phrase "I am," beginning with Lear's metaphorical description of his tormented state: "I am bound / Upon a wheel of fire." It continues with his confusion as to where he actually is—"Where am I?"—and an assertion of his own victimization, "I am mightily abused." This is followed by a kind of breakthrough in self-perspective with the most humble yet objective statement Lear has so far been able to make: "I am a very foolish fond old man" (IV.7.59). Lear's gain in perspective and sanity deepens into the paradoxical awareness of his own mental instability, "I fear I am not in my perfect mind," and in his acknowledgment of his confusion, "I am doubtful," and "I am mainly ignorant," yet his speech concludes with the assertion of his simple humanity: "as I am a man, I think this lady / To be my child Cordelia" (IV.7.68–69). Lear's grasp of his own basic "I am," his own fundamental identity, is met and affirmed by Cordelia's reply, "And so I am, I am," and the scene concludes with a resounding echo of Lear's earlier line of self-recognition, "Pray you now, forget and forgive. I am old and foolish" (IV.7.84). With this sense of himself within his deliberate possession, now free of pride and self-indulgent guilt, Lear at last can free himself from the constraints of merely trying to endure and the chains of unrealizable self-imposed silence—"No, I will be the pattern of all patience. / I will say nothing" (III.2.37–38)—and both ask for and accept forgiveness. As if born anew as a child learning to walk when Cordelia asks him, "Will't please your highness walk?" Lear also has begun to learn a new language of restoration and humility.

Having reconciled with Cordelia, Lear is literally in a state of ecstasy—he is outside of himself—and though this state resembles madness in its departure from ordinary reality, yet it is the opposite of madness in its higher, even divine, sanity. Although Lear and Cordelia are captured by the enemy forces, and Cordelia understands their predicament with exact and worldly irony—"We are not the first / Who with best meaning have incurr'd the worst" (V.3.3–4)—Lear's blissful mood remains unaffected as they are led off to prison, and Lear accepts his new fate, "Fortune's frown" as Cordelia gently calls it, as if it were his own choice:

> Come, let's away to prison.
> We two alone will sing like birds i' th' cage.
> When thou dost ask me blessing, I'll kneel down,
> And ask of thee forgiveness. So we'll live,
> And pray and sing, and tell old tales, and laugh
> At gilded butterflies, and hear poor rogues
> Talk of court news; and we'll talk with them too:
> Who loses and who wins, who's in, who's out;

> And take upon 's the mystery of things,
> As if we were God's spies; and we'll wear out
> In a wall'd prison, pacts and sects of great ones
> That ebb and flow by th' moon. (V.3.8–19)

Like Job, after God reveals himself in the whirlwind as the unfathomable creator, whose creation is both beautiful and cruel, Lear now sees the world as a spectacle, a source of song and story, and he sees it as if not only from outside himself, but also from beyond the world, from a divine perspective: "As if we were God's spies" (V.3.17). Neither Job nor Lear is given a vision of ultimate justice or the redemption of wrongs and suffering; rather, their visionary detachment is rewarded with the quality of laughter. Political intrigue and struggle, "Who loses and who wins," no longer seem urgent or important, but merely become part of "the mystery of things" which are of no more importance, from this timeless perspective, than the image of "gilded butterflies" (V.3.13). The worldly condition that makes such a vision possible for Lear, that connects his individual fortune to the impersonal transcendence of his fate, is his ability to exchange blessing and forgiveness with Cordelia. That ability alone, which is not dependent on events but on attitude, can transfigure suffering into a kind of divine laughter. This moment is Lear's realization of Hamlet's wish to become one who "in suffering all, that suffers nothing" (see "On Empathy," 159), and it is directly comparable to the jubilation in God's response to Job in recounting the origination of the created universe when "the morning stars burst out singing / and the angels shouted for joy!" (79).

Cordelia and the fool have both served as curative forces within Lear's mind, Cordelia as the potentiality and power of forgiveness and the fool as Lear's inspired madness, his conscience. The fool vanishes mysteriously in the middle of the play, after having replied to Lear's line, "We'll go to supper i' th' morning," with the equally enigmatic, "And I'll go to bed at noon" (III.6.85), suggesting that he knows his death is imminent. Since the fool has completed his accusatory work in the depths of Lear's mind, it is appropriate that he be replaced by the soothing spiritual powers of Cordelia. And so when Cordelia dies, the figure of the fool—"And my poor fool is dead" (V.3.303)—merges with her in Lear's mind as he symbolically bears witness to his own death, for they both have been part of Lear's psyche. Because the deaths of the three of them are inextricably bound and because Cordelia's death appears to Lear as a new and unanticipated betrayal of what should be the natural continuity of time in which children survive parents, Lear's ecstatic vision of himself and Cordelia safely outside of time and beyond worldly fortune is shattered. Thus, Lear responds to Cordelia's premature death in terms of absolute negation:

> And my poor fool is hang'd! No, no, no life!
> Why should a dog, a horse, a rat, have life,
> And thou no breath at all? Thou'lt come no more.
> Never, never, never, never, never! (V.3.303–6)

The empty nothingness of time seen as unrestorative in which loss is absolute and eternal provokes the question Lear now asks of existence; it is in essence identical to Job's questioning of God as to why the "wicked prosper" and good goes unrewarded. As an unanswerable question, it exposes the moral nothingness at the foundation of Lear's universe. Immediately after the above lines, the interminable repetition of "Never," Lear asks Albany to undo a button on Cordelia's blouse because Lear's hands are trembling as he kneels over her breathless body:

> Pray you, undo this button. Thank you, sir.
> Do you see this? Look on her! look! her lips!
> Look there, look there! O, O, O, O. (V.3.307–9)

Here, each "O" is filled with the emptiness of loss, filled with the palpable love for his unregainable daughter; the "O" that had earlier been an emblem of himself—"Now thou art an O without a figure" (I.4.196–97) as the fool had declared—returns to the original silence that preceded human speech. We, the audience, are confronted with a nothingness more absolute than Cordelia's silence when she refused to respond with no more than the words, "Nothing, my Lord," to Lear's demand that Cordelia force her feelings of love into public declamation.

In another early scene that is comparable to the "Nothing, my lord," "Nothing will come of nothing" exchange between Cordelia and Lear, Edmund is "ostentatiously reading a letter" that supposedly his brother Edgar sent to him to suggest that the brothers together plot to kill their father in order to get his inheritance without further delay. Gloucester readily falls into the trap the treacherous Edmund has set for him and asks: "What paper were you reading?" Edmund, echoing Cordelia's words, replies: "Nothing my Lord." Gloucester's angry rejoinder reveals the same blindness of understanding that characterized Lear's response to Cordelia:

> No? What needed then that terrible dispatch of it into your pocket? The quality of nothing hath not such need to hide itself. Let's see. Come! If it be nothing, I shall not need spectacles. (I.2.33–36)

At the end of the play, faced with death, and seemingly miraculously cured of his own hatefulness even, astonishingly, by the love of Goneril and Regan ("Yet Edmund was belov'd") as Lear is cured by Cordelia's love, Edmund attempts to redeem himself out of his own nothingness. In a reversal of character as radical as any Shakespeare ever offers his audience, Edmund, fully aware of his own transformation, cries out: "Some good I mean to do / Despite of mine own nature" (V.3.247), but though Edmund has succeeded in redeeming himself (as had Cawdor in his death in *Macbeth*), he fails to prevent the death of Cordelia which he had ordered. Shakespeare's irony is immense. Even the reversal of nothing collapses back into nothing.

Faced with ultimate nothingness, Lear's heart, having endured so long, now breaks. And yet we, the audience, cannot tell for certain whether it is grief that kills Lear or—like the parallel moment in which Gloucester dies ("his flaw'd heart / . . . 'Twixt two extremes of passion, joy and grief, / Burst smilingly" [V.3.196–99])—a joyous illusion that he sees movement on Cordelia's lips. At this culminating moment, everything and nothing appear as inseparable and interchangeable. If it is indeed the illusion that Cordelia is alive that mercifully kills King Lear, we do not know whether to regard this illusion as the final irony of the play—as the ultimate failure of the hero of patience and reconciliation to endure the ultimate truth—or as a kind of triumph of the fictive imagination to impose itself, like a work of art, upon mere reality. Lear's imagination asserts love here in the extremity of pain, like a work of art, in a universe of unheeding gods that begins and ends as a moral void. Like the epilogue of the Book of Job in which we are allowed a fantasy of restoration, Lear, too, is relieved of having to die with the absolute certainty of Cordelia's death. We, the audience, exhausted ourselves from having to bear witness to what now surely feels like the ultimate betrayal of love by Fortune—whether sponsored by the gods or as a contingency of the indifference of nature—may wish to see Lear's last moment as one in which it is fitting that he enjoy Prometheus' gift to mankind of "blind hope." To Lear's earlier question to Edgar—"Coulds't thou save nothing?"—the answer at the play's conclusion would appear to rest for the survivors as an interpretation of an illusion, a willingness to accept a fiction as its own kind of truth.

Statements about the power of fictional art, like the imagination which "gives to airy nothing / A local habitation and a name" (*A Midsummer Night's Dream* [V.1.16–17]) appear in many of Shakespeare's plays, but none is more succinct and telling than Edgar's final response to having witnessed King Lear's agony: "The weight of this sad time we must obey; / Speak what we feel, not what we ought to say" (V.3.321–22).

Edgar's words, which emphasize the importance of connecting feeling with speech so that language does not betray
meaning, directly echo the words of his father, Gloucester, in
condemning the "lust-dieted Man" who "will not see / Because he does not feel," so that, at last, son and father are indeed connected, and the son, in spirit and language, becomes
the father's true inheritor. As Edgar's words have echoed
Gloucester's, so, too, have Gloucester's words—

> Heavens, deal so still!
> Let the superfluous and lust-dieted man.
> That slaves your ordinance, that will not see
> Because he does not feel, feel your power quickly.
> So distribution should undo excess,
> And each man have enough. (IV.1.66–71)

—echoed Lear's most empathetic speech about the need for
feeling: "Expose thyself to feel what wretches feel, / That
thou mayst shake the superflux to them and show the heavens more just" (III.4.34–36). In Edgar's final "Speak what we
feel," then, all three of them are united in spiritual brother-
hood and across the generations as a healthy version of the
poisonous uniting of Goneril, Regan, and Edmund who, in
the moment of death, confesses: "I was contracted to them
both. All three / Now marry in an instant" (V.3.228–29).

Art, as impassioned speech—speech that unifies motive
and expression—ultimately must be concerned with human
endurance and survival. In so directing itself, felt speech
must face and confront truths so terrible that they may seem
to be unspeakable. And yet for both Job and Lear, the intrac-
tability of natural cruelty, seen as an inescapable aspect of
creation itself—as if God's betrayal of mankind were the
cause of the betrayals among brothers and friends, of children
by parents which in turn generated the betrayal of parents by
children—seems nevertheless to leave room for human invention out of moral and spiritual nothingness. For Job, that
invention is the openness of wonder in the spirit of humble

acceptance at the beauty of nature when no moral demands are made upon nature and its creator. For Lear, that invention is empathy, even more powerful because it exists only by virtue of the human will, for the suffering of others; thus empathy engenders love beyond self-love and the temptations of betrayal. Edgar's assertion of the need for endurance to his own father: "Men must endure / Their going hence, even as their coming hither. / Ripeness is all" (V.2.9–11), underlies his affirmation of honest human speech as a power that can enable us to confront chaos and the original void with a ripeness that is not merely an analogy to harvest time and natural endings, but the fictional consummation of the human imagination as it asserts itself hopefully in the hopeless face of nothingness.

INDEX